"An extraordinary vision of what might happen in the future as neuroscience digs ever deeper into our brains."

Henry Marsh Neurosurgeon
Author of NYT bestseller 'Do No Harm'

"It's a world where synaptically oppressed citizens are expected to surrender property rights to their own memories! Shulman's work is uncannily provocative and topical."

John O'Mahony
Critic and feature writer, *The Guardian*

"An audacious novel which blends courtroom Grisham with bleeding-edge neuroscience fiction."

Simon Pitts
Writer/TV producer

"Axion does what some great Sci-Fi can do: take you to the not-so-distant-future to confront the next harrowing 'what if'."

Daniel Biro
Founder, Sargasso Records

AXION

The Memory Rights Uprising

DAVID SHULMAN

AXION:
The Memory Rights Uprising
by David Shulman
© 2023

ISBN 979-8-35091-883-0

eBook ISBN 979-8-35091-884-7

ABOUT THE AUTHOR

David Shulman is a BAFTA and TV Academy Award winning documentary producer and director. Originally from New York City, David moved to London in 2000 in the context of a U.S./UK Fulbright Fellowship. By 2005, he became one of the few Americans to gain a staff position at the BBC where for 10 years he produced and directed science, history, and arts programs.

David conceived the format and directed the first two seasons of the long running 'Reality TV' series Rough Science which was produced by the BBC in association with Open University scientists. It became one of the most successful and acclaimed science series in Open University history and is distributed globally.

A graduate of the School of Visual Arts in NYC, as an artist and experimental filmmaker, David has long been driven by a deep curiosity about how social systems work and a passion for social justice. His earliest experimental films focused on linguistic dimensions of memory, cognition, and consciousness – and were exhibited at the Whitney Museum, the Museum of Modern Art, the Anthology Film Archives, and the New Museum. They were distributed by Castelli and Sonnabend Galleries.

David has made acclaimed feature documentaries about racism in American Network news coverage of urban violence – Race Against Prime Time (PBS), the pivotal role of Black landowners in Mississippi during the civil rights revolution of the 1960's – Dirt & Deeds in Mississippi (Smithsonian Channel), stories of resistance inside Nazi concentration camps – Auschwitz Untold: In Colour (Channel Four/History Channel), a BAFTA winning portrait of the artist Jean-Michel Basquiat – Basquiat: Rage to Riches (PBS/BBC) and a feature documentary about digital art on the blockchain – NFT:WTF? (Netflix)

'AXION: The Memory Rights Uprising' is a story that combines several areas of passionate interest to the author: memory, social justice, and notions of property rights.

SCENES

AXION: THE MEMORY RIGHTS UPRISING

He who learns must suffer. And even in our sleep, pain that cannot forget falls drop by drop upon the heart, and in our own despair, against our will, comes wisdom to us by the awful grace of God.

Aeschylus
(c.525 – c.455 BC)

The future ain't what it used to be.

Yogi Berra
(Yankee catcher 1946 – 1963)

Encryptions of episodic neuron ensembles to last a lifetime

The sky over the canyon is a primordial blue. It's a distinctive hue from a timeless palette which seamlessly drapes your field of vision.

A helicopter is flying past ancient limestone cliffs above a turbulent snaking river. Suspended from the helicopter are several 2 metre long stainless steel cylinders. As the helicopter slows to a hover, the cylinders begin to descend. A spectacular view of the Grand Canyon is welcoming them.

The rising sun refracts off the glistening cylinders as they are greeted by several Park Rangers situated on a dramatic precipice. The Rangers detach the cylinders from the cable hoist and move them into a secured position on a glass bottomed tourist platform.

The glass platform is about 20 meters wide and protrudes about 6 anxiety inducing meters over the canyon and features two long rows of vertical stations each equipped with a stylish clear plastic face mask. The Rangers begin to attach one of the cylinders to a distribution valve which feeds a network of tubes which connect to the vertical stations which hold the masks. A sign appears in the center of the platform:

Welcome to the Grand Canyon.
A view to last a lifetime.

Just beyond the platform, a calm orderly queue of about 100 tourists is patiently waiting in the crisp morning air for the opening of the viewing platform at one of the most popular tourist attractions in the world.

Through the thick underbrush of the Sabangau rain forest in Borneo, an elderly gamekeeper is leading a group of two dozen sharply dressed eco-tourists who have come a long way and paid a lot of money in the hope of catching a glimpse of the worlds last Orangutan living in the wild.

Each tourist is wearing a plastic face mask with a tube running from the mask to a small stainless steel cylinder kept in a holster which hangs from their waist. The gamekeeper takes them towards the cluster of tall trees where the Orangutan has a treetop nest. The visitors are expecting an unforgettable glimpse of a soon to be extinct species.

At a military base in Galveston, Texas, several dozen soldiers are wearing face masks with slender tubes that connect to a central network. They are sitting at bare desks in a military hanger all facing a large membrane screen. A gruff drill sergeant is barking out instructions.

"Listen up doll faces. Glue your eyes to the screen. In the next one hundred and twenty seconds you'll receive complete operational instructions for the latest front line, self-assemble, self-op, multiple targeting, high kinetic energy assault system. There is a pencil and paper on each of your desks – I don't think you will need them, but you can send love notes to each other if you wish."

The Sargent goes to his tab and clicks. The training video which details the complex assembly process unfolds at a steady and metronomic pace before the fresh recruits.

About two dozen primary school children funnel into a brightly illuminated classroom and scramble to find a seat. There is some initial confusion because this is not their usual classroom and the seats are haphazardly arranged. A double door entrance through which they entered is ominously shut and sealed behind them by a teacher's assistant.

Inside a closet adjacent to the classroom, valves on a row of silver cylinders are being opened. The hiss of gas can barely be heard as it exits vents in the ceiling above the children. Some of the children appear deeply anxious.

The normal buzz of children at the start of a new lesson is subdued. On the outside of the double doors to this classroom is sign which reads:

Putting the E into Education
Eidetic Industries, a subsidiary of Cortx

The teacher begins the lesson,

"Please open your story books children. Today, Timmy and Kylie play with their pet dog Pixie – as they learn to shop..."

In a bleak industrial estate, beyond CCTV cameras, motion detectors, and a 4 meter high fence with an electrified razor ribbon along the top, is a vast storage depot where thousands of stainless steel cylinders holding compressed gas are stored. Each cylinder is less than half a meter in diameter and 2 meters in height and has a Cortx logo beneath a valve. Cortx is an industry leader at the forefront of neurotech and nootropic research and development. It ranks at the top of the Ntech100 stock index.

Production, sales, and marketing of their proprietary nootropic gas formula is only one sector of the Cortx empire but the company is relentless in its efforts to expand it. The conglomerate is planning a spectacular plunge into the global family entertainment market. A growing list of countries and their regulatory regimes have given a provisional nod of approval to an ambitious scheme which the Cortx PR machine claims will revolutionise the cinema going experience.

Morning, trials and tribulations

To say Gil Hinchliff has not been sleeping well is a monumental understatement.

Sex with his girlfriend Dena is still a welcome soporific, but she is very close to leaving him. He's either got too much on his mind to notice or he's in denial about the deteriorated state of their relationship – or both.

Dena is frightened, alienated, and helpless in response to Gil's recent bouts of nightmares, cold sweats, spasms, shouts, and morning hallucinations.

Even before Gil's mental health went into freefall after his recent visit to a Cortx lab in Central Asia, Dena and Gil were drifting apart. Gil has been reluctant to talk in any detail about what happened to him during this trip which only adds to Dena's alienation.

An alarm clock goes off on a bedside table at arms length from Gil. It's making a loud squawking sound. Appearing above the base of the alarm clock is an animated hologram of a parrot.

Gil's face is half buried beneath the sheets. Dena is trying to bury her head under her pillow as the ghostly parrot begins to speak in its parrot like voice the reminders Gil programmed the night before:

'Six-fifteen' (squawk)

'Complete opening statement' (squawk, squawk)

'Confirm witness' (squawk, screech)

'Fuck Cortx' (screech, screech)

Gil's eyes open then shut. It's the vivid and harrowing morning horror show that has been flashing in his head with variations on and off over the past couple of months. It is exacerbated by stress. Gil opens then closes his eyes. It's a kitsch film scene from a Soviet era musical. Peasants astride a tractor sing in unison as they harvest crops. Gil's eyes blink open and shut. A grisly film clip of World War II POW's being executed against a church wall by a Nazi firing squad. The ear splitting sound of gunshots causes Gil to spasm. His vivid mental flashes are brief, jolting, and surreal.

The hologram continues to screech.

Gil sits up in bed, takes three deep breaths and gently props his eyelids open with his fingers. He discovered that this simple intervention helps to mitigate the morning horror show.

He waves his hand through the hologram to silence the squawking.

Trying not to disturb Dena, Gil stumbles out of bed and heads into the bathroom where he swipes a plastic card on a wall mounted sensor and starts to take a shower.

After a few seconds the water cuts off,

"'FUCK! Fuck, fuck, fuck, fuck, FUUUCCCK!'"

Gil jumps out of the shower.

Naked, wet and cold, he rushes back to a pile of clothes next to his bed. He finds another card in a trouser pocket. He returns to the wall sensor next to the shower and swipes it. Nothing happens,

"Aaaaahhhh fuuuck..."

Gil wraps himself in a towel as he runs out of the bathroom into the kitchen.

Amidst piles of used plates and a kitchen table cluttered with empty takeaway containers and stacked with odd printouts and court documents, Gil shouts into the air,

"Dial (UNDER BREATH) *fucking* bank."

The shout triggers electronic dialling sounds.

'What service please?'

"Transfer 50 E-ren to Aquanet (UNDER BREATH) *ripoff artists.*"

'Mr. Hinchliff, your request for a – fifty E-ren debit to – Aquanet – has been received. If this is correct please say 'yes'.'

Gil shouts,

"Yes."

Then mutters under his breath,

'*Motherfuckers!*'.

'Your transaction is complete. Thank you.'

Gil can't restrain himself,

'Fuck you completely.'

Approaching the bathroom sensor again, Gil swipes his card again. This time the the shower jutters to life. Gil continues to mutter as he steps into the stream of hot water,

"Mootheerrrrfuuuckkeeerrrs..."

Dena is slowly coming around but she is simmering. She's glancing at images on one of the bedroom walls of Gil's world. Some images resemble geothermal imagery of earth captured by high resolution satellite cameras.

Dena knows exactly what they are. They're high resolution scans of Gil's brain taken in a public neurogram kiosk.

It's one of Gil's hobbies to collect scans that reflect a range of his emotions. There are subtle visual differences between them. Each image also has a word hand scrawled in bold letters upon it. One scan has the word 'ANGER'. Another scan has the word 'LAUGHTER'. A third scan has the word 'GRIEF'.

On the same wall with the scans are some of Gil's family photos. Gil as a toddler with his smiling mum. A photo of little Gil with his older brother Stephen. Gil when he was about 6 sitting inside a large amusement arcade rocket. There is a man's hand on his shoulder, but the half of the photo with the man has been torn away. There's also a photo of Gil in a mortar board next to his mother on graduation day. His mother's expression is proud, but there is sadness and anguish in her eyes too.

Back in the shower, Gil taps his shower curtain twice with two fingers to activate it as a computer screen. A menu of options becomes visible through the cascading water. Gil taps the 'Breaking News' menu item.

A female news anchor appears on the shower curtain and her news report is heard clearly above the sounds of the running water,

"Is memory lane being turned into a toll road?"

The same news report is playing on a tab screen in the back seat of a limousine travelling through Central London. The anchor continues,

"...A landmark legal battle begins today in a London courtroom..."

Sitting in the back seat of the Limo with a pile of folders beside him is Ken Marshall the lead attorney for Cortx. Marshall is in his early 40's and a slick dresser wearing a custom tailored light grey suit, a peach coloured shirt and a dark blue tie with thin silver diagonal stripes. The news report on his screen continues. There's a montage of shots which include tourists kitted up with clear masks at the Grand Canyon, a pyramid in Giza, and the Eiffel Tower.

"It started out as a one-time premium charge at some of the world's top tourist attractions...

"...But Cortx, the neurotech entertainment conglomerate will be introducing an unprecedented payment scheme at their new chain of cinema's for a film going experience they promise to be literally unforgettable.

"Cinema-goers face permanent micro-charges for film memories Cortx claims remain their intellectual property. But a group of memory rights activists are challenging this controversial scheme as well as the safety of what they refer to as 'memory steroids' developed by Cortx. If beaten in court, Cortx faces a devastating financial setback."

The news report is showing the buzzing excitement of people in a queue outside the cineplex with a marquee which reads 'Welcome to the Eidetic Cinema'. Also on the marquee is the title of the film to be screened on opening night. It's a re-release of one of the most successful films in cinema history. Cortx takes shameless pride in showcasing a film which romanticised slavery in the American south. It has been retitled for the occasion:

GONE BUT NOT FORGOTTEN WITH THE WIND

The news report features vox pops which were supplied by Cortx PR.

Young woman,

"It's amazing. I've never experienced anything like it!"

Young man,

"It's like, the colours, the music all remain so vivid."

A young couple. One speaks,

"The charges? They're practically nothing."

Both together,

"It's definitely worth it"

The news anchor continues,

"Memory rights activists describe the Cortx plan as the world's first 'memory tax.'"

A ringtone and blinking light indicate an incoming call. Marshall activates a second tab embedded in the back of the front seat. Norman Palmer the CEO of Cortx appears on screen from another car. Palmer is meticulously dressed with perfectly cropped salt and pepper hair. He has a commanding voice and a tanned façade which conceals a dark core,

"Good morning, Mr. Palmer."

"Morning Ken, how's Margaret and the kids?"

"They're all fine Mr. Palmer, thanks for asking."

"Ken, do you think that bastard has anything from the lab that can hurt us?"

"I doubt it Mr. Palmer. We have him by the balls."

As Palmer's limo navigates towards the courthouse, it passes incidental evidence of how memory-centric the culture has become. A digital billboard for a travel agent promotes a surf and sun filled holiday package to the Arctic as 'a precious deposit in your memory banks'. Up market restaurants conspicuously display their number on the Michelin 'MI' or 'Memorability Index'.

An advertising trend in the popular culture has become 'memory shaming'. It is used to sell everything from computer games to health supplements and a wide range of mental exercise apps which all claim to improve your sex life, your wealth, and your intelligence – by boosting your embarrassingly inadequate memory. Memory shaming has long eclipsed fat shaming as a source of anxiety among teenagers and young adults.

Another Neurogram Kiosk is passed. 'NK's' as they are commonly called, are more ubiquitous and popular to use than photo booths of the previous century ever were.

The neuro-circus begins

Outside the Crown Court is a vociferous assortment of protesters. Most of whom are affiliated with the MRA – the Memory Rights Alliance. They are shouting in unison, 'Keep your claims out of our brains!'.

Separated by a LVPC (low voltage police cordon) is a smaller contingent of pro-Cortx demonstrators who are likely paid to be there by Cortx. They are a fake 'grass roots' coalition whose job is in part to confuse the public about the issues being raised by the MRA. They call themselves Citizen's for Memory Liberty or the CML.

There are also a handful of neurogeeks. Neurogeeks love anything and everything to do with neurotech. They've been agitating for decades for neural implants and can be heard shouting 'Jack us in'. They travel to the Grand Canyon, not for the view, but to take deep breaths of nootropics while viewing hard core porn on their tabs.

Also outside the courthouse is a large turnout of international media. There are reporters from India, China, Australia, France, and America and lots of them are busy filming their news reports.

With protestors in the background and a stream of people entering the building, a reporter from India begins her report,

REPORTER

'Are memories that don't fade
worth fees that never end?'

A reporter from China can be overheard,

REPORTER

'Your memories will remain the
property of Cortx...'

As Gil's taxi navigates the London streets on his way to the court-house, he makes a desperate call to Sophie Hudson,

"Sophie, this is Gil. I'm still running a fever. I've had no real sleep for weeks. I'm getting death threats. Please call me back."

The interior of the Crown Courtroom is state-of-the-art. There are large floating membrane screens on each side of where the Judge presides. Smaller screens are located where the attorneys sit and on the Judges' elevated bench.

A web of nearly invisible overhead filaments guides a network of camera's which are no bigger than Brazil nuts to provide dynamic live coverage akin to that of a rock concert or a football match. Live coverage of the proceedings are fed to the membrane screens.

As with most judicial reviews, coverage will not be streamed live on the internet but the entire proceedings will be made public at the conclusion of the review.

Ken Marshall is opening his briefcase and removing documents.

Sophie Hudson enters the courtroom and walks past Marshall on her way to a seat. He greets her with a tone of familiarity,

"Dobraye utro Sophie."

Sophie responds plaintively,

"Good morning to you too."

"I didn't expect to see you on opening day"

"Nor did I."

Professionally, Sophie has always taken great pride in her meticulous and conscientious work as a programmer. Her acquired and obligatory social skills disguise the fact that at heart she is an introvert. She has never been further outside of her comfort zone than taking a seat on a hard bench in this courtroom chamber on this morning.

Sophie cannot stop asking herself how and why she let herself get sucked into this madness. She has never been more conflicted in her life. But to everyone else present, she appears a study in poise.

A Memory Rights Alliance colleague of Gil's, Graham Calder, is sitting on the opposite side of the courtroom to Sophie who has settled in near Ken Marshall.

Norman Palmer and several Cortx executives are clustered together behind Marshall sharing a private joke. The courtroom is also packed with reporters, supporters of the MRA, and a handful of neurogeeks.

Gil enters the courtroom getting a dagger stare from Palmer. As he walks past Sophie, he says her name with a slight dip of his head by way of saying hello,

"Sophie."

Sophie stiffens and glances towards him, but doesn't respond.

Gil glances back over his shoulder as he passes and blurts out,

"They don't own you."

Sophie shoots back,

"Neither do you."

The court clerk announces the arrival of the presiding Justice.

Everyone stands as Justice Jason Henderson enters the chambers. Nearing retirement, his hair is dishevelled, his robe looks like he sleeps in it, and he has an air of eccentricity.

On his resume are several landmark cases from decades ago including a high stakes battle over intellectual property rights when biotech giants made audacious claims of ownership of helical strips of real estate on the human genome.

Henderson settles into his chair. The clerk asks the court to please be seated.

Henderson makes his introductory comments,

"This Judicial Review has something to do with human memory and may well be contentious. Well, here's something I'd like everyone in theis courtroom to remember: This humble court has zero tolerance for any disruptions."

The judge glances toward the spectators who are likely supporters of the MRA and the plaintiff,

"Consider this a menacing glare!

"The plaintiff in this case – the Memory Rights Alliance – is challenging a patent decision that has enabled the defendant Cortx Enterprises to claim a human memory as their intellectual property. Also being challenged are several recent regulatory decisions including the approval of Cortx nootropics for human consumption and the decision to allow permanent charges for a new class of supposedly unforgettable memories.

"Mr. Marshall, Mr. Hinchliff, are you ready to upload?"

Marshall and Hinchliff respond in unison,

"Yes M'Lud"

"God's speed."

The two attorneys simultaneously approach the bench.

What appeared to be a solid wood veneer on the front of the Judge's bench slides open to reveal various computer ports and displays.

Marshall and Hinchliff simultaneously insert memory sticks into two separate but adjacent ports.

Two parallel light strips begin to glow with a bright expanding green line of light. The uploads appear to be in a race to the finish line.

All of the membrane screens in the courtroom come alive with flashing images of documents, charts, and photographs as case related materials are ingested.

Gil's upload finishes first. Henderson interjects,

Not quite a photo finish. Normally, I allow the Plaintiff to give the opening statement, but Mr. Marshall, you have made an urgent appeal to open. I will allow you to proceed. Surprise me.

Marshall thanks Henderson, but proceeds to fumble with the pile of documents in front of him. Henderson wastes no time becoming impatient.

> *Editors note: The hearings before Judge Jason Henderson took place in Chamber 3 over a 4 day period. The plaintiff called a total of 8 witnesses to testify, the defendant called 5 witnesses to testify. An edited version of the transcript and visual coverage of the hearing is available via the Chancery Court website.*

Judge Henderson,

"OK, Mr. Marshall, the egg timer is ticking."

Marshall has convinced himself that his opening gambit will be a legal grenade that will knock out the memory rights case in the opening minute of round one,

"M'Lud, I have here in my hand and have also uploaded for the record documentation which substantiates that counsel for the plaintiff has engaged in illegal acts of industrial espionage against the defendant Cortx and that his actions have endangered public safety, violated international laws, and brought dishonour to the profession and this court. I make a motion that the counsel for the plaintiff be immediately suspended pending a disciplinary hearing and that the case against Cortx be dismissed with prejudice."

Gil gritted his teeth, held his breath, and kept his nerve as Marshall made his plea to Judge Henderson. Gil was expecting the possibility of a Cortx bomb thrown in his direction at the outset. As soon as Marshall finishs his plea, Gil's eyes dart to Henderson.

Henderson leans back for several seconds to digest what has just been lobbed his way. His eyes glance upwards. It's not clear if he is accessing a thought or rolling his eyes,

"Mr. Marshall, do you think there is something of which I'm unaware regarding the circus of events surrounding this case?"

Sheepishly Marshall responds,

"No M'Lud."

"Well, until that disciplinary hearing, get on with it."

Marshall takes a deep breath,

"Yes M'Lud."

Gil is more than prepared to defend the actions that Marshall alluded to, but that is now another battle on another day. In the meantime, Gil is taking quiet satisfaction that Marshall's tactic is so summarily tossed aside by Henderson.

Marshall looks down at his notes for a moment then looks back up.

"The byproduct of years of research at a cost of billions, a nootropic breakthrough was achieved by Cortx which will likely lead to a Nobel Prize in neurochemistry for our extraordinary team of scientists.

"Cortx has secured patents for the manufacturing process of our unique nootropic atmospheres. We own the IP linked to the nootropic atmospheres we produce and significantly with regard to this challenge, we have secured the intellectual property rights for the unique neuro-protein formations which constitute the consolidated ensembles of neurons which are the episodic memories formed with the use of our value-added nootropics."

Henderson interjects,

"Just to be clear, for the record Mr. Marshall, Cortx is claiming ownership of a memory inside a consumer's head?"

Marshall gives a well rehearsed answer,

"M'Lud, in science and history, and I might add in law, a paradigm shift is always controversial. It can be counted on to be resisted fiercely, and debate, disorientation, and hostility can be expected until the science gets more widely understood, a change of world-view takes hold, and what was at first unthinkable becomes the new 'common sense'. What we are discussing is a milestone of enhanced human memory capacity.

"The answer to your question M'Lud is yes. Cortx by virtue of the intellectual property rights does have ownership of the memory inside a person's head – if that memory was consolidated by virtue of our nootropics. These are value-added, atemporal, protein encryptions."

Henderson interjects,

"Atemporal?"

"Yes M'Lud, 'atemporal' in that they will not fade in time."

Marshall allows the point to sink in, then continues,

"In our daily lives of being bombarded by deadening streams of frivolity, enduring acute information overload, and atomised attention spans, 'unforgettable' has become a rare and precious commodity.

"Also, given the transformative impact of AI on the worlds job markets, millions of people have more leisure time on their hands and nootropics offer a gratifying and enhanced entertainment experience.

"We not only have a fiduciary responsibility to our shareholders, but if we cannot generate a significant return on our formidable research investments, the ground-breaking work of Cortx would be impossible. It is important to see our supplemental cinema charges in that context.

"This case is about the fundamental rights of a corporate entity M'Lud. Our innovative payment model of 'micro-charges' is an extension of one of the most sacrosanct principles of modern society, the protection of private property."

Gil is doodling the letters P P P.

"The plaintiff will claim that nootropics are not safe. The plaintiff will argue that our established intellectual property rights violate some fuzzy notion of personal identity and a person's physical sanctity. The plaintiff will argue that our payment model violates consumer rights.

"We have uploaded for this court a 400 page report which contains the findings of our clinical trials which also includes the ruling of the NOC – the Neurotech Oversight Committee.

"Our product has been determined to be safe and reliable. Its societal and personal benefits have also been established. There has never been a Cortx product which has received closer scrutiny and oversight than our nootropic atmospheres.

"I would like to add M'Lud that this product has provided huge benefits to families with loved ones suffering from neuro-degenerative disease, it has helped to boost the reading scores of disadvantaged school children and it is playing a growing role in our national security.

"It's a new product rapidly achieving broad popular acceptance. Our customer satisfaction surveys provide data-sets to be proud of."

As Marshall continues, the court 'skycam' does a sweeping rock concert camera move from over the shoulder of Henderson into a close up shot of Marshall delivering his opening comments.

Off camera, sweat is pouring down Gil's face as he listens to Marshall's opening statement. He mutters under his breath,

"Yeah right, one conglomerates' property rights are another person's mind fuck."

It's clear to Gil that if the Cortx legal strategy of discrediting him from the outset didn't succeed, they would present their case as an expression of the inevitable march of scientific progress that only a raggedy group of neuro-Luddites would waste their time to stand in the way of.

But the Cortx payment model of micro-charges was less motivated by an act of fiduciary responsibility than it was born out of sheer fiscal panic by an over leveraged and deeply indebted conglomerate down on its R&D luck.

But nootropics and micro-charges weren't the issues that initially fired up Gil and gave birth to the memory rights movement.

TWO YEARS EARLIER

The Cortx neuro-moonshot

Outside a handsome Georgian building which is home to the Royal Society in London, are armed police with visors down holding large plastic shields and keeping watchful eyes on a couple of hundred boisterous protesters brandishing placards. The police are from the much despised 'Metropolitan Police Data Unit'.

The protesters are shouting:

Stop the torture NOW!
Free Alex! Stop the torture NOW! Free Alex!

The transparent shields of the police 'Data Unit' are designed to also display text or images. They are wirelessly linked to a central data base which in turn gets a feed from the body cams worn by the police. With the use of facial recognition and voice recognition software a protestor who is heard or comes within the field of vision of a cop will in a matter of seconds see their name, address, date of birth, national insurance number and banking details including their current bank balance displayed on the shield. It's a most effective tool of intimidation. Unless you cover your face and eyes and remain mute, the software will likely ID you.

The fortified line of police act as a barrier between the protesters and a long meandering queue of families and children who are slowly snaking their way into the Royal Society building. Amidst the families and children is Gil Hinchliff.

Overlooking the scene on a rooftop opposite the Royal Society is a billboard size membrane screen with changing ads. One is for FACEBANK with the tag line:

*'For all your friends and family,
financial security is just a click away'.*

The long queue leads into a spacious room with ornate wood panelling which houses a large sleek stainless steel cage in which a single parrot lives.

The bird with its red tail feathers and grey plumage has an odd but attractive knit cap on its head held in place by a fine strap. The bird cage is surrounded by CCTV cameras and directional microphones. As the line of people flow by, Gil manages to pause long enough to press his face against the stainless steel bars of the cage and make eye contact with the intriguing creature inside.

Meet Alex, mascot for the neurotech revolution. He's an African Grey parrot with a memory chip in his brain. At first, most neuroscientists thought he was a hoax. But Alex is for real, a parrot who recites Shakespeare.

Every utterance of Alex is recorded for posterity but it's hard to predict when Alex will talk or what exactly he will have to say. His sentences can come out a bit fragmented and he's beginning to sound hoarse. But this afternoon, what he has to say will be clearly intelligible to anyone familiar with Richard II, Act III, Scene 4. Alex clears his throat as loquacious parrots with chip implants tend to do, then begins,

*"Oh pressed to death... through want of speaking... How dares thy
harsh rude tongue...sound unpleasant news..."*

Gil is dumbstruck. He's pushed along by the sudden crush of people wanting to get a better shot of Alex on their icams.

Soon after leaving the Royal Society, Gil meets up with his co-conspirator Tovy and together they manage to circumnavigate the protestors and police and make their way into the building opposite the Royal Society.

They manoeuvre past security on the pretext of visiting one of the businesses upstairs. As they are climbing stairs in a darkened stairwell, Gil is talking on his mobile,

"I'll be by the hospital tonight. I'm sorry, I can't make it any sooner. (His voice cracks) Tell mum I love her."

Gil and Tovy make it onto the rooftop, position a small wedge to keep the roof top door ajar, and make their way to the base of the large membrane screen.

One of the policemen in riot gear below looks up and sees two silhouettes moving along the rooftop. He gets on his walkie talkie.

Tovy pulls out a toolkit from his rucksack. Gil pulls out a micro-memory card with a reader. Tovy unscrews the cover to a box at the base of the electronic billboard where a feeder cable passes.

They are almost done cutting and splicing the feeder cable to the micro-card reader as two cops are entering the building.

Gil and Tovy hold their nerve. They complete the splice then hurry back to the roof door, remove the wedge, close the door behind them and start to race down the stairwell. Just as they get below the landing of the top floor, the lift door opens and two cops emerge with stun guns in hand and start climbing the stairway to the roof.

Tovy is a hacker with an anarchistic streak and is always up for an adventure. Having recently passed the bar exam, Gil is taking a risk of flushing his nascent career as a lawyer down the drain.

Among the protestors, there was little notice when the membrane screen initially went black. Then someone points and heads turn to look up.

On the billboard, a series of grisly images of dead, mutilated parrots start to flash by. A bold text message rolls up,

> *Whilst 1000 parrots mutilated*
> *by the whores of neurotech. Nay spoketh a word!*

The video appearing on the hijacked billboard is met with hoots of approval and applauds from the protestors.

There was hardly a mainstream e-zine cover that didn't feature Alex – in fashion, news, or sports. From *Cosmo to Vogue*, from *Time* to the *Economist*. Even the top consumer e-zine *Try* had a sexy pull out centerfold of Alex. It would be hard to exaggerate the international frenzy and controversy generated by a birds' brain.

The shareprice of Cortx went through the roof. Sci-fi had been fantasizing about intelligence expanding neural implants for so long it was a tired cliché. But, it was a tired cliché seemingly on the cusp of being imitated by life. Alex was a neurotech 'moonlanding' moment and the harbinger of the next great epistemological leap for humankind.

Cortx and other neurotech giants were known to be experimenting with chip implants and neural interfaces for years, but Alex was seized upon as proof positive of a potential neurotech killer app. He was a finance leveraging, market share boosting, neural implant marketing super bird. A new parrot paradigm.

One of the satirical British e-zines had the headline,

> *Alex Asks Humanity a Question,*
> *TO BEAK OR NOT TO BEAK?*

The permanent memory revolution was off to a flying start.

While the earliest commercial uses of nootropics began to stir concerns and scattered opposition, it was Alex who was the catalyst for bringing a number of groups together and laying the groundwork for a memory rights movement and fightback.

The 'Ah ha!' moment for Gil was reading an e-zine essay by a group of culture jammers in New Zealand who called themselves the 'Yes Brainers'. They were really smart and writing about the early marketing of nootropics by Cortx and their goal of turning tourists into memory junkies at heritage sites.

Politically, they critiqued the approval process of nootropics and discerned conflicts of interest, they raised troubling questions about their potential neurotoxicity, and on the legal front, given the long term unknowns of so called permanent memories, questioned the validity of 'informed consent' by those who consume nootropics.

Gil and the 'Yes Brainers' were united about Alex. This African Grey was undoubtedly an extremely smart creature to begin with, was not made any smarter as a result of a chip implant, and he was a shocking example of animal torture and cruelty run amok. They were also affronted by the marketing of nootropics and the Cortx spin on neural implants promising 'memory supremacy'.

Cortx was eagerly trying to sign up early adopters and take deposits for the nano-surgery to implant the neural interface. It was just what a deeply polarized society needed, technology that would eventually lead to a new memory underclass. It was not a big leap to a new social divide between memory have's and memory have not's.

About a dozen groups, including NeuroWatch, Genepeace, Advocats Sans Frontiers, and the All Creature Rights Collective – started to talk to each other about principles to organise around. They were queasy about nootropics and deeply disturbed by chip implants. The issues were only just beginning to hit a public nerve.

What broke things open was a young researcher at a Cortx lab where the neural interface was being developed. He was so distressed by what he witnessed, he made contact with Gil Hinchliff and passed on a memory stick with hundreds of photos of mutilated parrots. The stick also had sketchy data about ongoing experiments on humans at the Cortx 'K-Lab' in Kyrgyzstan.

Gil and Graham gave copies of the photos to all the media. Most of the mainstream press were reluctant to publish them fearful they would be sued by Cortx. But, they flooded the internet and a bottom up backlash against Cortx was brewing.

Memory crucible

It's the early evening as Gil arrives at the hospital waiting room outside the ICU of the London Central Infirmary where his mother is being cared for.

To Gil's surprise, Dena is sitting there quietly looking at a magazine. She looks up at Gil with watery and empathetic eyes.

"Dena, you didn't tell me you were coming..."

Dena's response was to give Gil a big gentle hug. It was a lingering hug he really needed. Dena then whispered into Gil's ear,

"You better go see your mum. I'll see you later."

Gil kissed Dena on the cheek and she left him alone in the waiting room.

The sounds and smells of the ICU are embedding themselves in a deep niche of Gil's unconscious. His brain is imprinting them with traumatic emotional associations that will exist in buried or not so buried form for the rest of his life.

As Gil enters the ICU he sees his mum surrounded by monitors displaying vital signs and ensnared by a web of tubes. A doctor is shining his penlight into her eyes – just another patient on life support. Gil can just make out that her pupils are not reacting to the light. The blood drains from Gil's face. He feels a deep chill.

Gil has a tightness in his chest which triggers a physical memory of the panic attacks he used to have as a child which felt like a waking nightmare accompanied by a terrifying and buzzing anxiety. He would be unable to catch his breath. It was as if he was drowning. He didn't know what they were as a child. He was always alone when they happened.

Tears are welling up in Gil's eyes. It was always his mum who came to the rescue. It was always his mum who would talk him down, calm him. It was always his mum who would instruct him to take three deep breaths and hold him close to her.

Approaching Gil and the doctor from behind is Gil's older brother Stephen. Stephen is in his late thirties and in contrast to Gil, very conservatively dressed in a dark suit and tie. The atmosphere is grim.

Gil asks the doctor if there is any change. The doctor responds to them both,

"I'm very sorry boys. The stroke caused massive damage."

But Gil persisted,

"There must be something that can be done…"

The doctor spoke quietly,

"The damage is in the brain stem. Most involuntary functions are affected."

Gil's brain was not ready to accept what it was hearing,

"What about neuro-regenerative stem cells Doc? Does this hospital have capacity for synaptic nano-repairs?"

The doctor looks down to the floor then glances back up,

"There is a counselling service here which any immediate family member of a patient may access. There's also an interfaith chapel on the ground floor. Your family will need to make some decisions on your mother's behalf. You can always reach me. Sorry, Mr. Hinchliff, boys, I need to see another patient now."

Stephen thanked the doctor as he clipped his penlight into a shirt pocket and left the ICU.

Stephen rounded on Gil,

"Dad was here earlier. He couldn't wait forever for you to show up."

Gil wasn't having it,

"Too bad".

Stephen persisted,

"You need to call him."

Gil asked,

"Why?"

His brother shot back,

"You're ripping his heart out."

Gil wasn't moved,

"That's a laugh. I didn't know he had one."

Stephen defaulted to older brother,

"When are you going to grow up?"

Gil defaulted to rebellious younger brother,

"All I need is a job at the Treasury like you, right?"

Stephen had enough,

"Screw you Gil."

For Gil and Stephen, growing up translated into growing apart.

As children they were always verbally or physically sparring until one or the other started to cry.

Stephen is convinced that Gil once tried to impale him with a fencing sword which belonged to their father. It was one of the two swords which always hung as a crossed pair in the center of their living room wall above some fencing trophies.

It's funny how two memories of the same event can be so dramatically different.

Stephen recalls an act of attempted fratricide. Gil recalls a well timed symbolic gesture made with a sharp projectile to protest an injustice. What that injustice was has long since been forgotten.

They were chasing and screaming at each other and running over couches and knocking over lamps when Gil did grab one of the swords off the living room wall. Stephen fled to their bedroom and as the bedroom door was closing Gil launched the sword.

The sword embedded itself with a 'boing' into the hollow panel wooden door and hung there cartoon-like bouncing up and down. When Stephen felt the coast was clear, he emerged to see the unambiguous evidence of attempted murder.

But Gil has always maintained that if crime scene investigators took a casual look they would see the obvious, that the sword had entered the door at a near perpendicular angle. That is unambiguous proof that the door was almost fully closed at the time the sword was launched and of no actual danger to Stephen. Such an investigation might still conclude that children should not play with very sharp swords.

The hole in the bedroom door remained there for years as a memento of childhood battles that run amok.

Gil's brother also has very different memories of their father. Stephen recalls their father spending lots of time with Gil when he was a toddler – that he was always playing with little Gil on the kitchen counter top, so much so that he was jealous. Gil has no memories whatsoever of his father playing with him in the kitchen or anywhere else. His main memory of his father was of him being AWOL as a parent.

When the time came to think about the possibility of university, with his fathers wholehearted approval, Stephen studied macroeconomics with an aspiration to be an actuarial or an investment analyst. Gil wanted to study philosophy with an aspiration to – study philosophy. He wanted to be a full-time philosophy student. But there were no universities left where an undergraduate could do that. It was one of the rare times that Gil's mother half heartedly sided with her husband about the insecurities of such a career path.

Gil's father was Mr. Tough Love about philosophy and made it clear that even if Gil could find some anachronistic place that offered philosophy as a full-time major, he would not pay for such a useless indulgence. His father laid down the law, and the law was – law. Gil could study philosophy as a minor if he majored in law.

Gil hemmed and hawed and finally gave in. But his dad wasn't too pleased that Gil's graduate thesis was on the structural inadequacies of criminal justice systems in prosecuting transnational corporate crimes against nature.

———————————————

Memories not meant to be

Gil arrives back home from the hospital looking very depressed. Dena welcomes him with a bottle of wine and a pizza ready to throw into the thermawave.

Initially, there is a loud silence. Dena knew better than to ask Gil how his mum was doing, but she eventually does ask,

"What is your family planning to do?"

Gil stared off into the mid-distance for close to half a minute, then responded,

"I don't know for sure. It's not looking good. Do I believe in miracles? I don't know. I'd like us to wait a couple of days before making a decision."

Gil and Dena Sustrand met at university several years before at a presentation made by Advocats Sans Frontier which had been organised by the student body – not by the university itself.

ASF talked about the legal work they were doing in mostly non-western countries in the aftermath of wars, natural disasters, and in places where there are unfolding crimes against nature.

Dena has a streak of idealism which drew Gil towards her and was the initial bond between them. After graduation, her first serious job was at a law firm specialising in mergers and acquisitions. More conservative values and a cynical streak began to emerge.

Politics has become more and more a wedge between them and Gil's very recent battles with some form of psychosis was causing a deepening fracture in a relationship which was breaking apart.

They had polished off the bottle of wine. Dena walked over to the fridge hoping to find more wine inside. On the fridge door were photos of their first big adventure driving across Eastern Europe together which they did soon after they started to date.

One of the photos on the fridge is from inside a 4x4 looking out the front windscreen. The water level of a deep stream or shallow river is almost to the top of the windscreen. Tipsy from the wine, Dena starts to riff,

"I'll never forget that trip. I thought we were goners. I thought we really were gonna drown to death".

For Gil, the memory that photo evokes is a peak adventure moment, not a near death experience.

Even without nootropics, neither will forget the helpful strangers, hostile locals, the suspicious officials, the food poisoning, sleeping with mountain goats, and the forging of that stream in a mad Romanians' 4x4. At that moment, as they watched the water level rising almost to the top of the windscreen, when almost the entire car was underwater – Gil did not feel panic, he had the presence of mind to take an unforgettable photo. Dena was expecting her life to begin flashing before her eyes.

Gil is further depressed by the wine and beginning to slur his words,

"I don't deserve to have any memories – none, nothing."

Dena gives a quizzical look,

"What do you mean Gil?"

Gil has entered a very dark place,

"I really don't think I should even exist."

It isn't that Dena lacks empathy, but she has never heard Gil talk like that before. She doesn't have a clue as to where it is coming from and her first impulse is flight – not engagement.

With the anguish of a broken soul Gil then said,

"I should never have been born, I should never have been born"

Dena is taken aback,

"That's pretty heavy Gil."

Dena is feeling emotionally cold. In the early days of their love affair, she asked herself if he was the one. But tonight, she has lots of her own anxieties on her mind about work and her father's health. Her aspirations for a family are on the back burner.

Gil has lately been on another planet. Dena doesn't have a clue as to where Gil's comments are coming from. She thinks it's the wine talking. Dena knows that Gil needs some kind of help, but she is not going to put up with another night of Gil as psycho and she as psycho-therapist,

"Gil, I hope you don't mind if I don't spend the night. I'm going to head back to my place, but we can speak tomorrow. I'm so sorry about your mum."

With that, Dena gave Gil a half hearted hug and left.

Parrots and PR disasters

At a news kiosk outside the office of the Memory Rights Alliance, the morning tab has a photo of Alex below the headline:

ALEX CHIP LEAVES
LONG TRAIL OF DEAD
PARROTS

The story included several grisly photos of decapitated parrots. It was a PR disaster for Cortx.

By mid-morning, Gil is sitting quietly at his desk at the MRA office. The office is bathed in morning light but the mood is surprisingly subdued given the level of excitement the previous day at the Royal Society protest and given the publicity that the release of photos of mutilated birds has generated.

There is a flood of morning emails. The MRA is being congratulated by groups in dozens of cities, more people want to join the MRA, and there are several emails promising significant donations.

Their actions have inspired plans for more anti-Cortx rallies at Cortx regional offices from Seattle to New Delhi.

Gil stands up from his desk and turns around to review his 'Neurotech Corruption Flow Chart'. It is one of his pet projects. The chart is about 3 meters long and has names and photos of company execs, regulators, politicians, and university department heads.

Gil and Graham have been discussing the possibility of a lawsuit against Cortx. If not a lawsuit, then a Judicial Review if they can make a convincing case that existing laws are inadequate or have been abused. But in either case, it's an uphill battle. Petitioning for a Judicial Review is not too expensive and they have nothing to lose for trying.

Graham slowly approaches Gil,

"So sorry to hear about your mum, Gil."

Gil doesn't look to Graham,

"Yeah, thanks."

Graham is being very sympathetic at first,

"Are you sure you want to be here?"

Gil turns towards Graham,

"Not sure where else to be."

Gil steps back from the flow chart he was just adding a name to,

"There you have it! The Cortx game plan for the end of human memory as we know it – or should I say, as we remember it."

In a rapid-fire delivery, Gil summarises the chart,

"Cortx endows neuroscience departments at major Uni's. Courses get re-designed to better fit Cortx R&D priorities. Retired Cortx execs get appointed to the neurotech regulatory and oversight committees. Cortx lobbyists write the regulations and work as bag men for the MP's who champion and pass the neurotech friendly laws.

"I'm sure Cortx could get LSD approved for pre-schoolers if they wanted to."

Graham knows how passionate even strident Gil is on matters of neurotech, but there has been a blinking orange light in Grahams head about Gil which started blinking red following the recent protest and it's finally coming out,

"Gil, please don't stitch us up."

Gil was not expecting that,

"Excuse me?"

Graham elaborated,

"Your heroics could stitch us up and destroy our credibility, and you'll end up disbarred."

Gil was indignant,

"Heroics? Credibility? I suppose it doesn't mean much to you that our exposé of Cortx has made the front page of the tabs? That we're getting friendly emails from potential donors?"

"What if they trace the billboard back to you meaning us? Cortx would love nothing more than to see us branded as neuro-terrorists. We were about to release those sick photos to the press anyway. We need you as a lawyer, don't throw that away. Why would you jeopardize that? What you did could have really backfired. I would love to have had the opportunities you've had Gil."

"What fucking op...?"

"I wish my Dad had 'forced' me to get a law degree."

"Keep my goddamned father out of this."

Gil gestures to the flow chart,

"We're being stitched up all right, but not by me."

Augmented bird brain

For Cortx, the animal cruelty stories in the tabs is like a bad dream. It's very unpleasant while it's happening, but likely to fade quickly in the morning and soon to be forgotten.

Overall, the suits at Cortx are thrilled about being part of a neurotech revolution that is promising to deliver a new era of human enhancement with its superstar Bard spouting parrot as trailblazer.

A lot is riding on the back of a bird with an augmented brain. Cortx has invested billions in developing the interface for neural implants. They expect to use the hype around Alex as leverage to raise more capital, boost share price, and bring about a leap in human cognitive capacity.

Looking back, neural implants of previous decades were marvels in their day but primitive compared to the K-Lab neural interface. In the past, neural implants successfully controlled epileptic seizures, restored motor neuron activities to injured limbs, functioned as brainwave activated commands to turn a washing machine on or a light off, or give binary 'yes' or 'no' commands via a computer interface. The 'mind reading' implants which actually read subvocalisations are pretty cool but they are only one way and not augmented memory. Alex left all these in the dust.

Relative to their huge investment in Alex, Cortx was banking on monetizing dozens of patents developed in the course of their R&D. They were also acquiring patents the easy way by buying up small start-ups doing ingenious work.

One start-up which Cortx bought and was crucial to the success of Alex was doing pioneering work in the rapidly advancing field of 'neurofibrology'. It's the art and science of weaving together and fusing neurons to conductive polymers. It was estimated that a minimally effective interface for an implant would require a linkage to at least a hundred thousand carefully chosen ensembles of neurons in the hippocampus fused with as many ultra thin conductive polymers on the interface. The weaving and fusing is done with AI guided nanobot surgery. A brilliant neuroscientist at K-Lab designed an endogenous method to power the implant by tapping into the chemically generated electricity of the brain.

For close to two years, executives at Cortx HQ in London received a steady stream of upbeat news and exciting progress reports from hyper-ventilating middle managers at K-Lab.

As a multi-trillion E-ren conglomerate, Cortx was the darling of the Ntech100 on the Shang Hai stock index. It was unthinkable to the Borg mindset of Cortx exec's that Alex was a Cortx breakthrough that could lead to its downfall.

In the immediate aftermath of the public debut of Alex at the Royal Society, the Cortx chief financial officer prepared a report for CEO Norman Palmer. As it turned out, the PR disaster was the least of their corporate worries.

The CFO's report was blunt. While crunching all the numbers related to the R&D of Alex, she found it hard to see the other side of a mountain range of debt.

Unless the Alex breakthrough could be rapidly monetised on a large scale, the Alex enterprise was in danger of bankrupting the R&D division with catastrophic knock on effects for annual earnings and stock valuation. In the hope of stimulating this new market, Cortx had the bird insured for a billion E-ren. The premiums were of no big financial consequence and as a publicity stunt for a press release, it was an occasion to trumpet Alex as the most unique and valuable bird who ever lived.

Fiscal projections of even best case scenarios were sobering. Based on projected costs of nanosurgical implantation of a remotely programmable endogenously powered memory augmenting chip, only the top 1% of the population were likely to be able to afford the procedure. A survey of potential early adopters within that demographic indicated that only about 3% of the 1% would consider having the procedure done.

That percentage would be expected to grow over time with effective marketing, testimonials, etc., but for the short and medium term, the vast majority of the target demographic still preferred reading a tab edition of Shakespeare's collected works over brain surgery.

The truth about how the human trials were going was grim news.

Rumours and reckonings

In the cherrywood corporate boardroom of Cortx, CEO Norman Palmer is swiping through a tab. He stares at the headline about Alex then throws it down on the conference table in disgust – nearly cracking the tab screen.

On a trophy shelf behind him is a larger than life bronze statue of a parrot with its wings fully extended. Its sharp beak open wide as if to screech or perhaps make a speech.

Palmer called for the meeting as a matter of urgency. The CFO report has really rattled him. Rumours about how the human trials are going is causing deep anxiety. He needs information. Decisions need to be made.

Present is Ken Marshall, Sally Zhao from PR, the CFO Patti Harrison, and the manager of K-Lab Dr. Marcus Van Trotta.

Palmer starts things off,

"Thank you all for coming. We have a lot of ground that needs to be covered – and please don't feed me bullshit."

Palmer asks Van Trotta for a K-Lab update,

"We were euphoric when Alex happened. We really thought we had cracked it."

Palmer stares intently at Van Trotta.

"All the right neurons were fused seamlessly. It was really incredible, but, the scale of a bird's brain was very difficult to work with from the outset... We had trouble duplicating the results."

Palmer looks down and starts to fiddle with a pen. He then repeats three words,

"Trouble duplicating results?"

"I wouldn't go so far as to say Alex was a fluke, but the margin of error on the scale of a bird brain which is 1/100th the size of a human brain is extremely tight. We all felt, and I believe rightly so, that moving ahead to human trials was justifiable and gave us much better odds at refining and perfecting the selection and neuron fusion process. The results of human tests have not been as encouraging as we had hoped."

If the results weren't as bad as they were, Trotta would be merely embarrassed to read the results, but as they stood, Trotta was actually scared to read out a summary to Palmer, so he handed him the document and points to the section which summarises 'side effects'.

Palmer reads out loud,

"...A high probability of seizures, strokes, extreme migraines, aphasias, blackouts, and in some cases tumour formation."

Palmer puts the document down,

"Oh, this sounds just great. Let's not sugar coat it. What else?"

"Well actually Mr. Palmer, there were salt deposits starting to coat the polymers as a result of the electric current which was contributing to some of the side effects, but we fixed that. There were also cognitive difficulties initialising the implant."

"Initializing the implant?"

"To be able to successfully access the implant, there's an early stage when you have to cognitively 'find' it. It's akin to trying to recall a memory. You have to learn to steer your intentionality to the neurons that connect to the implant. You're chasing a cluster of a hundred thousand neurons out of 100 billion. It's like trying to find a micro-needle in a mountain sized haystack. It's a very frustrating process for most subjects. We see lots of long blank stares. But once the implant is 'located', it becomes easier to access."

"Would it help to up the scale of the fusing?"

"At present the recipients must be sedated for between 2 and 3 days to complete the surgical process. To fuse another 100 thousand neurons would mean much higher costs and likely mean a higher mortality rate."

"I did not hear that! Jesus Christ."

While Cortx publicly gives lip service to the recently revised Helsinki Accords on human experimentation, the truth is, K-Lab is where it is in Central Asia in an effort to evade as much as possible existing Ntech oversight frameworks. To their credit, some Cortx neuroscientists pushed back hard on the decision to begin human experimentation. But the pushback to the pushback was even harder.

A cart of sandwiches, coffee, and snacks is wheeled into the board room by two Cortx hospitality workers. They begin to serve the coffee.

Palmer is looking pale,

"Folks, let's take a bit of a break... I need to digest what I'm hearing."

Sally Zhao wanders over to Palmer and they begin to chat. Palmer has always liked Sally and while she's not a scientist, he thinks she's the smartest of the lot.

Sally is trying to lift Palmer's spirits,

"I wouldn't be so down about the interface Mr. Palmer. Think of all the good that was achieved by the retinal implants. Giving a person their sight back is something to be hugely proud of."

Palmer puts a half teaspoon of sugar into his coffee, some cream, and stirs,

"I am proud Sally, but to be honest, it's extremely niche. Had the CFO not proposed the 'PAYS' model, I don't think it would have been cost effective to be in the business of curing blindness. It's too narrow a corporate vision to have."

Palmer takes a sip,

"Sally, after our break, can you give us an update on what you've been up to? I've heard you've been revisiting the nootropics."

"For sure Mr. Palmer."

Palmer puts his cup down and in a confiding tone says to Sally,

"We may have to cut our losses on the implants. I have to decide on whether or not to pull the plug."

Alex was supposed to be the opening act of the next big revolutionary thing from Cortx. The plans for a lateral move into family entertainment and the use of nootropics in cinemas had been put on the back burner.

Palmer was now desperate for something to boost revenues in the next quarter. He needed something with less risk, something big, and something that might deflect from the implant fumble.

After the coffee break, Sally prepares to give an update to the others. She is petite, fashionably dressed, and lives and breathes market research. She shuffles her papers, clears her throat, takes a sip of water, removes her eyeglasses, and begins her presentation at warp speed,

"I still have a great deal faith in the potential mass appeal of our nootropics. What's so neat about them is that they put an end to memory shaming. They make people feel super smart and without any need for surgery. Our surveys indicate that lots of people are squeamish about the idea of surgery. That is definitely a hurdle to the growth potential and revenue potential of implants.

"Nootropics are needed now more than ever."

"A recent university study done by a neuroscience department has documented that the average size and weight of the human hippocampus in adults between the ages of 25 and 40 is shrinking.

"As you know, the hippocampus is that part of the brain where most memories are processed. Attention spans which have been shortening for a century have fallen off a cliff. From a marketing perspective, studies also show that there is a diminishing cognitive capacity to recall commercial messaging both consciously and more importantly – unconsciously. I don't need to spell out how scary and potentially catastrophic that is for the economy. But in this cognitive crisis is opportunity.

The nootropical good ol' days

Long before Cortx bribed UN officials with massive 'donations' to allow the nootropic experience to be commercially introduced at World Heritage sites such as the Grand Canyon, nootropics, funnily enough were free.

Cortx nootropics were rolled out stealthily upon an unsuspecting public literally under their noses in marketing campaigns for a variety of fashion designers, auto makers, and perfume companies.

More than half a century ago, 'Scratch & Sniff' stickers made their olfactory debut in magazines as a gimmick for marketing perfumes. But a few years ago, under the radar of regulation or oversight, Cortx introduced and aggressively pushed a novel twist on this quaint device. They were called SSR's and they promised to improve between five and tenfold the efficacy of 'Scratch & Sniff' for sales. It was akin to 'Scratch & Sniff' on steroids. The SSR stood for 'Scratch & Sniff & Remember'.

They quickly caught on. Today, to the extent you can still find printed magazines, it's hard to find one that doesn't have an SSR or two or three.

For better or worse, governments, political parties, and all kinds of hucksters have also started to use SSR's. A simple design modification was introduced to activate the nootropic effect by simply pulling apart two pages in a magazine.

Even if you didn't want to scratch and sniff a sticker, merely turning the page could activate an SSR on a recruitment ad for the army or a real estate scammer selling agricultural land with planning permission to build in the arctic.

Gil enjoyed following the antics of the 'Yes Brainers' who were so ahead of the curve on memory rights issues. At the peak of SSR usage, they demanded government regulation and organized a protest outside a Cortx office in Christchurch, New Zealand. They hired a dump truck to unload a vast pile of horse manure in front of the entrance. On the top this hill of horseshit, they planted a big sign which had a Cortx logo and the message:

SCRATCH AND SNIFF THIS!

In the Cortx boardroom, Sally is taking a sip of water and about to finish her cheerleading for nootropics,

"There is a paradoxical flip side to micro-attention spans. My research has also detected across the demographic spectrum of ABC1 that there is a significant craving for more lasting, vivid, and pleasurable memories that break through the sensory clutter."

Palmer thanks Zhao for her nootropic pep talk and invites the Chief Financial Officer Patti Harrison to speak,

"Patti, what are your thoughts?"

Of everyone in the room, Harrison has been with Cortx the longest. She's managed numerous Cortx shit storms in the past and knows that Cortx is now facing one of its biggest. Harrison is aware she has the good will of Palmer and not solely because she knows where the bodies are buried. Palmer thought the PAYS model which Harrison suggested for retinal implants was absolutely brilliant.

To have a Cortx retinal implant is extremely expensive. For extremely rich people who are blind or going blind receiving the implant is invariably akin to a miracle. There is even the case of a middle aged heiress who has been blind from childhood who received an implant and wrote Cortx into her will.

Suffice it to say these are people who wouldn't necessarily blink at any price to have their sight restored.

The PAYS model is a payment innovation for people who were blind or close to blind as a result of degenerative eye disease or injury who had undergone the retinal implant surgery developed by Cortx.

Cortx owned the intellectual property of the physical implant. They had patents for specially designed surgical tools used to do the implant. They owned the intellectual property of the software that operated the surgical instruments. They owned the intellectual property of the retinal protein maintenance delivery procedure and they owned the intellectual property of the synthetic proteins that needed to be maintained. So, Harrison's suggestion was rather than charge a flat rate, Cortx could charge an up front fee covering the costs of the procedure with a colossal mark up and then on top of that, lease the eyesight rights back to people who had their vision restored on a monthly or annual basis. It was a 20/20 win/win situation. 'PAYS' is an acronym for 'Pay As You See'.

There were endless tears of joy in spite of the astronomical initial cost and virtually no bitching about having to make exorbitant monthly payments to Cortx. The option of annual payments rather than monthly proved to be the preferred payment arrangement to keep eyesight in working order. These payments would continue for the rest of a person's life. PAYS is not an insignificant revenue stream for the Ocular Solutions Division of Cortx.

With the success of the PAYS model in mind, Harrison made her pitch,

"I couldn't agree more with everything that Sally was saying. Norman, I hear you loud and clear we need to fight our way out of this quagmire as best we can and as soon as we can. I was having a chat with Ken earlier about the feasibility of applying the PAYS model to nootropic consumption in the context of the eidetic cinema concept which has been on the back burner. Ken kinda lit up about it."

Ken interjects,

"I think it can fly, I think it's a great idea..."

Harrison picks up the thread,

"We batted some ideas around. Ken clearly thought it was defensible. I think we need to proceed carefully regarding what and when.

"In contrast to PAYS, rather than aim for massive ongoing charges from a small number of people, we go for very small charges from millions of people. Sally, can you do some chicken scratchings on this?"

This was something Sally was eager to jump on,

"By the end of this week I will have some pricing, growth, and income projections to be reviewed by Patti, I will speak with the back office about the feasibility of building a new payment platform to reduce if not completely eliminate processing of payment costs, I will conduct some focus groups, and have some initial ideas for marketing."

Palmer was feeling buoyed by the discussion,

"Sally, Patti, Ken, you guys are brilliant. Not sure if we want to proceed carefully or boldly! let's take it to the movies."

Palmer's colleagues were not expecting the outburst from Palmer which followed,

"Fuck Alex. I want every movie goer to love it, I want every teacher to need it, I want every army to require it, I want every pathetic tourist to gag on it."

As they all got up to leave the conference room, Palmer turned to the bronze statue of the African Grey and said under his breath,

"Sorry bro."

Rattling the cage

Gil and Graham are sitting in a corner booth sipping on pints at a very noisy and very packed London pub on a Friday night. They have come down off the high of the Royal Society protest and the black eye the MRA gave to Cortx in the tabs.

Sitting near Gil and Graham with his back to them is Geoff Weyland. Geoff is in his mid 20's with neatly trimmed short black hair and wearing a white shirt and wire rimmed eyeglasses. He looks extremely nervous as he stares off into the distance. His right leg has the shakes.

It's not entirely out of context that Geoff would be sitting with his back to Gil. Gil doesn't look directly at him but acknowledges his presence,

"Hey Geoff."

Gil is met with silence.

Graham has met Geoff on only one previous occasion but can sense something is wrong,

"Are you OK?"

Graham is also met with silence.

Gil and Graham take a couple of more sips expecting the silence from Geoff to eventually crack.

It does. Half muttering to himself Geoff begins to talk,

"This is it guys. The Gestapo is grilling all the lab workers. IT has brought in a forensic team. They're out to crucify whoever released those parrot photos. I can't help anymore..."

Geoff puts down his pint and leaves the pub.

As Geoff leaves the pub, a photo is taken of him via a telephoto lens.

Inside the pub, Gil and Graham are assessing the loss of a crucial inside source. They are at a loss to come up with an alternative. Geoff's help was invaluable. Graham puts down his pint,

"I hope he'll be OK."

As Gil and Graham leave the pub, photo's are taken of their departure.

Opening inoculation

The court camera is slowly moving in for a close up on the lead attorney for Cortx – Ken Marshall – as he continues his opening argument. It's standard for an opening to anticipate your opponents strongest case against you and to 'inoculate' the judge, jury, or magistrate in advance.

"The plaintiff will argue there is no legal precedent for our claim to own the rights to a human memory and that we should never have been granted a patent in the first instance. That argument M'Lud is clearly moot.

"For the record, there are important legal precedents I would like to reference..."

As Marshall speaks, Gil is in a cold sweat. He's struggling to stay focused on Marshall as his attention drifts to a childhood memory of his mum trying to talk him down from one of his panic attacks.

Her voice and demeanour is very quiet and gentle as she asks Gil,

"Tell me my precious little monkey, is there something you have seen that has upset you, is there some bad thought that you can't get out of your head?"

Gil is tearing up and wipes his face with a damp tissue.

Marshall is close to concluding,

"...So while the Supreme Court did rule that BioRaid Pharmaceuticals could not claim ownership of a naturally occurring genomic structure they discovered, the court did rule that their intellectual property rights for the gene structure they had modified were legitimate..."

Gil knew the case well,

"Objection M'Lud. That is a distortion of the Supreme Court ruling. The modified gene structure in question was not inside a person's body but used externally and solely for diagnostic purposes."

It's traditional courtroom courtesy not interrupt or object when either side is presenting their opening comments. But Gil is not feeling especially compelled to show such courtesy.

Marshall wasn't phased. It was a legal parry that he was more than up for,

"M'Lud, whether that modified gene structure was inside or outside a person's body is not relevant. The legal requirement for a patent is for the invention or creation to be adjudged 'a new arrangement of matter'. There is no specificity that this new arrangement of matter be internal or external to the human body.

"It was a modified version of a naturally occurring gene structure which received the patent and it was upheld on appeal. This is only one important precedent to draw the courts attention to..."

Judge Henderson interjects a question,

"Lets say I have a memory that I will never forget. For example, let's say it's a fantastic memory of the day I caught an 11 kilo Rainbow trout fishing in Scotland. Except for some form of brain disease which I dare not wish upon myself, I will never forget that day, that moment.

"How does the structure of that memory compare to the kind of 'indelible' memories you are supposedly creating and marketing with the use of nootropics?"

Marshall appreciated the Judge looking at the matter in a personalized way, but was anxious that the question take him out of his comfort zone as a mere lawyer,

"M'Lud, it's a good question with a complicated answer. It might be preferable for a Cortx neuroscientist to respond in more detail. But I'll take a stab at it. I think the simple answer is they are both very similar and very different.

"What Cortx has achieved is a neurochemical short cut to memory consolidation into long term storage. This applies to both episodic and semantic memory.

"Neuroscientists have an expression, 'neurons that fire together wire together'. And if they fire together often enough the encryptions become more engrained among the neuron ensembles which constitute that memory and the memory migrates to a different part of the brain for long term storage. The Cortx nootropics accelerate the memory consolidation process and dramatically boost the strength of the encryptions. The migration process into long term storage or LTS, is almost immediate.

Henderson is listening intently as Marshall continues,

"When you caught that Rainbow trout, the unforgetableness didn't happen all at once neurochemically. It was a number of factors which combined – emotional, associative, replaying that moment in your head again and again for the pleasure it gave – all these things added to the strength and embeddedness of the memory.

"All those processes take a bit of time and require an emotional charge. For example, you brain probably released endorphins when you caught that jumbo trout. Endorphins are known to enhance memory encryption.

"Our patented formula works to establish protein structures that mimic the neurochemical structure of unforgettable memories."

Henderson has another elephant in the room type of question,

"And what if a film screened at the so called Eidetic Cinema is a turkey? What if a viewer would rather forget they ever saw it?"

Marshall was not surprised by the question nor did it appear to throw him off his stride,

"A good question M'Lud. Of course this is something which is getting careful and ongoing editorial attention from the production subsidiary of Cortx.

"But please consider the Eidetic cinema in the broader context of nootropic uses which are mostly utilitarian for example, educational uses, training uses, learning new skills, etc. It's mostly a case of dramatically transforming a slow learning curve into a sharp learning spike. In the case of our Eidetic cinema's and films we produce or format for them, we have a strict code of practice to promote family values and offer family friendly entertainment.

"As for any acquired content, we would not for example consider screening any episodes of a B-Movie franchise such as 'Chainsaw Masseur'. Of that you can be reassured.

"Importantly M'Lud, a viewer retains full cognitive control over whether or not they choose to recall a film or what scene in the film they wish to review. Eidetic film memories are accessed like an 'On

Demand' service. They are accessible whenever your intentionality is to retrieve them. Our post screening consumer surveys indicate a high level of customer satisfaction and value for money.

"M'Lud, apart from the entertainment uses, on matters regarding the administration of justice, nootropics could potentially have a revolutionary impact. Any defence lawyer knows that memories of witnesses can be unreliable. The memory of events gets distorted. Human memory is fallible. When nootropics are more widely used and accepted by the culture, nootropically embedded memories are likely to have enhanced credibility in a court of law.

Marshall took a few steps closer to the spectators. The court camera started to widen out from a relative closeup to reveal the packed courtroom which Marshall was addressing.

"In closing M'Lud, Hollywood, Bollywood, Nollywood, and Chollywood – have all been referred to as 'dream factories'. But more accurately, they are memory factories. Their movies are the vehicles that deliver the memory products which come off the cinema production assembly lines.

"The Cortx use of nootropics in our new chain of cinemas is a natural step in a progression to deliver the vivid and pleasurable dreams that millions of people crave. We are confident that consumers will enthusiastically seek out our products and express their approval of our funding model at the box office. Thank you."

As Marshall begins to walk back to his seat. Judge Henderson throws him a question,

"Excuse me Mr. Marshall, you may sit if you wish, but I've been hearing about bootleg versions of nootropics used by the so called adult entertainment industry. What is your companys' position on that?"

Marshall chooses to remain standing and drifts back to where he was for his opening comments,

"M'Lud, nootropics are only licensed for use in strictly monitored and approved environments.

"We support all efforts to shut down the flow of illegal and possibly unsafe counterfeit gases for uses that were never intended. The use of nootropics by the pornography industry is abhorrent. We maintain a strict code of usage and support all efforts to keep nootropics out of the hands of all unauthorised users including minors, criminals, and drug cartels. Furthermore, personal use for events such as birthdays and weddings are not condoned and run counter to our stringent guidelines for use.

"M'Lud, almost any drug however safe it may be in its recommended usage has the potential to be abused. Cortx is doing everything in its power to work with the agencies that are responsible for curtailing these illegal operations."

Judge Henderson leans back in his chair,

"Thank you Mr. Marshall. This court will recess for lunch."

Lunch hour at Courthouse Square is the best time for protestors to make their voices heard. It's also when journalists do voxpop interviews, pieces to camera, grab miscellaneous visuals, and upload their rushes.

Formulation of principles

Since the publication of their principles only days before the start of the Judicial Review, the MRA has been taken much more seriously by the traditional media. These principles are the outgrowth of weeks of discussion between member organisations, consultation with funders, and much internal debate about priorities and future directions.

These are the principles as they first appeared on the MRA website.

WE ARE THE MEMORY RIGHTS ALLIANCE

1. We oppose any intellectual property claims that infringe on the sovereignty of a person's body or mind.

2. The 'right to forget' is a sacred universal human right. Artificially induced unforgettableness is considered a mental health hazard to be opposed.

3. We oppose any forms of employment discrimination or job penalties against any worker who refuses to subject him or herself to nootropics in the course of training or work activities.

4. We are opposed to any mnemonic driven ideologies which promote ideas of 'memory supremacy'.

5. We are opposed to any human experimentation which does not fully comply with the revised Helsinki Accords which mandate verifiable and independent oversight.

6. We are opposed to the use of animals for any neurochemical and/or neurotechnical research or experimentation.

7. We oppose neurotechnical products and interventions which are likely to exacerbate social divisions by creating a class of 'memory have's' and 'memory have not's'.

8. We oppose all forms of marketing or advertising which embodies or promotes 'memory shaming'.

9. We oppose any form of permanent memory surcharge.

10. If a corporation is receiving permanent fees for so called 'permanent' memories, consumers of such memories should be

entitled to and receive premium rate optic nerve transit fees in perpetuity.

Since the publication of the MRA principles, Gil and Graham have begun to lobby the UN Human Rights Council to establish a Special Rapporteur On Memory Rights and promote a charter for 'universal memory rights'. Beyond formulating new principles, its role would be to investigate and advise on all the current and intended uses of nootropics by Cortx including independent oversight of nootropically related defence contracts.

After the MRA formulated its core values, Cortx PR went into overdrive with the objective to deliberately confuse the public with the creation of a similar sounding 'coalition' to do battle on the side of consumers and their 'memory rights'.

Separate from the MRA supporters in front of the courthouse is the well dressed group of professional looking picketers pretending to be part of a 'grass roots' movement calling itself 'Citizens for Memory Liberty'. They are a Cortx PR fabrication or 'astroturf' coalition. Their creation is in response to the MRA and corporate anxiety about losing the battle for hearts and minds in the wake of revelations about Alex. The CML lobbies legislators with the goal to 'liberate' the neurotech industry by diluting what little government oversight there is.

The CML also does intelligence gathering for Cortx. If they aren't sending people to disrupt public meetings of the MRA, they get people to join the MRA and its affiliates around the world.

The MRA knows all this because they do the same to them. The MRA tries to have someone in attendance at all public meetings of the CML. If someone attends often enough and expresses enthusiasm for the CML agenda, they may be asked to spy on the MRA.

Most of CML's funding comes from a consortium of neurotech companies led by Cortx and a think tank called The Granite Foundation. Granite has a well cultivated profile on social media. They are prolific at spewing out a steady stream of distortions and disinformation about the MRA. They claim the MRA gets most of its funding from care home oligarchs who profit from warehousing people with dementia and have no interest in reversing the upwards curve of degenerative brain disease in the general population. Members of the MRA have been slandered as brainwashed anarchistic memory absolutists.

The Granite Foundation has been pushing the libertarian line of 'cognitive choice'. ANY restrictions on the privatisation of human memory is an infringement on personal liberty. They fund the campaigns of politicians, give generously to memory sports competitions, they successfully lobbied for memory sports to be a new Olympic category, and they recently helped draft legislation that would expand markets for nootropics i.e. more opportunities for land grabs in the cerebral cortex.

A court officer is standing near the Judge's bench in front of the chambers and directing people back to their seats. He then announces,

"Please rise."

Henderson, carrying a cup of coffee, is walking towards his seat. Even before he sits down he is gesturing for the crowded courtroom to be seated.

The Judge is ready to get back to business,

"Is the plaintiff ready with his opening comments?"

Gil, in a heavy sweat, is looking distressed. Henderson has noticed,

"Mr. Hinchliff, are you OK?"

Sophie Hudson and Graham Calder are staring at Gil. Graham closes and opens his eyes then looks up at the ceiling. Ken Marshall appears somewhat bemused.

Henderson is still waiting for a response,

"Mr. Hinchliff – is anyone home? Opening comments anyone?"

Gil snaps out of it,

"Yes M'Lud."

Gil wipes his forehead with a tissue as he stands and approaches the center of the courtroom. He takes a deep breadth, then begins,

"For centuries, people have fought to protect freedom of expression against all forms of tyranny. But however brutal and repressive a regime might be, the one thing they could never control, curtail, or deprive people of was freedom of thought.

"Now, for the first time in human history, a corporation makes a claim that thought itself should not be free.

"The Cortx claim to property rights on a memory of yours or mine is the thin end of the wedge of a cerebral land grab. The gradual privatisation of human memory is where the Cortx memory tax will inevitably lead."

Marshall jumps up,

"Objection M'Lud. It is not a tax! Only governments can levy a tax."

Henderson agrees,

"Sustained."

Gil continues,

"The grounds upon which a judicial review such as this is granted is on the basis of a perceived illegality, procedural impropriety, or irrationality.

"With regard to Cortx nootropics, their claim of safety, their claim to memory ownership, and their scheme of permanent charges – we will demonstrate that their claims are either fictional, illegal, or irrational.

"Mr. Marshall rightly predicted that the plaintiff would claim that their nootropics are not safe."

Gil holds up the thick 400 page Cortx report which contains the data and conclusions of the clinical trials which was the basis of getting regulatory approval for consumer use of nootropics,

"On the basis of this, the documentation of their clinical trials, Cortx nootropics received approval from the Neurotech Oversight Committee. This report is a great work of fiction. There has not yet been an assessment of the safety of nootropics by an independent body. If allowed, the Cortx nootropic formula has the potential for doing harm to the cognitive processes of millions.

"On the face of it, the process of receiving approval did not have integrity..."

In spite of a tradition of not interrupting opening comments, Marshall doesn't restrain himself,

"Objection M'Lud. The NOC is completely independent and they make their decisions with integrity. The plaintiff is mud slinging."

Henderson first addresses Marshall, then turns to Gil,

"Mr. Marshall, it is a bit rude not to allow the plaintiff to complete his opening comments without interruption. Granted, the plaintiff interrupted your opening comments as well.

"Having said that, Mr. Hinchliff, I trust there is more substance to your comments you will be sharing with us shortly?"

Gil put down the thick clinical trial report he was holding on his table,

"Yes, M'Lud.

"Cortx applied for and received fast track approval from the NOC for their nootropic formulas citing an urgent need to help people with dementia and other neuro-degenerative conditions in spite of the fact that Cortx has never formally claimed that nootropics have a capacity to stop, slow, or reverse any degenerative brain diseases. Nootropics effect healthy sections of the memory forming centers of the brain and its long term impact hasn't adequately been studied."

Marshall cuts in again,

"Objection M'Lud. Assessing the long term safety of the nootropics was a precondition of having received NOC approval."

Gil barely misses a beat,

"For a drug that claims to have a permanent impact on memory formation, there has not been adequate longitudinal and latitudinal studies of both the long term effects on different age groups or genders nor people with various underlying medical, neurological, and psychological conditions."

It would be simplistic to regard Cortx as a neurotech ogre without any redeeming achievements. For all the billions of E-rens spent in R&D, they have made some commendable medical advances that have delivered some good. One of the start-ups they acquired did allow Cortx to advance pioneering work in the field of neurofibrology. The advanced techniques of neuron and nerve fibre fusions successfully helped people with specific types of spinal injuries to walk again. And some people who lost their sight as a result of injury or degenerative eye disease have been enabled to see again. But these were not significant profit centers for Cortx. The R&D in these areas was scaled back dramatically. They still have the shameful PAYS revenue stream, but about 3 years ago, they turned to higher risk projects in the hope of satisfying the expectations of major share-holders for revenue growth.

Corporate hubris drove Cortx to take a huge financial gamble on the viability and popularity of neural implants which they appear to have lost. The aggressive marketing of their nootropic formulas to institutions both public and private – including the military, education, and the entertainment market is driven in part by financial desperation.

Cortx is loath to let independent oversight or regulation throttle down the pace of their R&D. Otherwise, a breakthrough with the potential to generate billions in profits might be stymied. But ironically, over the past year, Cortx spent more on marketing nootropics than on R&D related to combatting degenerative brain disease. That's according to their annual report.

Gil continues his opening comments,

"The five member panel of the NOC which reviews clinical trials and makes the final decisions regarding consumer safety and approval for commercial use has several members who are retired Cortx executives. How can that instill trust or be seen as an independent assessment of a new Cortx product?

"We look to this court to hold Cortx to legal and ethical account in their determination to turn millions of consumers into unsuspecting nootropic guinea pigs as they distort the nature of human consciousness in the process.

"On the matter of permanent micro-charges for so called 'fade proof' or eidetic memories, they are an unethical circumnavigation of the intent of consumer protection statutes.

"Pity the consumer who rates an eidetic movie a rotten tomato. Cortx doesn't offer a 'delete button' or a refund."

At this point, Marshall jumps in with a specious R&D update,

"M'Lud, Cortx is in the process of developing a safe neutralising therapy so that in the future, nootropically enhanced memory proteins can be converted back to regular protein structures and subject to fading and forgetting as with inferior memories."

Gil decides not to take the bait regarding Marshall's reference to 'memory inferiority.' But he has heard rumours about this initiative.

"M'Lud, Mr. Marshall is referring to an even bigger can of worms. I have heard about these experiments, but what I have also heard is that if successful, Cortx would still continue with micro-charges for the neutralisation process. So the consumer would in effect still be paying a monthly charge NOT to have a fade-proof memory."

"Objection M'Lud, that is simply not true."

Of course Marshall objects. The Judge orders that the contentious claim of Gil be deleted from the record.

Gil continues his attack,

"The micro-charges are a clever and insidious payment model akin to having a cancerous growth on your bank account. Cortx is betting that these small subtractions from the bank balances of millions won't be noticed or felt financially. But the steady drip of deductions will add up over months and years and not just for the Eidetic Cinema movie buffs who Cortx Entertainment is counting on to see every new release."

Ken Marshall appreciates what is financially at stake.

If the micro-charge payment model can fly, for neurotech investors they are virtually recession-proof and a hedge against neurotech market instability. What at first appears to be a meagre projection of annual revenue of about 1 billion E-rens belies their medium and long term value as a weatherproof revenue stream that can be collateralised by a factor of 30. They are likely to outrun inflation and have locked in growth potential as micro-charges continue to rise with every film viewed at a nootropic theatre. It's not a goose that lays a golden egg, it's a flock of geese that lay an endless stream of golden micro-eggs.

Gil is intent on hammering away at the insidiousness of the micro-charge concept,

"These small seemingly insignificant monthly charges which start out as low as .01 E-ren per month are akin to a racketeer skimming off the top of a person's earnings. They are worth billions of E-rens to Cortx.

"If Cortx can get away with this payment model for their Eidetic Cinema, what's to stop them from introducing such a charge for millions of tourists at world heritage sites?

"M'Lud, such a charge is unprecedented..."

Marshall was anticipating this argument and was ready to spring up like a jack-in-the-box,

"Objection M'Lud. There has long been a precedent for such a payment structure. This precedent and framework has existed for a couple of hundred years..."

Henderson could not contain his curiosity,

"Mr. Marshall?"

"M'Lud, what we have structured by way ongoing monthly charges based on usage is very much akin to the payment model of a utility company. Furthermore, I'm pleased to inform this court that a sub-division of Cortx has recently been granted the status of a utility by the Public Service Utilities Commission. We will become the world's first 'memory utility'."

Gil is completely blindsided, utterly incredulous, and totally flummoxed by this little bit of breaking news. It's actually more evidence of the sea of political corruption which Cortx swims in.

The judge was also puzzled,

"Mr. Marshall, why are we hearing about this new status now? I read nothing about this in the documents submitted to this judicial review?"

"M'Lud, the final decision to approve the utility status was made only several days before the start of this hearing. In an abundance of caution not to prejudice the decision making process of the Public Service Utilities Commission we felt it prudent not to include reference to their deliberations in the documentation we submitted earlier.

"We are about to submit to this court the updated documentation which covers all statutory requirements relative to this new status.

"The PSUC will provide an additional layer of oversight and regulation of nootropics and set standards for service, customer satisfaction, and billing."

> *Editors note: To view the newly established regulatory framework for the EMPEC (Enhanced Memory Protein Encryption Charge) visit the Neurotech Regulatory Administration (NRA) website and search 'EMPEC'. As a newly established utility, customer service obligations and payment plans can be viewed at the Public Service Utilities Commission website. Search: 'MICRO-CHARGE PROTOCOLS/MEMORY'. It is worth noting that a newly licensed utility will likely qualify for significant government subsidies.*

Gil and Graham stare at each other in disbelief. Marshall is taking his objection and expanded it into a triumphal speech. He is hoping to steal some of the thunder of Gil's opening critique,

"The description of our charges as unprecedented is clearly a stretch. The objection to being permanent charges per se is misleading. Our rates are commensurate with use. Consumers want enhanced protein encryptions for added value and entertainment with 24/7 convenience. This is akin to any subscription or streaming service. We have successfully developed, tested, and delivered enhanced protein encryptions for a wide range of audio video content, priority data, and..."

Judge Henderson interrupts,

"Mr. Marshall, would you be kind enough to allow Mr. Hinchliff to complete his opening comments?"

"Of course M'Lud."

Gil is staring off to the mid-distance and trying to think on his feet. He pivots towards Henderson,

"M'Lud, I would like to quote Alex the Shakespeare quoting parrot,

'I have no spur
To prick the sides of my intent, but only
Vaulting ambition, which o'erleaps itself,
And falls on th' other...'

"Alex was citing Act 1, Scene 7 of Macbeth.

"Macbeth is trying to rationalize in his head his intent to murder a King. His higher self realizes it would be an immoral act and he can't find any justification to kill an otherwise good ruler other than his overriding and overwhelming ambition.

"M'Lud, the Neurotech Oversight Committe is compromised. It cannot provide ethical guidance nor unbiased evidence based assessment for safety and nootropic use. The ambitions of Cortx if left unchecked, will likely have injurious consequences for countless consumers. Cortx nootropics are not a ground-breaking achievement in quote unquote 'human enhancement', they are a threat to the mental health of millions. Thank you."

Exhausted and deflated, Gil walks over to sit down with Graham.

Judge Henderson calls for a short recess.

Spectators are standing up and beginning to drift towards the exists.

Graham offers Gil his off the cuff diagnosis,

"That was a bombshell, but I'm not sure what it really means."

It's clear he is referring to Cortx being given utility status.

Gil is still reeling,

"Curiouser, and curiouser. Hopefully, we will be able to return the favour."

It never crossed Gil's mind before that very moment in the courtroom to quote Alex quoting Shakespeare.

He is impressed with himself that he actually remembered a relevant passage from Shakespeare's tragedy. It was a bit of a cheat because he isn't certain that Alex has yet gotten around to quoting that particular passage. It just magically bubbled up from some distant bout of binge reading Shakespeare when he was at Uni.

As Gil exits the courtroom he unsuccessfully tries to make eye contact with Sophie.

Outside the building, Gil is dodging breath clouds in the chilly air emanating from people he is passing as he looks for a quiet spot to try again to call Dena. A virus savvy population has adopted the urban choreography of avoiding other peoples dissipating plumes of exhalation.

Still no luck getting through to Dena. The sinking feeling that Dena does not want to talk with him has found an oxygen starved place in his heart. Gil would feel even worse if he knew that Dena's father was lobbying hard for his daughter to end her relationship with him.

Major the Myna

When Gil first encountered Alex at the Royal Society, Alex triggered a flood of poignant memories of Gil's first pet, a Myna bird which his mother gave him for his 9th birthday.

The Myna which Gil named Major, had a yellow patch on its head, dark feathers, and orange feet. Gil would spend hours talking to it and carry on imaginary conversations. He occasionally read it bedtime stories before the cloth was put over its cage for the night.

Major didn't make Myna sounds for anyone else but Gil. And when it did, it was a magical sound like a long descending note on a calliope.

In spite of the buzz of the crowd at the Royal Society, Gil could hear the sound made by Major loud and clear in his memory.

Some child psychologists recommend that parents give their children a pet so they will learn about mortality, death, loss, and grief on a supposedly manageable scale to better prepare them for the emotional jolts that inevitably come in life. That may have been the thinking of Gil's mum when she bought Gil a pet bird.

Gil loved Major so much, he asked his mum if it would be OK to let Major out of the cage to join the other birds outside. Gil's mum tried to explain that Major didn't grow up free and wouldn't know how to feed itself, it would have no friends, it would be picked on by bigger birds and if it didn't end up a meal for a cat, would almost certainly die.

It was very hard for 9 year old Gil to get his head around the idea that setting a bird free – allowing it to fly – would mean its death. Gil began to feel sorry for Major and guilty that he lived in a cage. Gil was coming to realise that Major was a creature that had never been in control of its own fate.

The morning that the 11 year old Gil found Major lying motionless at the bottom of its cage was followed by one of Gil's worst panic attacks and a week of inconsolable grief.

The neuroanthropologist

After the court was called to order and Judge Henderson took his seat with coffee in hand, Gil proceeded to call his first expert to testify,

"M'Lud, I would like to call Professor of Neuroanthropology Abidemi Okafor of the Sociogenic Research Laboratory at Oxford University."

Gil had once audited a class of Professor Okafor and was pleased he was willing to take the time to prepare a presentation for the judicial review. Okafor was horrified, bemused, and fascinated by Cortx plans for the Eidetic cinema and all the issues it raised.

Gil continues,

"The purpose of Professor Okafor's testimony will be to put nootropics into a broader historical, cultural, and neuroanthropological context, and in so doing explain the multiple hazards which are likely to accompany their use now and in the future. The stakes are very high and the decisions of this judicial review will likely be of long term consequence.

"Professor Okafor, would you please explain the focus of your work as a neuroanthropologist?"

The professor begins with a very wide and engaging smile,

"That would be my pleasure.

"Broadly speaking, the brain gives rise to our culture and our culture influences our brain. In effect, our brains and our culture co-evolve. I study that interaction historically and I study that interaction today."

Gil knew what the professor was likely to say and knew he was a great storyteller. And for better or worse, Okafor was likely to be nuanced and reflective rather than hyperbolic. Knowing that, Gil was hoping that the professors high minded presentation would be perceived in stark contrast to Cortx as barbaric, brain stem sucking mind-fuckers!

"Professor, can you please give some example to illustrate this interaction between culture and the human brain?"

The professor's smile became even broader,

"Surely."

The professor removed his glasses and placed them in his vest pocket,

"I have spent much time researching, analysing, and writing about the profound cultural and neurobiological transition from an oral tradition to a written tradition in both Greek history and African tribal societies.

"In Greek mythology, Mnemosyne was the goddess of memory. She was traditionally paid homage to in the first few lines of many oral epic poems. She receives honourable mention in the Iliad and the Odyssey. The memory of this goddess of memory would typically be invoked by storytellers to assist in the accurate recall and performance of the epic poem about to be recited.

"It's hard for anyone today to fully appreciate the ancient oral tradition paradigm. No books, no movies, no phones, no tabs, no icams. The storyteller was a main source of news and entertainment – no pressure!

"In Greek literature, Mnemosyne was regarded as a 'Titan' because memory was so fundamental not only to the oral culture but was considered the key building block of civilization. Memory was essential for the preservation of the creation myth of the culture.

"In ancient history, the verbal power of kings and poets was attributed to their special relationship with their muses and with Mnemosyne. Power, leadership skills, and memory were interconnected.

"Enter Hesiod. Hesiod was a Greek poet and a revolutionary in his day about 700 BC. He was a contemporary of if not mates with Homer. Hesiod was a poet who bridged the transition between the oral tradition and written poetry. He took the oral tradition about the origin of Greek gods and put it down on paper – or to be more accurate on papyrus. What an incredible and world changing thing to have done!

"With the gradual transition to a written culture, the absolute dependence on people with prodigious memory capacities began to decline. The human brain would evolve accordingly.

"Forensic archaeologists who have studied the skeletal remains of thousands of bodies from one and two millennia BC and compared them to skeletal remains from one thousand AD concluded that human brains may have become slightly smaller on average.

"The hippocampus is that part of the brain where much of human memory is processed and where neurogenesis – the production of new neurons takes place. The hippocampi of the poets and storytellers in the oral tradition were likely to have been larger than the average hippocampus of their contemporaries by virtue of the demands of their day job as the storyteller and the sheer scale of what they committed to memory.

"In the 17th century there were fanciful experiments by scientists attempting to determine if memories had physical weight. Now that may sound laughable, but a recent study by the Sociogenic Research Lab where I work in Oxford, used cerebellum data-sets from the mid 20th century – the era before the internet and before the precipitous decline of western human attention spans – and compared those data-sets to cerebellum data sets over the past decade and the evidence was striking. The human hippocampus where most memories are processed and where neurogenesis takes place has actually on average gotten smaller. Now those 17th century scientists might be gratified to know that their supposedly laughable question does actually have a quantifiable response.

"The evidence of a smaller hippocampus could make a case that on average human memories weigh less today than they did a mere hundred years ago. The point is, our cultural and neurobiological capacities co-evolve."

The good news for Gil was that Henderson did not appear to be squirming in his seat. He appeared to be listening and taking it in as he sipped his coffee. Gil proceeded,

"Professor Okafor, what relevance to you as a neuroanthropologist does this have regarding Cortx nootropics?"

Okafor took his specs out of his pocket and put them back on,

"Well, I would make an important distinction between invoking the deity Mnemosyne vs. exposure to nootropics.

"Firstly, with regard to episodic memory – memory of events in your life or film memories for that matter which are also episodic memories – some people clearly have better memory abilities or memory skills than others.

"People with good memories have historically been associated with having higher intelligence. Surveys show that the vast majority of people wish their memories were better than they are. That having been said, the 'idea' of nootropics is very appealing to many. It's no surprise that Cortx nootropics are finding a growing market. But memories that are synthetically enhanced may also create a distorted sense of their intrinsic worth.

"Remembering by virtue of chemical intervention and remembering by wilful act of intentionality are two very different things. Apart from what nootropics may be doing to human neurometabolism, nootropics..."

To Gil's surprise, Marshall hadn't completely tuned out and was listening attentively to what Okafor was saying,

"Objection, M'Lud. The professor is speculating about a link between neuro-metabolism and nootropics, an area he has no qualifications to speculate about."

Henderson was quick to respond,

"Mr. Marshall, I did not hear the professor make any specific claim related to the neuro-metabolic effects of nootropics. Please continue Professor."

"...So, apart from what nootropics may or may not be doing to neuro-metabolism, and what that might mean for the neurogenesis capacity of the hippocampus..."

Marshall is on his feet again,

"Objection M'Lud, the professor is clearly implying a connection between the capacity for neurogenesis and nootropics. The capacity for neurogenesis is not effected whatsoever by nootropics."

Henderson put his cup of coffee down,

"Mr. Marshall, given the nature of this review in which issues of oversight and safety are being questioned, I will allow Professor Okafor's comment to be part of the record."

Henderson turns to Okafor,

"You can proceed."

The broad smile returns to Okafor's face,

"...In my humble opinion, by short-circuiting the consolidation process and side stepping intentionality or wilfulness and the effort to commit something to memory, nootropics may in effect be cheapening the intrinsic value of human memory. It may also be introducing an element of memory rigidity, allow me to explain..."

Marshall is dismissively shaking his head but not interrupting Okafor.

The professor continues,

"...I have not used Cortx nootropics, but as I understand them, Cortx promotes an eidetic memory experience. The concept is a powerful one and I understand its appeal. To see a complex image or sequence of images and be able to close your eyes and see the same image in all its detail, or to able to absorb new information rapidly, that is a powerful ability and a seductive idea. But there is a price to be paid given the fixed and somewhat rigid nature associated with that.

"The African griot or the Greek poet choose to remember and their memories have a fluidity not a rigidity. They can tailor a story to an audience, the memory will even evolve in time. It's not a totally fixed and locked down thing."

At this point, Okafor took his specs off, placed them back in his vest pocket and turned to address Judge Henderson directly,

"From my perspective as a neuroanthropologist, the important difference with nootropics is that we don't have a nootropic memory, that nootropic memory has us."

Okafor paused. His last comment seems to resonate. You could almost hear the echo of his comment bounce between brains in the packed courtroom.

Gil allows the moment to reverberate for a few seconds before asking his next question. He phrases it as neutrally as possible to avoid obvious editorialising on a matter that is horrifying to him,

"Professor Okafor, you may be aware that nootropic atmospheres are not solely intended for use in a new Cortx cinema chain. In addition to UN World Heritage sites, there has been a trial use by six private primary schools over the past year where children as young as five years old are exposed to nootropics.

"From your perspective, what are the possible upsides or downsides to such a trial among adolescents?"

The broad smile which appeared to be a permanent fixture on Professor Okafor's face – dissolved,

"Our childhood memories are our own individual 'creation myths'. They live and breathe, get buried, transmute, become distorted, or exaggerated, or forgotten – by the complex interaction of psychological factors during the ebb and flow of our emotional growth and constantly shifting neurochemical tides.

"Children, if subjected to nootropic chemicals in unpredictable circumstances, given uncertain effects, could have an unquantifiable impact on identity formation."

Marshall interrupts,

"Objection and clarification M'Lud. The Ministry of Education approved and carefully monitors our pilot program with school children. We have begun the study with a half strength formula of nootropics. School officials and representative parental committees are involved in oversight. We are not talking about 'unpredictable circumstances' we are talking about reading lessons.

"I hasten to add that in the preliminary results, the introduction of nootropics has helped raise reading scores among early learners by 30%. The schools in question were astounded and children's parents were delighted."

Henderson first turns to Marshall,

"Mr. Marshall, your clarification will be part of the record. We are talking about a trial use of nootropics among young people. There are clearly unknowns, or why the need for a trial? Professor, please proceed, but please try to limit your speculation,"

Okafor responds,

"I will try Your Honour, M'Lud, sir, but the point I was beginning to make is that we are talking about an extremely sensitive dynamic involving children with much that is unknown.

"Mr. Marshall questioned the idea of 'unpredictable circumstances' that it was only a reading lesson. That is not how I see the situation. 'It is only a reading lesson' is from the point of view of the teacher, not the point of view of the child. To the child so much else may be going on.

They may be happy or miserable to be at school. It's possible they are being bullied by a classmate or, they may be coming from tremendous turmoil at home.

"Given the power of nootropics to effect multiple areas of the brain, and given the complexity of the psychological forces at work in children, there is an intrinsic danger that reading lesson or not, a negative aspect of a passing stage in a child's development could be reinforced. The truth is, we do not yet know for sure if this could feed or reinforce a latent neurotic tendency or even a psychosis..."

Marshall makes a loud noise as he picks up then forcibly drops back down a pile of documents in front of him,

"Objection M'Lud. The Professor's comments are more than speculative they are demonstrably untrue. Preliminary studies were done with children even before the school trial began. The nootropics were proven to be 100% safe. The documentation of this study which preceded the school trial has been uploaded for this review."

Henderson is willing to give Marshall the benefit of the doubt,

"Ok Mr. Marshall."

Henderson then addressed the computer program which automatically produces and edits the testimony transcript,

"Please strike the last comments by the Professor from the record. The comments about intrinsic dangers and the possibility of reinforcing neurosis, etc."

"Mr. Hinchliff, is there more from the Professor?"

"Yes M'Lud."

Henderson notices that Okafor is sheepishly raising his hand like a kid in a classroom.

Henderson,

"Professor Okafor, you have a question?"

"Yes sir, if I may... I was curious if there is an age restriction on who is allowed to attend an Eidetic Cinema?"

The judge looks toward the defendant,

"Mr. Marshall?"

Marshall is initially caught off guard,

"...Ah, that is something we are discussing. But at present we do not anticipate an age restriction because of the family friendly nature of the content Cortx expects to be producing and distributing."

Okafor thanks Henderson and Marshall and is awaiting the next question from Gil,

"Professor Okafor, as a neuroanthropologist are you aware of any cultural precedent for someone to claim ownership of a piece of somebody else's brain?"

After a long pause, Okafor responds,

"Just a piece?"

There is laughter from the spectators. Gil is enjoying himself,

"OK, OK, a part or the whole of someone else's brain?"

Okafor is also enjoying what at first seems to be a very wacky question,

"I suppose you are not referring to aboriginal head hunters in the Amazon or the Panamanian rain forest, or the Sarawaks in Borneo, or Scythians of antiquity? They certainly acted like they owned other people's brains..."

There's more laughter in the courtroom. Even Marshall is trying to suppress a laugh.

Okafor continues,

"But I suspect that's not what you are asking me about. I would say if you look back at history, I think there certainly is precedent of property laws being applied to human beings in part or whole."

Gil is happy to supply all the leading questions needed for the occasion,

"Property laws applied to human beings?"

Professor Okafor is no longer smiling. He's staring straight at Gil with a stern expression,

"Yes, property laws applied to human beings. It's called slavery. The slave..."

Marshall strenuously objects,

"M'Lud, must this court indulge such a far fetched and inappropriate analogy? There is no comparison to a voluntary purchase by consumers of a life enhancing experience..."

Gil tries to hold his ground,

"M'Lud, I think Professor Okafor is making a simple and relevant point that property laws – which encompass intellectual property laws and patent ownership – have had a tainted history in relation to how they have been used in the context of human exploitation of another human being. They've been used to negate another person's humanity and violate another person's physical integrity.

"M'Lud, I think this is the principle we are looking at. If Cortx is allowed to stake their claim of ownership on a cluster of your neurons, it is a violation of your physical integrity and a trespasses on the gray matter that makes up your humanity."

Marshall is nearly apoplectic,

"M'Lud, this is inappropriate, irrelevant, delusional, prejudicial, and..."

With the hint of a smirk, Gil interrupts Marshall,

"M'Lud, I have no further questions for Professor Okafor."

The murmuring courtroom spectators seem to be enjoying the show.

Henderson asks Marshall if he has any questions for the Professor. Marshall indicates yes.

As courtroom choreography unfolds, defendant replaces plaintiff as Marshall turns his attention to the neuroanthropologist.

One of the courtroom cameras does an arcing move from facing Marshall to sweeping behind him as he asks his first question,

"Professor Okafor, I did not hear you say that the intellectual property rights which Cortx owns was in any way unethical.

"Rather than the plaintiff putting words in your mouth to insinuate the moral depravity of Cortx for defending its intellectual property rights, I'd like to ask you about a fascinating article I recently read called, 'The Price Tag of Immortality'.

"Are you familiar with it Professor?"

"Of course. That was one of my first published essays about 20 years ago."

"What inspired you to write it at the time?"

"It was written for a panel trying to predict neuroanthropological issues a hundred years into the future."

"Can you please try to summarize for this court your intriguing essay?"

Okafor's eyes were glancing up as if to access a cerebral hard drive,

"It's complicated. I was speculating on the theoretical possibility of mind uploading. The idea was quite the fad at the time. I explored what it would mean for the culture and what the ethical issues would be. On a more practical level, I speculated about what kind of neurotech infrastructure would be needed and how much it might cost."

Marshall wasn't sure how far he'd be able to steer the testimony, but he was going to give it his best shot,

"And your conclusions about the costs of uploading a complete mind, and the trade-off's that might be considered?"

Okafor was actually enjoying being back in touch one of his earliest thought experiments,

"Well, the scenario went something like this, with advances in AI, a mind upload is theoretically possible if a digital counterpart could be efficiently produced molecule by molecule of the 85 billion or so neurons which exist in a human brain. The neurotech infrastructure needed would be monumental and the cost would likely be astronomical – at least in the early days of mind uploading.

"The premise is that if you can upload it – 'it' being your consciousness and everything that entails, you can eventually download it to a new recipient – voila, immortality.

"The early candidates for an upload and a shot at immortality would either be ridiculously rich, or someone with extraordinary abilities. It might be a brilliant scientist, artist, musician, leader, or genius in their field to make it worth the effort."

Marshall was honing in on the point he hoped to make,

"And Professor, in your essay you speculated about the trade-off that might be necessary if a brilliant or special person was to have his or her brain uploaded..."

Okafor remembers the essay as if he had written it last week, not 20 years ago,

"So, a neurotech company has created a digital copy of your brain. Who owns the copyright or intellectual property? The obvious answer would be the person who had their brain copied for upload.

"But what if the deal from the outset was that in exchange for your shot at immortality, the neurotech company is given the non-exclusive rights to own and market the part of your brain they consider special or unique?"

Marshall can also ask leading questions as good as the next guy,

"And in your essay, what was your conclusion about the ethics of a neurotech company hoping to negotiate ownership of an aspect of someone else's brain?"

Okafor hesitates for a moment,

"Well, the conclusion in the essay was that given the benefits that the company was able to provide, there would not be anything intrinsically unethical on the part of the neurotech company to own part of the brain, but..."

For Marshall, there was absolutely not going to be another syllable beyond the 'but'. The interruption fell like a guillotine.

"Thank you so much Professor Okafor for your insights. No further questions M'Lud."

Latte out on a limb

In the aftermath of the MRA exposé of animal torture by Cortx and the guerrilla actions by Gil and Tovy, Graham continued to chastise Gil about taking risks which could end his legal career or endanger his life.

Graham has known Gil long enough to identify self-destructive tendencies he does not fully understand.

One of Graham's theories has to do with Gil's fucked up relationship with his father. Maybe Gil wants to deny his father the satisfaction of being a successful lawyer. Hence, the subconscious lure of being a fuckup.

Coming from a hardscrabble working class background, Graham doesn't have a great deal of empathy for Gil.

In spite of Graham trying to discourage Gil's self-destructive tendencies, Gil is persuing a plan that will likely place him in extreme jeopardy.

Today is the first of several days during which Gil is doing reconnaissance on Cortx employees as they enter and leave Cortx HQ in Central London. He is making a list of the coffee shops and snack bars they frequent with their laptops and tabs to hang out, login, surf, and check emails.

Gil's knowledge of who's who at Cortx is informed by countless news clippings, the neurotech trade press, the Cortx annual report, their self-aggrandizing website, and other professional networking sites. Exec's in R&D, marketing, and legal affairs are priority targets.

A senior attorney in the company named Kenneth Marshall is frequently quoted in the tabs on a range of legal matters related to Cortx.

If there was a media report about a neurotech startup suing Cortx for copyright infringement, Marshall would be quoted. When Cortx was lambasted for a tax avoidance scheme by claiming an obscure island off the coast of Thailand as its Global HQ, Marshall was quoted. When the PAYS payment model for Cortx retinal implants was challenged in court, Marshall led the Cortx legal team and won the case.

For his intelligence gathering operation, Gil purchases a quasi-legal little toy called an A-cam. It was bought on the ZillaWeb which is dark corner of the internet where illegal, quasi-legal, and obscure spyware that most governments would prefer you not have access to – can be acquired.

It's an unregulated netherworld which thrives on secrecy and a paradox: most things on the Zillaweb are not illegal to sell or buy, they're just illegal to own or use – especially if you are an unlicensed non-governmental entity or individual.

Gil buys two early model A-Cams aka Antcams. Their batteries don't last very long and they are not rechargeable.

As the name suggests, they look and move like a very small insect. They have the capacity to 'crawl' on almost any surface. The head of the 'ant' has a micro 7mm lens which is extremely wide angle. Via its 'antennae', the device is capable of transmitting and receiving signals up to a 45 meter distance.

An A-cam can crawl up to 1 meter in sixty seconds. It's battery can last up to 3 hours and it's a relatively inexpensive piece of sophisticated spyware – about 300 E-rens for the early model.

Gil is sitting in a distant corner downing his third coffee inside the café with the most Cortx employee traffic.

Several customers wearing their Cortx ID's have ordered coffee. One of them sits down by a wall close to the front counter with his tab as he awaits his order.

Gil's heart is beginning to pound as he approaches the countertop with the sugar and utensils which is about 2 meters from where the employee is sitting.

Gil activates the A-Cam which he tested at home the night before. If a target is sitting near a wall, that's ideal. The most crucial moment for using an A-Cam is its initial positioning and traction onto a surface. If you drop it, or it falls off, you may be unable to recover it.

The technique to position the A-Cam is to place the activated device on a piece of paper first and then allow the paper to press against and curve upwards upon the surface of the wall. Let the A-cam crawl up and off the paper onto the surface of the wall. Gil practiced this transition at home. He can now do it in about ten seconds.

The A-cam has been navigating the wall and recording over the shoulders of several customers for a couple of hours with uncertain results.

A customer who looks like it might actually be Ken Marshall is spotted being handed a coffee at the front counter. He then makes his way to a plush chair against a wall in the middle of the café.

Gil is stationed in a quiet corner with the A-Cam software on his tab. The camera is already legging its way along the wall towards towards the latest target. Gil's heart is pounding harder.

The video feed from the A-Cam is disorienting. As it moves along the wall the entire room is seen lopsided and the surface of the wall looks like a moonscape.

In less than two minutes, the A-Cam arrives on the wall within a meter of Marshall's tab and just behind his field of vision. He appears to be checking some sports scores. Gil hits 'record' on the software. The heading of an email being opened begins, 'Hi Ken...'

Asynchronicity

Gil is back home listening to Dena on the phone as he simultaneously begins to scan the video catch of the day from the café.

"...It felt like they were taking me for granted. If they sent me one more gigabyte of overdue compliance documents to sort out, I would have screamed bloody murder at the top of my lungs, maybe even walked.

"But my boss called me into his office today and said he was really pleased with my work. They're giving me a promotion to Deputy Compliance Officer and they're giving me a raise Gil..."

In spite of his attention being elsewhere, Gill was pleased for Dena,

"That's really great Dena, congratulations! You deserve it"

Dena responded in a very seductive voice,

"I was thinking of picking up a bottle of champagne and coming by later and we could stay in and celebrate?"

Gil is scanning some of the footage as she says this.

Dena can tell Gil's distracted,

"Gil, are you listening?"

Gil hits pause on the software,

"That would be great Dena. Can we celebrate tomorrow night? I've had a really stressful day..."

Dena isn't ready to give up,

"I've had a stressful day too Gil. We can engage in special relaxation techniques, don't you think?"

Gil was on another planet,

"I'll make it up to you De. Can I take you out for dinner on Friday and we can have a real celebration? That would be fantastic..."

Dena's mood and tone changed abruptly,

"We'll see Gil, I'll talk to you later."

With that, she hung up.

The guilt Gil was feeling quickly evaporated.

He resumed reviewing the footage.

Gil was watching and replaying, pausing, enlarging, and trying to catch login id's and passwords.

Using a chained connection of encrypted proxy servers, Gil is ready to attempt to log into a Cortx email account.

That may prove the easy part. Accessing the content of encrypted attachments is more of a challenge.

Tovy showed Gil how to access a site called the 'Flophouse Supernet'. It's an under the radar distributed supercomputer with over the top capacity and lots of attitude. It's used by some renegade academics but mostly short traders looking for an edge.

Gil logs in, activates a cracking program which probably has Tovy's tag embedded in it somewhere, and feeds it the link.

A dalek voice is heard,

"Decrypting binary algorithms utilising more than 1,000 primes requires patience."

Gil mumbles under his breath,

"Take your sweet time darlin.""

Glutamate Instability and Potentiation Variables

It's about 3am later that night and Gil is finishing up a long hot shower in spite all the water credits going down the drain.

He wraps himself up in a towel and walks over to his computer just in time to hear the dalek voice,

"Decryption complete. No problemo."

Gil dries his hair, puts on his shorts and a T-shirt, makes himself a cup of Sage herbal tea, places a cushion on his chair and settles down to open the freshly cracked Cortx document.

Gil's eyes widen.

The document has an ominous militaristic sounding classification:

CORTX

DELTA LEVEL:

RESTRICTED CIRCULATION

Gil mutters to himself,

"This...looks...good."

Gil clicks to the next page. The title of this highly confidential research document is revealed,

PROJECT AXION
Memory Protein Structures &
Patents
by Ken Marshall

Gil turns his phone off and takes another sip of his Sage tea as he begins to scrutinize the document and its table of contents.

Gil continues to mutter and read to himself,

"...K-Lab Report... Kyrgyzstan Research Parameters...

"...Neurogenesis and Rapid Consolidation of Episodic Memories...

"...Augmented Film Memory Neuron Ensembles and Molecular Property Rights...

"...Glutamate Instability and Potentiation Variables..."

Gil had stumbled upon the Cortx Kama Sutra for mind fucking.

Tchaikovsky, Cortx, and Kalashnikov

A helicopter passes over a dramatic mountainous landscape in Central Asia. A clear blue lake below has the distinctive shape of a human eye.

As the corporate helicopter comes in for a landing, two black-clad security guards carrying the latest model Kalashnikovs position themselves near the helipad. The newest model Kalashnikov is half the size but has twice the firepower of the original classic Kalashnikov assault weapon. They've been nicknamed 'Kalashnikids'.

A group of men in suits including Ken Marshall disembark. Their jackets are flapping furiously in the propeller's down draft.

Incongruously, less than 50 meters from the helipad, Sophie Hudson, wearing a white lab coat with her hair tied back in a pony tail, is maintaining a garden vegetable patch. She's wearing headphones.

Tchaikovsky's Symphony No. 4 accompanies her activities pruning some plants, pulling up some weeds, and picking several ripe tomatoes.

A clear plastic breathing tube appears clipped to the base of her nostrils. The tube runs to a miniature steel canister in her lab coat pocket.

After looking up from the vegetable patch, Sophie removes the tube from her face and is staring off into the distance. She's been in Kyrgyzstan for over a year. She took the position at K-Lab not long after her husband Ian died from a cancerous brain tumour.

The helicopter blades stop spinning soon after the engine is turned off.

Sophie was persuaded to come to Kyrgyzstan to work as a programmer on the Axion project. It took her several months to adapt to being so far away from home and friends but the dramatic change of scenery and break of routine has helped her cope with her grief.

The suits are crossing the helipad and heading for the Encore Foundation Laboratory which everyone refers to as K-Lab. The facility is a sprawling two acre site and looks like a big glass sandwich. It has a concrete base a little over 1 meter high and a cantilevered concrete top and lots of green tinted glass in between.

As Marshall and the entourage approach the K-Lab entrance, they pass a very small beautifully manicured park with benches. A group of about 8 lab workers on a break appear to be talking to each other in very animated fashion. They are all in white lab coats.

Several men seem to be hamming it up and reciting lines from some script or play in perfect unison,

"That's what's wrong with you Scarlett. You should be kissed and often and by someone who knows how."

The several women present respond in unison,

"And I suppose that you think that you are the proper person?"

The men respond in unison,

"I might be, if the right moment ever came."

The women,

"You're a conceited, black-hearted varmint, Rhett Butler, and I don't know why I let you come and see me."

The men,

"I'll tell you why, Scarlett, because I'm the only man over sixteen and under sixty who's around to show you a good time. But cheer up, the war can't last much longer."

Ken Marshall recognizes the dialogue and fills in his colleagues,

"I think that's 'Gone With The Wind'!"

Two of Marshall's colleagues respond in unison,

"It is!"

They all have a big laugh at the coincidence.

Some lab workers have formed an impromptu film memory club and amuse themselves reciting lines of classic movie dialogue.

The entourage pass a plasma sign:

Guests enter a long narrow glass chamber that funnels them towards the main reception. Curiously, the long entrance chamber is not physically attached to the reception area. There is a half meter gap where the long chamber ends and the reception area begins with automatic doors on either side of the gap.

The gap is narrow and momentarily outdoors. There are no enclosures on the sides nor above. In that half meter gap you can look up and see the unobstructed sky and even get wet if it's raining.

The gap is crossed thousands of times each week with rarely a thought about why it exists.

This subtle architectural conceit is intended to mimic the synaptic gap between neurons.

Standing in the reception area awaiting the arrival of Marshall and colleagues from Cortx HQ is Dr. Marcus Van Trotta the laboratory manager at Encore. He's in his late fifties, about 6ft tall and wears bifocals.

Sophie Hudson approaches him carrying a basket of vegetables,

"Marcus, I've been waiting weeks for that diagnostic report. Is there any..."

Van Trotta cuts her off,

"This isn't a good time, Sophie. Besides, the preliminary report was uploaded two days ago."

Sophie was surprised to hear this,

"Really? Why was there no email notice?"

Van Trotta is making eye contact with the arriving guests,

"Sophie, I have to welcome our guests."

Van Trotta introduces himself to all the visitors. He then escorts them one level up to a conference room for orientation. It's an elegant polarized glass enclosed lozenge shaped chamber.

Van Trotta takes quiet pleasure at introducing visitors to the extraordinary work at K-Lab,

"There's coffee, juice, water, and some biscuits – please help yourselves."

"You can call me Marcus. I've been facility manager here for about six years.

"I'm very excited to report that Project Axion is on the home stretch. When I started working here 6 years ago there were doubts that this project would ever be completed – at least, not in my lifetime."

With theatrical understatement Van Trotta continues,

"Axion is *only* the most ambitious mapping enterprise in human history.

"All of the major breakthroughs by Cortx over the past decade are in debt to greater or lesser degree to Axion.

"The birth of a new field of neuroscience – neurofibrology, the historic work on chip implants and the amazing Alex, and the transformative nootropic products would likely not have come to fruition if not for Axion.

"Axion has led to no less than 157 patents which are the gold reserves of Cortx."

One of the visitor's leans over to whisper in the ear of Ken Marshall,

"So this is why the boys in intellectual property have been creaming in their pants."

Van Trotta continues,

"When complete, Axion will be a realtime computer model of all cognitive functions of the human brain. Think of it as an A to Z of a 100 billion neurons.

"To put Axion in historical context, in the early 20th century it took a scientist 15 years to complete a map of every neuron in an earth worm. Beginning in the late 20th century and with the use of super-computers of their day, it took 25 years and 4 successive teams of scientists to map the brain of a mouse which is 1/100th the size of a human brain.

"The ambition to map a complete human brain was originally a university based initiative that began in the early 21st century. But resources were limited, continuity of personnel didn't exist, funds dried up and at the rate they were going it would have taken 500 years to make some real headway – excuse the pun.

"About a decade ago, Cortx bought out all previous work which had been done on brain mapping. Using AI, we developed, adapted and integrated a form of nanotography, threw an exaflop of computer power on top of it, and gentleman, against all odds, we are here today on the cusp of an historic achievement."

Van Trotta is gushing with pride,

"Project Axion is a hundred thousand times more complex and ambitious then the mapping of the human genome.

"Each neuron may connect to approximately 10,000 other neurons via 1,000 trillion synapses. We're mapping quadrillions of connections.

"It's kinda mindblowing to even think about it. And Sophie Hudson here is our programming guru."

Sophie wasn't expecting to be put on the spot,

"Sophie, would you please give a bit of background on our exaflop computing for our guests?"

Sophie was not inclined to give dumbed down explanations of extreme scale parallel computing to a bunch of suits.

Van Trotta nudged,

"Sophie, for our guests, just how big is an exaflop?"

Sophie expressed her appreciation with a hint of sarcasm in her voice,

"Just delighted to Marcus.

"An exaflop computer is capable of 1 million trillion operations per second. That's a million times faster than the fastest IBM supercomputer. Our exaflop computer is roughly comparable to the molecular processing capacity of one human brain.

"The program for Axion runs off deep memory hierarchies and complex interconnect topologies..."

Sensing that this was over the heads of the guests Van Trotta tried to interject some humour,

"Suffice it to say, programming Axion was a bitch."

Sophie grunts, then continues,

"There certainly were code sustainability issues..."

Van Trotta then asks,

"What about power use Sophie?"

Sophie reached over to grab a tomato in her nearby vegetable basket, before accommodating,

"In the early days of exaflop computing, systems almost needed their own nuclear power station to operate.

"We only use about 10 megawatts to run Axion. That's relatively low power consumption and barely enough to power 6,000 homes."

With the press of a button by Van Trotta, there is a dramatic transition of lighting inside the conference room. The polarized windows make a transition as one section darkens to block the exterior light and another section becomes more transparent to reveal the vast laboratory on the level below.

There are arrays of monitors, computer nodes, and gurneys being wheeled about. At the center of the action are a dozen lab technicians attending to six people who are harnessed into form fitting body units. These units are tilted back with the subjects inside facing monitors above their heads. Van Trotta has turned on a microphone that picks up the sounds from the lab. Audible is the hum of all the equipment and the faint sounds of a movie soundtrack.

"After lunch I would like to invite you all to come with me and Sophie down to the lab and be among some of the first people in history to witness in real time the memory formation process taking place in a person's brain."

Rather than join the group for lunch, Sophie retreats to her sprawling computer domain. She is eating a slice of ripe tomato and reading a Cortx report on one of the screens in her constillation of computer terminals. It's the supplemental report on nootropics which she was pestering Van Trotta about earlier.

She's skimming the table of contents of the report and notices that 'Revised Safety Parameters and Diagnostics' is pages '96-110'.

She's about to click on the update when she gets a call from the lab floor. Technicians are about to initialise a network of computer nodes and need her to be present. Sophie takes her half eaten tomato and makes her way to the lab floor. As she arrives, the first of a new group of 'memory donors' is being wheeled into position and four of the technicians are starting to do the prep work.

Two of them are holding syringes as the other two are preparing to brace the donor.

Ken Marshall has managed to find his way to the lab floor and walks up to Sophie.

Sophie is taken aback,

"You shouldn't be here Mr. Marshall, you should be with the group."

"My curiosity got the better of me Sophie. May I call you Sophie, Ms. Hudson?"

"I think it would be better if you were with Marcus and the others. I've got some boring computer stuff to do and there's some sensitive prep work going on right now."

Marshall made his plea as charmingly as he could,

"Please don't chase me away, I'll behave, I promise."

Sophie relents, then gives a nod for the technicians to get on with what they were doing.

Marshall is fascinated as he follows the procedure. A memory donor is securely harnessed into a unit that swivels on a universal axis. The middle aged man with dark hair is turned around, tilted back until almost upside down and his head is lowered towards a pool of rapidly swirling silvery fluid. A video monitor is poised to the side of the donor but not yet in position above the donor's head at an optimum angle for his viewing convenience.

The prep work on the first 'memory donor' continues. Several more donors arrive.

Had Marshall already had his lunch he might be in danger of losing it. He places a hand over his mouth at the scene he is witnessing.

One of the technicians is inserting a syringe into the corner of an eye of a memory donor. Another technician is inserting a second syringe into the passageway of an ear.

With his hand still to his mouth and trying not to reveal how repulsed and horrified he is, Marshall asks,

"What – are – they – doing?"

Sophie has long since recovered from her own initial shock and almost forgotten her first reactions to seeing this process unfold. Her answer is matter of fact,

"There's a technique K-Lab has pioneered called 'nanotography'. The technicians are introducing nanoscopic transmitters into perceptual pathways."

The heads of several memory donors are within millimetres of the swirling silver fluid. Each has a video monitor positioned at an accommodating angle for viewing.

Film classics are about to be shown to the donors. 'Casablanca' or 'Gone With The Wind' make for archetypal episodic memories.

While Axion is mapping all dimensions of human cognition, for episodic memory, it is using films as the template. With picture, sound, and emotional associations, films do a pretty good job of mimicking the protein encryptions of real life experiences.

Once the nanoscopic transmitters are injected and the video files begin to play, the only thing missing from the movie going experience is the popcorn.

The transmitters are carried along the nerves and neurons by the endogenous electro-chemical charge. To breach the synaptic gaps, they attach themselves to sodium molecules and continue their neuron surfing journey at about a hundred feet per second.

If a comparison was made between the brain and the whole earth, the images of brain activity on vintage MRI scans is comparable to viewing activities on earth from a satellite. Axion is real time mapping and visualisation on the surface of the planet. Its software is tracking, metadata collecting, and modelling in molecular detail all the topography, flora and fauna.

Marshall finally drops his hand from his mouth,

"Is that mercury spinning? What's it doing?"

While Sophie is a computer scientist and programmer, she is not a neuroscientist, yet, she's picked up the gist of things,

"Good try. It's not mercury. It's liquefied silver. It's the most conductive material known to science. It's used to create a hyper-sensitive magnetic field which can detect and register the locations and movements of the transmitters as well as other neurochemical data.

"This design replaces the need for an 8 meter dish antenna to pick up a myriad of extremely faint signals from a donor's brain. The scientists here have adapted frequency amplification technologies used by deep space astronomy in its search for extra-terrestrials. Is that not super cool?"

Sophie gestures to the computer visualisation screen.

Marshall moves to the screen to catch a glimpse and his jaw literally drops.

Signals from the brain are flooding in. The realtime processing power is vastly beyond anything ever attempted or achieved in computer history.

It is an extraordinary hyperkinetic display. It's Formula 1 meets acid trip meets lightning storm meets Jackson Pollack action painting on steroids.

An adjacent screen is receiving satnav type metadata from the nanoscopes. The timing and location of the signals is a window into the memory configuration and consolidation process.

The software allows an operator to 'zoom in' and observe the traffic on individual neurons. To follow the neurochemical trail on that scale is akin to looking out of a car window as it drives across the width of Australia at hypersonic speed. To record, playback, and study in slo-mo the detail of this process would take days to get from stimulus input to consolidation.

Sophie is not a company person per se, but like Van Trotta, she too takes much pride in her work,

"We are accumulating the largest datasets in history. The datasets on Axion are more than a million times larger than datasets used for predicting global weather patterns."

Marshall is transfixed by what he is seeing.

Signals are arriving en masse to the hippocampus. Offshoots head to the frontal cortex. A frenzied migration of glutamates takes place out of cellular cytoplasm. The walls of tens of thousands of nuclei are being breached by the glutamates. A new visual memory is being encoded.

Axion is a peep show into the epicenter of human cognition. It's a window into the process which underscores the human condition. All human experience in all of human history has been made possible by the same raw ingredients in dynamic motion – enabling everything that has ever been seen, heard, felt, thought, and remembered.

What Sophie and Marshall are witnessing is possibly the most close-up and most concrete expression of the most ephemeral phenomenon which philosophers and poets have long pondered and been transfixed by: the NOW. And how the NOW is being transformed into a THEN, a human memory.

Sophie is having trouble reading Marshall. She is still awed by the visualisations. He's been relatively quiet. He's either completely awestruck, or his head is somewhere else.

He finally blurts out,

"Sophie, would it be possible to see a visual comparison of a film memory made without nootropics with a memory of the same film made with nootropics?

Sophie was surprised by the question,

"Possibly. Why?"

"It's to do with a patent application."

"A patent application?"

"That's my specialisation, I'm an IP lawyer. But my background is entertainment law."

Suddenly, one of the memory donors goes into violent convulsions.

Sophie mutters under her breath,

"Shit. Not another..."

Two technicians bolt into action to extricate one of the memory donors from the viewing harness. Sophie appears alarmed yet resigned to what is going on.

Marshall is genuinely horrified – again,

"What's happening?"

Sophie wearily responds,

"Neurons and nanoscopes don't always mix."

"What do you mean?"

"Some nanoscopes don't make it across the synapses, so there's a tail-back, then seizures, convulsions..."

The donor is requiring the forceful efforts of two lab assistants to be restrained and to prevent him from harming himself. There's foam coming out of his mouth.

Sophie is keen to shift Marshall's attention,

"So, what's your mission in beautiful Kyrgyzstan?"

"I'm preparing a legal brief regarding mnemonic property."

Sophie can't restrain her sarcasm,

"Well, I hope you're enjoying the show..."

The two technicians inject a sedative and strap the donor to a gurney. He is now moaning and writhing and his legs are shaking as he's being wheeled away.

In spite of the unfolding drama of human experimentation gone awry, Marshall is still focused on nootropics,

"Would it be possible to allow me to take a glimpse of where the nootropic research is taking place?"

Sophie is incredulous,

"Haven't you seen enough trailblazing research for the afternoon?

"I will escort you back to Marcus and the rest of the group who are probably in the cafeteria wondering if you've been kidnapped."

But Sophie is a softie,

"...The zone doing nootropics is on the way to the cafeteria"

As Sophie and Marshall arrive at what lab workers jokingly refer to as the 'NooZoo', Marshall scans across a group of 10 human guinea pigs in a semi-circular array with a control station in the middle.

The subjects are not strapped into units or swivelled topsy turvy. They are encased in body conforming clear plastic pods. Inside the pods, each person is wearing a cap with dozens of electrodes to measure neurometabolic rates and other brain activity.

One of the lab assistants is in the process of latching shut one of the pods. The assistant walks to the control center and activates the input of the nootropic formula atmosphere which feeds into the pod. The sound of a pump starting up can be heard.

Marshall is curious,

"So what exactly is the...?"

Sophie answers a question she thinks she's about to be asked,

"They're still tinkering to get the ideal nootropic mix for the maximum number of people. Different brains, different neurometabolic rates, different effects, etc..."

Marshall is surprised to hear this,

"But nootropics are already available to the public?"

Sophie doesn't have much of a vested interest in nootropics and it shows,

"I think you need to talk with Marcus and marketing about that – some mantra about 'first to market'. I think they were worried that Z-Napse might beat them to the punch with something similar."

On video screens conveniently positioned for each person in a pod, more movie classics are playing. On console displays in the center of the group, neurometabolic rates are being monitored.

One person is having her pod chamber opened. She is having a loud conversation in Russian but not with anyone in particular.

The lab technicians are removing her electrodes and making some entries into a database.

Marshall makes an off the cuff comment,

"Is she giving a film review?"

Sophie fills Marshall in otherwise,

"Probably not. I've seen something like this before and I've asked a supervisor about it. He just fobbed me off. I spoke instead to one of the technicians. Apparently, in a very small percentage of noo users, if the dosage isn't right it can trigger a schizoid episode.

"They may hear voices, maybe triggered by some association made while watching the film. Anyway, its gotten a lot better. I haven't seen this happen for a while."

Marshall appears indifferent. He looks at his watch,

"Sophie, would you join me tonight for some 'plov'?"

The plov thickens

Ken Marshall is escorting Sophie to her flat after a very pleasant night out at a popular restaurant in Bishkek which Sophie recommended. They're both drunk and stumbling their way to the steps of her Soviet era dormitory complex. The taxi driver is asked by Marshall to await further instructions.

Sophie is slurring her words,

"That was the first time I had the courage to order Kumis."

Marshall is boisterously loud,

"Not a bad kick for fermented mare's milk!"

The moment for Sophie to make a decision has arrived. Drunk or not, she can think along parallel paths simultaneously.

There was once a great American baseball player named Yogi Berra who was famous for making wonderfully illogical statements that seemed to have mystical resonance. He was giving career advice to some new players one day and was quoted as saying, 'Always be sure that when you come to a fork in the road – take it.'

Sophie is at an emotional fork in the road. She is trying to tune into her thoughts and feelings as she ascends the stairs to her flat with key in hand and a guy who seems charming enough.

Sophie has not been with another man or woman for that matter since her husband Ian died. Is she allowed to be? Does she want to be? Will she allow herself to be? How guilty or not will she feel if or when it happens? All those questions are crossing Sophie's mind when she blurts out,

"I'm dreading the hangover!"

Marshall is still on about the mare's milk,

"Great for washing down mutton."

Sophie appreciated all the choices,

"Mutton soup, mutton stew, mutton everything."

Marshall expresses mock disappointment about desert,

"I was shattered that they were out of mutton ice cream!"

"Remind me Ken to order rabbit next time!"

"It was all 'ochen fkoosna' Sophie"

"Yup, just delicious."

Ken Marshall holds out his hand to shake Sophie's hand goodnight. Upon grasping it, he pulls her in for a kiss on her cheek. They separate for a few seconds still holding hands, eyes locked, smiles wide, and alcohol levels still up.

They kiss each other again, full on.

Carrying a large bouquet of flowers, Gil enters the hospital room where he had last visited his mother. But the bed she was lying on is empty and all the tubes and monitoring devices are gone.

Family, finality, farewell

Large clumps of dirt mixed with rocks make a thunderous and heart stopping sound as they are thrown onto the coffin of their mother by Gil and his brother Stephen in turn.

It may have been ancient happenstance or the great wisdom of those who designed burial rituals in the distant past – but the sound of rocks and earth hitting the surface of a wooden coffin six feet below creates a reverberating and unforgettable bass note of finality – if not closure.

It's a sound that can be counted on to provoke a paroxysm of cathartic wailing among assembled mourners who are near and dear to the departed.

The rent-a-priest provides a requisite homily,

"Remember thine own mercy, when others forget to appeal to it. May the souls of all departed, through the mercy of God, rest in peace."

Tears are running down Gil's cheeks. Additional thunder of rocks and earth trigger more bursts of weeping among family and friends.

Dena has also been crying. She was not very close to Gil's mum, but she had been over to her house on several occasions for a holiday meal. She grasps Gil's hand and holds it tightly. She will always remember how caring and sensitive he was when she lost her mum three years before. The funeral for Gil's mum has rekindled the memories of her own loss and grief. She barely says a word to Gil the entire afternoon nor does she need to.

Stephen walks over to Gil and they put their arms around each other.

The door to a car is heard slamming shut. A limo is seen driving off.

Stephen says to Gil,

"Dad has invited everyone to his house tonight."

Gil, lost in his grief, merely sighs.

Stephen drifts away from Gil. He takes a few steps over to a very small headstone about 5 meters from his mother's burial site.

The name engraved on the headstone is Eva Hinchliff. Stephen picks a wild flower near by and places it atop the stone marker.

Its been many years since either Stephen or Gil joined their mum on her annual pilgrimage to Eva's grave. Their mum preferred to be on her own anyway.

Eva was Gil's baby sister who he never met. She died as an infant before he was born. Stephen has the faintest of memory fragments of his baby sister. He was only two and a half when she died.

Gil learned that he had a baby sister by accident. He was only about 4 or 5 years old when he was playing hide and seek with Stephen and came across some photo's in a draw of his mum holding a baby and asked her if that was him.

A darker turn

A young man with short black hair is walking along a deserted London street in Soho. A dark blue sedan is following him at a matching pace but remaining about 10 meters behind.

The passenger door of the car opens and a man with a heavy build in a dark suit calmly exits the car, reaches the pavement, and in two seconds is behind the young man.

The dark suited man is holding a taser. He lunges forward and discharges it at the base of the neck of his target.

The young man falls to the ground in convulsions. His mouth begins to foam. Another discharge of the taser takes place only this time, it's to his chest. There are more convulsions lasting about 10 seconds and then his breathing stops.

The attacker turns the man over, rifles his clothing, and removes a wallet and keys.

The person sprawled on the pavement is Geoff Weyland.

At the MRA office Graham Calder is on the phone with his third neuro-affairs editor of the morning. He's trying to drum up interest in a series of memory rights actions that are being planned for the weeks ahead.

He sounds calm but looks distraught.

"I thought the investigative story you guys ran last week about bootleg nootropics was brilliant. I'll send you our press release about what we're up to and hope to speak with you again soon..."

Graham hangs up.

On Graham's desk is his tab showing a headline:

'*Young Computer Scientist Killed in Street Robbery*'

When Graham looks up, Gil is staring at him and looking extremely distressed.

"We are dealing with murderous fucking thugs."

Graham is still in a state of shock and denial,

"We can't be 100% certain what happened. Maybe..."

Gil was convinced beyond any doubt that what happened to Geoff was retribution and a message.

"They are monsters, they are true, sick, fucking monsters. They must be even more desperate than I thought they were."

Graham is considering cancelling the meeting planned for the afternoon which he and Gil have been preparing for for a couple of weeks.

"Maybe it's not too late to reschedule..."

Gil doesn't agree,

"I don't think we should cancel. I think it's all the more urgent."

Graham was to chair the meeting,

"I just don't think I have the stomach to go ahead with it."

Gil can almost taste fear. His mouth is dry and he hasn't eaten a thing for many hours. The news about Geoff just keeps going in circles in his head. A feeling of guilt threatens to overwhelm him,

"I hesitate to say this, and it may sound sick and self-serving, but I think we are lucky in some way that Geoff came to us and wanted to help. We didn't go to him and ask him to take some kind of risk. He knew he was taking a risk."

Graham continues the thought,

"Yeah, he knew he was taking a risk, but not a risk of being fucking killed."

"If we go ahead with today, let's push the petition for a judicial review."

Gil's anger and frustration is being vented at Graham,

"Fucking petition. What about Molotov fucking cocktails?"

Graham did not react.

Gil continues,

"We must make those motherfuckers pay."

"At any price? I believe in what we are doing, but I'm really feeling sick. We need to draw a line or at least I need to draw a line. I can only do what I can do."

After a long pause, Graham wondered out loud,

"If it wasn't 'just another street robbery', should we go to the police? Should we make contact with Geoff's family?"

Growing a global alliance

The monthly MRA meeting is taking place in a small Victorian era theatre above a pub in Central London. There are close to a hundred MRA members present. They are mostly young but maybe a quarter were over 40 and about a half dozen were elderly. You're a member if you've registered on the MRA website, subscribed to the newsletter, and gave a donation of at least 25 E-ren.

The relationship between the MRA office in London and other individuals and affiliated groups around the world that have signed up to be part of the alliance is loose and not overly prescriptive. It has yet to encounter much in the way of divisiveness over strategy or tactics. In part that's because affiliated groups can do their own thing and because the MRA is still formulating its core principles.

Filling the entire height and width of the wall behind the front stage is a video screen receiving live feeds from at least two dozen MRA members in the UK and from cities around the world.

Graham is on stage with a mic,

"Our sources are telling us that what is being planned by Cortx is a true shocker even by Cortx standards.

"Using nootropics, Cortx is planning to convert cinemas into memory cementing gas chambers.

"And if that's not enough Cortx is planning to claim commercial property rights on its movie memories.

"The implications of this take a while to sink in. It's a profanity.

"If this is confirmed, we will launch an all out campaign to collect signatures and testimony for a judicial review. A judicial review can be very powerful tactic.

"We will get as much detail as possible about the Cortx plans and forward them to everyone. We will also be approaching the UN Special Rapporteur on Human Rights to make the case that memory rights should become part of their mission. Stay tuned."

There was a lot of crosstalk and incredulity about the news from Graham. There were questions neither he nor Gil had answers for.

"That's all I can report for now. I'm eager to get the news from you all and hear what you are up to.

"Hi Sandra, what's happening in Australia?"

Sandra from Australia is on the video screen,

"Well, we discovered, surprise, surprise, that a neurotech lobbyist in Canberra wrote most of the new tax code as it applies to R&D investments in neurotech.

"We put the info on-line and let The Sydney Times know about this and to their credit they did a great exposé. It remains to be seen what changes if any there will be to the tax law. That's the big story from down under."

"Thanks so much Sandra. Whatever happens, well done!"

The next affiliate for Graham's attention was in Seattle,

"I see you Beth, how are you?"

"Hi Graham, I'm fine. We're OK.

"We've been having a bit of a debate at this end about where we should be putting our energy. Some of us, including myself feel that our main focus should be on the regulators. Cortx and the other Ntech companies can only get away with what they are allowed to get away with by the regulators.

"So, we managed to set up a meeting with the industry ombudsperson in Washington State for next week. It's obvious that Ntech oversight needs oversight, but I'll let you know what if anything comes out of it..."

A few more updates were provided from other cities and then Graham wound things down,

"Great to see everyone. One last thing, before you all go... Gil and I are writing up a draft document of MRA principles, you know, along the lines of, 'we oppose all forms of mind fucking' etc. Please send us your suggestions. We'll circulate this as soon as there's something to circulate.

"Thanks to everyone for coming and see you all again next month."

Brain tax reax

Norman Palmer CEO of Cortx is gazing at the screen of his computer which sits atop his polished cherrywood desk in his neo-retro glass and chrome appointed executive office suite.

Palmers' jaw is clenched as he reads the article which accompanies the headline,

CORTX PLANS
'BRAIN TAX!'

Palmer is fuming.

Entering his office is Phil Thurgood head of corporate security and Sally Zhao from marketing. Thurgood is a tall, barrel chested, semi-intelligent brute. He's ex-SAS. In addition to overseeing security for CHQ, he takes on trouble shooting assignments at the direction of Palmer. Recently he liaised with the computer forensic team tasked with uncovering the rat who leaked parrot photos.

Palmer is talking to no one in particular,

"Are we running some kind of sieve? How the hell did this come out? It's also full of total bullshit. It says we are planning to screen midnight snuff films. For god's sake!

"Phil, I thought this was sorted?

"I thought so too Mr. Palmer."

"Well obviously not."

Nothing more needed to be said. Phil responds with military crispness,

"On it Mr. Palmer."

Palmer then turns to Sally,

"What does this do to the timing of our trailers and the rollout of the campaign?"

"Actually Mr. Palmer, I think we can exploit it. We can push forward the trailer buys and issue a press release rebutting the lies. I can get you a revised plan by this afternoon."

Palmer gives Sally a thumbs up,

"Sounds good, please do."

Sally stands up getting ready to leave Palmers office,

"Sure thing, Mr. Palmer."

Palmer glances again at the computer screen and shakes his head,

"That's all guys."

Zhao is leaving Palmers office with Thurgood two steps behind when Palmer signals him over. In a tone that could turn water into ice, Palmer adds,

"And Phil, wring somebody's fucking neck!"

In the London MRA office, Gil is overlooking his computer with co-conspirator Tovy. Tovy is a restless twenty-something with long curly hair, a tattoo of a pentacle on the back of his neck and the refined skills of a seasoned hacker. He's knocking back one coffee after another as he hammers away at Gil's keyboard. Gil and Tovy bonded doing the rooftop billboard hijacking at the Alex protest by the Royal Society.

Gil cranes his neck to get a better angle on the action. Tovy fills him in,

"You can use the encrypted proxies and easily modify the header and the return path so they would never know or be able to trace where the email actually comes from."

Tovy completes his demo with a flurry of keystrokes,

"Voila! This is their SMTP port. I do hereby pronounce the browser interface modified for the ease and security of your interdepartmental communications."

Gil is impressed,

"Tovy, you're a genius. Remember to donate your brain to Cortx."

Eidetic cinema scheming

Gil and Graham are sitting in the café of a cineplex near their office. Gil decided to share his plans for an intelligence gathering exploit with Graham and Graham is desperately trying to talk Gil out of it.

With tickets in hand they get up to join a queue. They soon arrive at screening room 14 and take their seats.

Following ads for Honda hydro-cell transport capsules, and Gitanes Vascularettes – the cigarette that promises to combat rather than cause heart disease – a movie trailer for the Cortx Eidetic cinema begins.

Hollywood legends Clark Gable and Vivien Leigh – the stars of cinema's all time greatest box office hit 'Gone With The Wind' have been brought back to life with the same AI software used for deep fake news reports that have started three wars over the past dozen years. They look and sound perfectly like themselves at the pinnacle of their stardom.

Clark Gable is the first up to speak,

"Do you ever wish you could remember ALL the dialogue of your favourite movies?"

Vivien Leigh walks into the shot and stands besides Gable,

"Or re-live the most romantic screen moments again and again and again?"

Clark and Vivien in unison,

"Or escape into spectacular widescreen beauty any time you wish by simply closing your eyes?"

The scene changes to Tara, the idealised Southern plantation maintained by slaves but romanticised in the Hollywood classic.

Gil and Graham are taking in the trailer and it's winding them both up.

Gil is pushing his plan to get inside the Cortx lab.

Graham is unequivocal,

"It's insane, it's suicidal."

"But Graham, if we are lucky enough to get a judicial review, there is no fucking way they would ever submit to the court information about what's really going on. They would never provide inculpatory evidence of any kind. Also, if we have information which really exposes them, we'd be much more likely to be granted a judicial review."

"I think the documents you managed to get your hands on should be enough, but we have to be extremely careful about if or how we use them, and how we explain getting our hands on them."

"But they are mostly legal documents, and say nothing about the trials, the human experimentation..."

"You'll end up in some Siberian jail, or worse..."

"Graham, Kyrgyzstan is nowhere near Siberia."

"It's not worth risking your life or your career Gil."

"We'll be fighting blind otherwise."

"You are crazy – C. R. A. Z. Y. – crazy, and it will backfire."

"OK, I'm C. R. A. Z. Y. So S. U. E. me"

There's a long pause before Graham says anything else.

"Look, I know the Cultural Attaché for Kazakhstan, maybe he..."

Gil cuts in,

"Kazakhstan ain't Kyrgyzstan. Besides, what use is...?"

Graham interrupts Gil,

"Don't do it."

A middle-aged woman sitting in front of them turns around, gives them a look that could kill, and tells them to shut up.

The trailer is finishing,

"Experience the Cortx Eidetic Cinema. *Unforgettable* screenings of the greatest movies ever made..."

The revised title of the Hollywood classic soon to be re-released for opening night at the Eidetic Cinema flashes across the screen,

'GONE BUT NOT FORGOTTEN WITH THE WIND'

Anxiety of the Yes Brainers

Gil spent several weeks exchanging encrypted emails with two key contacts among the Yes Brainers in New Zealand. He was extremely cautious at first and danced around the idea of somehow getting access into the main Cortx lab.

Gil had spoken several times in video calls with these two contacts and he trusted them – and apparently they trusted him too.

They confessed that they too had considered something similar to what Gil was alluding to. They had worked hard to cultivate a useful contact in Cortx corporate communications and felt they had concocted a credible cover story and could obtain the needed visa but in the end, they chickened out, perhaps wisely. But, they were willing to share their contact at K-Lab.

Gil knew he was taking a huge gamble just to be exchanging encrypted emails with the Yes Brainers. With eye watering processing power so readily accessible, cracking encrypted messages ain't much more difficult than steaming open a letter use to be.

Gil told Dena he was travelling to New Zealand to do research for the MRA but that was about all he told her. He gave Graham his travel itinerary and contact details. He would meet with the Yes Brainers in Wellington to pick up some kit, fly to Islamabad, and from there to Bishkek. Gil had his visa and most importantly, an email from the corporate communications department of Cortx saying that the manager of K-Lab would be expecting him.

Zigs and zags to Bishkek

If Gil travelled to Bishkek directly from London it would only have taken about 12 hours to get there. But with the global zigs and zags he decided were necessary, it would take him almost four full days to make it to this Central Asian city.

He travelled first to New Zealand, a 24 hour flight from London. He met his contacts at the Yes Brainers and hung out with them for half a day. They provided some professional photography kit as promised. They also provided a crash course on three point lighting for head shots.

Gil then took a 27 hour flight to Islamabad which was directly on route to Bishkek. Islamabad is the base for a production company that occasionally does PR work for Cortx. Unbeknownst to them, they were part of Gil's cover. To be able to say he's flying in from Islamabad is expected to add credibility.

From his Islamabad stopover, Gil completed his marathon journey arriving 19 hours later at the Manas International Airport outside Bishkek. The season was turning and the fabled Russian winter was approaching.

Gil knows hardly a word of Russian but translation visors have long reduced the linguistic stress of international travel.

The visor is akin to a clear facial safety shield. When activated, a menu allows you to select languages. Your speech is immediately translated into the language of your choice as text which appears on the face of the otherwise clear visor. When a person responds in their native language, it too is immediately translated and the text cleverly flops orientation and shrinks in size enabling the visor wearer to easily see and read it.

The lab was on the far side of Bishkek from the airport. Gil jumped into a taxi with several large black canvas bags labelled 'Fragile'. The trip from the airport would take Gil through the heart of town.

While snaking through Bishkek, Gil was pleasantly overcome by a wonderful bouquet of spice smells. Gil put on and activated his visor to speak to the driver who didn't otherwise understand a word of English. Gil wanted to know about the incredible smell. The driven said they were passing near the 'Osh rynok spetsiy', which translated to: 'Osh spice market'.

The driver, thinking Gil might be a tourist, offered to take him for 50 E-rens to the regionally famous Alpine lake which locals call the 'Blue Eye of Earth'. When asked about its name the driver explained the lake is called that because it's shaped like a human eye when viewed from planes or satellite. But Gil didn't schedule any time for sightseeing – even a chance to see the eye of the world.

Gil was listening to a Russian DJ on the taxi radio playing country western music. About a dozen Yurts punctuate the passing valley landscape. The driver informs Gil he is only minutes away from arriving at the lab. The medulla at the base of Gil's brain is beginning to secrete epinephrine – aka adrenalin.

After the 45 minute drive, the taxi arrives at the security gate of the Cortx lab facility. It feels as if Gil has circumnavigated the planet to get there – he has. ID is presented to the security guard in a booth and a barrier is lifted. Gil feels a rush of adrenaline.

The taxi drops Gil off by the entrance to the long glass corridor which channels into the main reception area. Gil walks along the corridor and crosses the symbolic 'synaptic gap' too nervous and burdened by his canvas bags for any architectural allusion to neural pathways to register.

Within a few minutes of arriving at reception, a PR official, Kees Ridijk is greeting Gil. Kees is tall, forty something, with short dark-ish blonde hair, very friendly, and he has a tic – his right eye occasionally twitches. Kees insists on helping Gil with his bags.

The warm reception by Kees has the effect of slightly reducing Gil's anxiety level,

"I received an email that you were coming Mr. Lynchfield. How was your trip?"

"The flight went very smoothly, thank you. Seeing the snow on the Celestial mountain range approaching Bishkek was beautiful."

"You have accommodations in Bishkek?"

"Yes, that's sorted."

"What are you photographing?"

"Just some head shots and exterior shots for the annual report."

"You are aware of course that no photography is allowed inside the lab?"

"I'm aware of that."

"Who are you photographing?"

"The lab manager Dr. Van Trotta."

"Who else?"

"And the lead programmer..."

"That would be Sophie, Ms. Sophie Hudson."

"Yes, and I also expect to photograph a couple of other scientists."

Kees directs Gil into a small conference room off the corridor,

"Leave all of your equipment here for now. It will be absolutely safe. I can take you on a quick tour, which you might find interesting."

"That would be great."

"And leave behind your phone and any other communication or photographic devices you have."

As Kees is escorting Gil down a long corridor, they pass the entrance to the infirmary.

Gil catches a glimpse inside. A delirious man appears to be yelling at someone but not necessarily the two men in lab coats who are restraining him. Gil wishes he had his translation visor.

Kees stiffens at first, then attempts to reassure Gil,

"It's not really serious. We try and help, but some volunteers are heavy drinkers."

Kees takes Gil up a flight onto a narrow balcony which extends around the lab perimeter. There is not a lot of activity on the lab floor below, but Kees points out the zone which contains the nootropic pods.

Gil can barely believe he is actually inside K-Lab. He can only take mental snapshots but starts to fire questions at Kees, careful not to come across as too prying, just curious.

Does he know how many volunteers have taken part in the research? How does a person qualify to be in the program? Does the lab stay in touch with the volunteers? Are the nootropics produced on site? Have you ever tried them yourself? Is it as amazing an experience as he's heard it is?

Kees gives only vague answers, but there were a few useful tidbits. Over time, he thinks there have been hundreds maybe around a 1000 volunteers, mostly from the immediate region. Lots of farmers, some university students. The local economy isn't very good, the lab must have had ten times more applications than needed. Kees refuses to say how much people were paid claiming he doesn't know.

They do have the capacity to produce small amounts of nootropics on site but only for the clinical trials. The location of the main production facility is not made public for security reasons. He has never tried the nootropics personally, but the Lab policy allows employees to sample the nootropics if they are willing to fill out a 12 page health report and sign a 15 page release beforehand and a 20 page questionnaire afterwards. Was the research on the nootropics complete? Kees was especially vague on that one.

Kees stays with Gil as he begins to unpack kit from his canvas bags. For unexplained reasons, there is delay in meeting up with the lab manager Dr. Van Trotta. It is approaching lunch time and Kees escorts Gil to the canteen and agrees to come back for him in about an hour.

There's already a long queue of lab workers with trays who are making their way towards the buffet. The walls are covered in a checkerboard pattern of white and black tiles and many of the fixtures including a row of maroon vinyl booths have the look of a retro American diner. One of the most charming features of the canteen is a large hand painted menu above the buffet with the greeting,

Rita's Far Far Away from Home Home Cookin'
The best you'll ever get west of Tibet!

While Gil is in the queue, he turns around to face two men in lab coats. He looks for any opportunity to strike up a conversation.

"Is the food here as good as it smells?"

The guy to Gil's left responds,

"If you've never had Rita's cooking, you're in for a treat."

"I haven't but I'm looking forward to it. Hi, I'm Gil."

"Hi, I'm Roy, and this is 'Birdbrain'.

Clearly there is some kind of inside joke going on here. Gil just smiles and reaches out to shake Roy's hand. He then reaches over to shake the hand of 'Birdbrain'. 'Birdbrain' is in his late thirties and wearing stylish glasses with a tortoise shell frame.

Gil notices a tattoo on the four knuckles of his right hand which are the letters A L E X. Gil shakes the hand of 'Birdbrain'. Roy and 'Birdbrain' clearly have a sense of humour,

"His real name is Yoshio, he's a very shy genius. He's the nanosurgical control pilot who did most of the neural fusion work on the Alex chip."

In spite of Gil's tirades against the animal torturers, he is awestruck,

"Wow! That is absolutely incredible. I can't believe I'm actually meeting the person who did that. What an honour to meet you."

Birdbrain responds by way of channelling Alex,

"*Moody beggars, starving for a time of pell-mell havoc and confusion.*"

Roy laughs and translates,

"He's trying to say we're late and he's very hungary! Anyway, nice to meet you Gil. Enjoy Rita's cooking!"

Gil is loading up his tray and in gregarious mode. He sees a woman in front of him loading her bowl with salad ingredients,

"That looks really fresh!"

"I grew these tomatoes myself."

"A neuroscientist with a green thumb?"

"Nope, a data slave."

"A 'data slave'?"

"Well, it feels like that. Actually, a programmer."

"So I wasn't a million miles off. A computer scientist with a green thumb. Hi, I'm Gil."

"Nice to meet you. I'm Sophie."

Gil's pulse rate just about doubles,

"Are you by any chance Sophie Hudson?"

"C'est moi. And how do you know..."

"May I join you for lunch? I'd be happy to explain how I know your name."

"Why not?"

Gil immediately warms to Sophie's unpretentiousness. With soil visible under her fingernails, there is literally and figuratively a down to earth quality about her.

They slide into one of the vinyl booths as a small group is leaving it.

Gil explains his cover story and that she was one of the Cortx lab personnel he hopes to take a photo of for the annual report.

"I don't think so. Nobody warned me about this and even if they did, I would say no thank you. I'm very camera shy."

"But, there should have been an email."

"I'm sorry, I don't recall seeing any email. Besides, my contract ends in a few weeks, so I don't see why they would want me to appear in the new annual report. I'll be heading home soon".

"Where's that?"

"London."

"If you don't mind my asking, where in London?"

"South London, near Wandsworth Common."

There was a momentary lull in the conversation as they

ate their lunch, then Gil went into mission mode cloaked as idle curiosity,

"As a programmer, were you at all involved in the development of the nootropics?"

"Well, let me put it this way, almost everything done here these days involves huge datasets that need to be managed. I would be involved with that. But most of the development related to the nootropics happened before I got here so, it was another team. What's your interest in nootropics?"

Gil was caught off guard,

"Neurotech, nootropics, it's just something I'm fascinated by, generally."

"Generally?"

Gil instantly realizes how lame that must sound. He tries to recover,

"Actually, I'm particularly interested in nootropics and heuristics."

Sophie seems to perk up,

"Heuristics?"

"Yeah, all that philosophical stuff about what is real knowledge and how we assign values..."

Sophie starts to smile and she puts down her knife and fork,

"My post-grad thesis was about heuristics and memory."

Gil was actually not faking it,

"I love it! More effort greater value, less effort less value."

Sophie was delighted,

"Bingo! Nootropics in a nutshell."

It is an intellectually bonding moment but the moment is cut short as Kees arrives with Dr. Van Trotta.

Kees was his friendly and smiling self,

"I see you've met Ms. Hudson. Let me introduce Dr. Van Trotta."

Gil and Van Trotta shake hands,

"Mr. Lynchfield, I appreciate how far you've come. We did get an email but haven't had a chance to confirm the details with corporate."

Gil swallowed hard,

"Is there a problem?"

Van Trotta was in back covering mode,

"There are security issues, lab hazards, privacy agreements, insurance restrictions, etc. Nothing is straight forward. I'm sure you understand.

"The exteriors are not a problem as long as there are no people in your photo's and certainly no car or travel pod license plates."

"And the head shots?"

"Tell me again, what exactly do you need?"

"I need a photo of you Dr. Van Trotta, ideally in the lab."

"Sorry, I cannot allow that."

"We don't necessarily have to do this inside the lab. You can be at the entrance to the lab and I can keep the background out of focus. It just makes for a more interesting picture. You can see any photo I take and approve it."

Van Trotta glances over to Kees. Kees gives a slight tilt of his head which is taken for a tacit OK.

Van Trotta looks at his watch,

"When do you want to do this?"

Gil is setting up two lights at the threshold to the main lab. There is very little activity in the background. He can see the harnesses used for the nanoscopes but no subjects are in them. Sophie Hudson is working at her console on the upper level overlooking the lab.

Van Trotta is on his phone not far from where Gil is setting up. Snippets of his conversation can be overheard.

"Look, I'm only the damned lab manager, I don't work for marketing. I'm telling you, London has its head up its ass about this..."

In a matter of seconds, Gil grabs several clandestine shots of the lab. A wide shot, the harnesses, the detail of an 'Emergency Vent' on one of the plastic pods, a row of syringes, a gurney with straps for arms, legs, and waist.

Gil shifts his attention to positioning a lab chair for Van Trotta just as he arrives for his photo,

"I really don't have much time. Will this take long?"

"Two or three minutes, tops. Please have a seat."

Gil is placing one of his camera bags just inside the threshold of the lab against a wall as he packs up his other kit and prepares to leave the premises.

Van Trotta escorts Gil to a waiting taxi.

"Sorry you didn't get everything you hoped for."

"Will I be able to get through security at 7AM – to photograph the exterior in the morning light?"

"I'll let them know. I'm in at 8, I'll look for you then."

Gil gets into the taxi.

Gil asks the driver if there is anywhere nearby with a nice view to watch the setting sun. In about 20 minutes, after ascending a narrow dirt track off the main road, the taxi arrives at a parking zone near the top of a mountain. There's a spectacular view of a valley and the jagged profiles of the snow capped Celestial mountains receding into the distance backlit by the setting sun. In the opposite direction, Gil sees the ancient mountains in the flattering orange light of the golden hour. He takes out his phone and asks the driver to take a photo of him with the gold lit mountains in the background.

To Gil's surprise, there is a phone signal on the mountain top. He sends the photo to Graham with a message,

"Greetings from beautiful Kyrgyzstan, so far, so good, Gil"

Gil kills some time taking a few more photos. The sun is setting, the temperature is rapidly dropping, and it's starting to get dark. He explains to the driver that he will need to wait a bit longer then return to the lab where he expects to meet someone. He would like the taxi to wait for him back at the lab but since he's not sure how long he'll be, he would like to negotiate a flat rate with the driver. The driver agrees.

It's dark when Gil arrives back at the K-Lab security gate.

"Hello. Yes, I was here earlier today. I forgot one of my bags. It has the key to my hotel room in it. I need to get back in to the main building just for a minute. Is there a security guard who can escort me?"

The guard at the gate responds in Russian,

"Odin moment"

He makes a call to another security guard.

"Someone to meet at reception."

The barrier goes up.

There is a security guard waiting for Gil in reception,

"Where is bag?"

"I think it's by the infirmary."

The guard stares at Gil for a moment. Gil doesn't blink.

The Guard begins to escort Gil through the building opening locked doors and walking down a long corridor heading to the infirmary. Gil notices the CCTV cameras that punctuate the path.

Upon entering the infirmary, Gil feigns looking around for his bag, then walks over to the man glimpsed earlier in the day who was behaving deliriously. The man is staring off into space. Gil glances at the foot of the bed and sees his name,

"Hi there, Askar! Are you feeling any better?"

The zombified man stares blankly.

"It was good to talk with you earlier!"

The guard is listening to Gil with incredulity,

"Did he really talk you?"

"Is that unusual?"

"Doctor's try days to talk to him."

"Maybe I just got lucky. What's his problem?"

"Talk doctor. Nano djavoli.

Gil did not understand much Russian,

"Djavoli?"

The guard tries to translate,

"Djavoli… ahhh, how you say, 'devil.'"

"And them?"

Gil gestures to several other patients in the infirmary.

The guard responds,

"Djavoli, djavoli. Find bag?"

"I thought I left it here, but I just remembered exactly where I left it. It's right inside the main entrance to the big lab."

As Gil and the guard navigate their way to the lab their movements are being monitored in the security control room. As they get to the threshold of the lab the guard gets a text message.

"Please stay. I be soon."

The guard walks off and Gil is left alone in the Axion lab not far from the body conforming plastic pods.

Gil's eyes dart about. His heart is racing. He looks over his shoulder then cautiously approaches one of the nootropic pods.

It's in the open position. There are plasma screens, feeder tubes, computers, and valves. He peers over to the syringes to see if he can glean any detail about what they are used for.

His camera in its softcase is slung over his shoulder. He's tempted to steal another photo but decides not to push his luck. He takes the camera and places it on the floor and walks nearer to the pod.

Gil wants to sit in the pod but dares not. He hesitantly reaches out to touch the cap which holds the leads for brain monitoring. Just as he's about to touch it, he almost jumps out of his skin. He's startled by a security guard standing close behind him.

The guard is actually smiling at Gil. His English is very good,

"It's OK. It's fascinating is it not? Please, feel free to check it out."

Gil hesitates in part because he is embarrassed and in part because he is caught so unawares. The security guard gives Gil a nudge. Gil climbs aboard.

A dozen questions begin the swirl in Gil's head as he considers what to ask the guard without raising undue suspicion.

Before Gil realises what is happening, the guard swiftly shut the pod and pulls the lever which locks and seals it.

A tidal wave of fear overcomes Gil. His amygdala launches into overdrive. A cerebral flood of cortisol and adrenaline coincide with a hard knot in the pit of his stomach.

Gil quickly realises he has no physical leverage whatsoever to try and push open the pod.

From inside the pod, Gil's voice is muffled,

"What the hell are you doing, let me out of here!"

Gil sees the back of someone in a lab coat about 15 meters away at a control panel.

Gil is trying to kick but he cannot bend his legs. He hears the sound of a pump starting and feels the pressure change inside the pod. The nootropic mixture is entering. It's not quite odourless. Amidst the fear and frenzy, Gil realises it has the very faint aroma of popcorn!

Gil is screaming and demanding to be let out. His breathing begins to tighten. He's having a panic attack. It's his first full on panic attack in more than 20 years.

The video monitor above Gil's head is swivelling into viewing position.

Gil can't catch his breath. He thinks he's going to die.

Outside the pod, computer screens and status indicators are lighting up.

A childhood memory returns to Gil about what to do in the event of a panic attack. Gil tries to take slow deep breaths through his nose.

Gil starts to hear white noise. The video monitor is coming on line. He hears a voice from a small speaker inside the pod,

"Welcome to K-Lab Mr. Hinchliff. We trust this will be a memorable visit."

Gil is terror-stricken and becoming disoriented.

He is shouting at the top of his lungs,

"Let me out of here you fuckers! Open this goddamned thing."

Gil is pushing and kicking and straining in vain,

"Fuck."

The video monitor is now only about half a meter from Gil's face and it's starting to play film clips. Some are contemporary, some are historic, and all horrific.

A man with his hands tied behind his back is standing at the edge of an outdoor pit. The force of the shots by a Nazi execution squad kills him and knocks him into the pit.

CUT TO

Distended bodies on a battlefield.

CUT TO

A prisoner being water boarded.

CUT TO

Assembly line killings of cows in an abattoir.

It's a smorgasbord of grisly horrors with sound and picture.

Gil is thrashing about and moaning. Not all the images are horrific. There are also clips from a Soviet era kitsch musical.

Men and women peasants wearing work overalls and red bandanas around their necks are dancing and singing astride a tractor as a corn crop is being harvested.

Gil is starting to sweat profusely. He has closed his eyes. He's no longer shouting but muttering to himself. He's completely exhausted,

"You motherfuckers, let me out of here."

Gil hears the voice that spoke to him earlier,

"We have a very special treat for you Mr. Hinchliff."

The man who was standing by the control screen has picked up a syringe. He begins to look inside a wall mounted cabinet which holds an assortment of drugs and solutions.

An amber light is beginning to blink above the pod where Gil is imprisoned. It's part of a pre-programmed safety protocol to limit exposure time in a pod filled with mind fucking gas.

Throughout Gil's misadventure, Sophie Hudson is working late making data entries for one of over 100 Axion computer nodes. The blinking light below catches her attention. She decides to head down to the lab floor to investigate.

Sophie glimpses the backs of two lab workers exiting the lab floor.

She's aghast to see Gil inside one of the pods.

Sophie immediately punches the emergency vent button. She lifts the lever and opens the pod. Gil is breathless.

"How the hell did you end up in there?"

Gil is barely able to talk. He raises a finger to indicate 'give me a moment'. Sweat us pouring down his face. He takes several deep breaths then speaks,

"Wrong turn at the cineplex."

"How long were you in there?"

"Too long."

"Didn't anyone brief you? Explain 'Otema'?"

"'Otema'?"

"'Otema' is the Russian word for 'cancel'. If for whatever reason you want out of the pod you say that word out loud, the system shuts down, and the pod case opens."

"The bastard who locked me inside forgot to brief me."

Sophie turns off the video screen and inspects the nootropic settings.

"Continue to breathe slowly and deeply. How do you feel?"

Gil is slow to respond. His face is still dripping with sweat. He places his hands over his eyes and then removes them,

"I feel like the subject of a snuff film."

"I don't understand how this could have happened, or why it happened"

Rather than wait for an answer, Sophie pulls over a gurney and insists that Gil climb aboard. She helps to steady him as he follows her order.

She wheels him to a nearby diagnostic scanner. While Gil remains on the gurney, Sophie is beginning to slide Gil's head into the machine,

"Please, please, please. Hold on. I don't think I can take any more of anything right now."

"It's just a scanner. You won't feel anything. You'll hear a faint hum that's all. It will help me to see what's going on"

"You mean, what does a mind fuck look like?"

Sophie positions Gil's head inside the scanner then activates a nearby screen. On it is a colourful hi-rez real time representation of the metabolic activity of Gil's brain.

"Your amygdala looks like its just been in a war zone."

"It feels like I was."

"The level of endogenous cortisol is off the chart."

"I thought you were a data-slave?"

"You hang out around the 'NooZoo', you pick this stuff up. You were watching things?"

"Pretty horrible shit. Killings, torture..."

"I don't believe this. Why the hell...?"

"It's a long story. Anyway, when it got to the abattoir, I don't know, I just closed my eyes."

"That was exactly the right thing to do."

"Maybe not soon enough. Maybe I managed to catch the best bits."

"Glad you still have a sense of humour."

"When I close my eyes the images return."

"That's awful, unbelievable."

"Is that your review as a film critic or a diagnosis of brain damage?"

"You really do make me laugh. It may be better for now if you don't close your eyes."

"That's just great."

Gil is slowly being pulled out of the scanner,

"My camera!"

Gil hobbles off the gurney and stumbles over to the pod and sees that his camera is gone. He looks over to the lab entrance and realises that the case he left there has also disappeared,

"Fuck, shit, piss."

Sophie walks over to the medical cabinet near the pod and rummages around inside until she finds what she is looking for. She heads back to Gil,

"You might want to take one of these."

"What's that?"

"Decertraline. It won't necessarily stop the images but if taken soon enough it will help flatten the spike of hormones that make a trauma *feel* traumatic."

"Jesus, how much of this stuff is needed around here?"

Sophie lets out a heavy sigh which speaks volumes.

Neuroterrorist on ice

Gil's head is face down in a basin filled with ice. He comes up for air after about 20 seconds, takes several deep breaths, then back down for another 20 seconds, and up again,

"That's all I can take. My thoughts have become icicles."

Sophie hands Gil a towel. They are in her spacious flat which is part of the dormitory complex near the lab.

"So, you're a neuroterrorist?"

"Yeah right! You saw what they did to me, and I'm the neuroterrorist?"

"You asked for it."

"Thanks."

"I've been here for almost two years. I see mostly good people trying to do good things. You lied to everyone. You're spying. I shouldn't even be talking to you – whoever you are."

"As I said, my name is Gil Hinchliff. There's a difference between spying and investigating."

"If I can believe anything you say."

"Why ARE you talking to me? Why are you helping me? I doubt your boss will appreciate it."

Sophie assumed the other shoe will inescapably drop – but in the morning.

"As I said, my contract ends soon. My head has already left the building. Whatever it is you are doing here or trying to do is wrong. I haven't a clue what's going to happen to you. I've not done anything wrong and there's not much they can do to me anyway."

The ice treatment helped but Gil is experiencing aftershocks,

"I just had a flashback. What's happening to me? When will it stop? Will it ever stop? What if it never stops!?"

"With an OD of that gas you can expect flashbacks, hallucinations, brain fevers, memory disorders, and possibly seizures..."

"Hallucinations? Seizures? What the fucking hell!"

"I was told that the latest formulas have less risk of serious side effects, but I've not yet seen the latest trial datasets."

"Great, how reassuring."

"Things should settle down in a matter of weeks, maybe a bit longer depending on the time you were in the pod. For the next few days – don't freak out and don't try to fight it. Don't close your eyes unnecessarily."

"Why the hell should I ever want to unnecessarily close my eyes?"

"If you're feeling feverish, the ice water should help. I think things will eventually subside, but stress can stir things up."

"Is what I got better or worse than the 'Nano Djavoli'?"

"Where did you hear that?"

It was clear from Sophie's tone she heard about 'nano-devils'. Gil wanted to be as honest as he could but was reluctant to admit he made his way into the infirmary,

"A graffiti in the men's room?"

At that moment, a heavily armed para-military unit smashes open Sophie's door. They're brandishing Kalashnikids and shouting 'Ruki werkh, Ruki werkh!'.

A terrified Sophie throws her hands over her head. A half second later, Gil does the same.

Orange jumpsuit blues

Gil wakes up in a faded orange jumpsuit with several days growth of beard. His cell is very small, dark, and filthy. There's one opening on a wall less than a foot square but too high to look out of. It has one thick vertical bar in the center.

En suite accommodations include a hole in the floor in one corner for a toilet and a sink with cold water only which is a little bigger than a soup bowl. At night there is heavy traffic of vermin.

It's the morning of day 3 in captivity. Gil's sense of time is disoriented by his surroundings and by his ill-fated encounter with a Cortx gas chamber.

He has not been allowed to make a call, send an email, or have any communication with the outside world.

The food is at the opposite end of the spectrum relative to Rita's home cooking. Meals might include a piece of black bread, a few ounces of steamed meat with a bone, some barley, and yesterday there was a bonus potato.

Gil is very worried about Dena being very worried. If he ever gets out of this, he knows Graham will be a one man chorus of 'I told you so's.'

The past two nights have been the nightmares that Sophie warned him not to freak out about. Insomnia turned out to be a preferable option to closing his eyes and trying to drift off and witness war crimes. Last night was a bit less feverish than the night before. He may have dozed off for half an hour without any cinematic atrocities.

As Gil lies on his narrow bunk staring up at the ceiling, he hears approaching footsteps and the opening of an outer steel door on the approach to his cell.

A guard is escorting James Mitchell-Williams an immaculately dressed grey haired middle-aged man to see Gil.

When Mitchell-Williams arrives outside the bars he introduces himself.

"Good morning Mr. Hinchliff. My name is Mitchell-Williams, James Mitchell-Williams. I'm from the British Consulate. Can we talk?"

The guard proceeds to begin to open Gil's cell door.

"Yeah, sure. I'd make you tea if I could, but..."

"No worries."

Mitchell-Williams enters the cell and remains standing. Gil sits up in the bed with his back propped up against the wall and his legs covered by a thick bristly brown wool blanket. The jailer locks the door behind Mitchell-Williams and walks away.

"When you missed your flight back to London, a friend of yours, Mr. Graham Calder became extremely anxious about your well being.

"He contacted me at the embassy in Kazakhstan and pleaded with me to look into your situation.

"Apparently, one of the corporate citizens of Kyrgyzstan wants to charge you with trespass, industrial espionage, and being some kind of terrorist. They would like to lock you up and throw away the key. Should they succeed at having you classified a terrorist, they'd be able to skip the nuisance of an open trial.

"Mr. Hinchliff, you really don't want that. I'm trying to convince your friends at Encore that they don't want that either.

"Over the past two years the Kyrgyzstan Ministry of Health has received several complaints from local families accusing the Cortx lab of conducting human experimentation in ways that do not conform to the standards established by the revised Helsinki Accords.

"I assume you know that the Helsinki Accords are the benchmark for conducting human experimentation within a strict ethical framework.

"For whatever reason, the Ministry has been dragging its feet about conducting a follow-up investigation.

"The British Consulate finds this disturbing but is less likely to intervene because the complaints are not coming from British nationals.

"Just how much pressure the consulate can or will bring to bear to investigate these allegations remains to be seen. Numerous lab employees are British and that could be a factor. It cuts both ways.

"If you were to be put on trial here, I made it abundantly clear to my counterparts in Bishkek that the British government would be forced to consider defending your interests as a British subject and that a trial could prove embarrassing to Cortx in unexpected ways."

Gil was listening intently but couldn't restrain himself from jumping in with a question,

"Would it be possible to get more detailed information about the complaints that were made?"

"My goodness Mr. Hinchliff, what cloud are you living on? Have you not noticed you are in a jail cell? You are in serious trouble. I don't think you realise how close you are to falling down a rabbit hole and never being seen or heard from again.

"They still want to see you in jail and disbarred. Apparently you are a lawyer for god's sake!

"If you agree to desist from any current or future legal proceedings against them they will consider dropping the industrial espionage charges against you. If you..."

Gil was already mounting his defence,

"What I was doing was not industrial espionage. I'm not working for a rival company and stealing secrets for a competitive advantage or trying to cause economic damage per se to Cortx. What I was doing was squarely in the public interest and defensibly so. They are no better than drug pushers marketing an unsafe product to thousands and they hope millions of people. They are politically corrupt and please believe me, they have blood on their hands."

"Mr. Hinchliff, Cortx has huge political influence here. If they press their charges against you here, you will – I can almost guarantee it – lose.

"They have made an offer. I suggest you seriously consider it. The rabbit hole otherwise awaits.

"The ball is in your court Mr. Hinchliff."

A fury too far

Dena is in the kitchen of her flat standing by the kettle with her back to Gil who is sitting at the dining table. She is shaking her head as she waits for the water to boil. She is replaying in her head a week of anxiety, fear, more fear, drama, relief, and now simmering fury.

"How could you? What were you thinking? Why didn't you tell me where you were going, what you were doing...?"

"Because you would think I'm crazy? Because you would try to talk me out of going? Because I didn't want you to worry..."

"Gilbert, what you did was crazy. I would have been crazy not to try and talk you out of it. You friend Graham also thinks you're crazy and said he tried to talk you out of going too. You wouldn't even listen to him. He was freaked out. At least you told him more than you told me.

"Do you have a fucking clue how worried I was? 'Going to New Zealand to do some research'. You lied to me."

"I didn't lie, I just didn't tell you everything. I'm sorry. I was..."

"I'm sorry? Sorry isn't enough. I'm just so damn fed up.

"I almost feel betrayed. Maybe I do feel betrayed. I certainly feel disrespected. I was so fucking worried, I couldn't concentrate on my own work. My dad could tell something was wrong. I told him you had disappeared. For all I knew you had been kidnapped. I feared the worst. He called the Foreign Office asking for advice. I couldn't sleep."

Gil feels tossed into a boiling stew of his own making. He can see clearly why he did what he did but at the same time feels deep regret at the fracture it has caused between him and Dena.

Like his mental turbulence, Gil hopes that Dena's fury will pass. But he saw no easy way to make amends. And, there was something else on his mind – Sophie.

Dena pours herself a cup of tea and begins to walk out of the kitchen,

"You can make youself a cup of tea Gil, if you wish."

Overflowing memory chamber

As Sophie enters the carpeted foyer of her home her eyes are tearing up. It's bittersweet to finally be back home.

Dormant engrams spanning 15 years of life here with Ian are being kindled, reactivated, vibrating. These bundles of associations were why she decided to take the job in far away Kyrgyzstan in the first place.

The taxi pod driver was kind enough to help her carry her bags to the door but politely declined her offer of tea. It wasn't a hollow gesture on Sophie's part. She was not looking forward to entering the empty house alone. Her home can be described as a Victorian era semi-detached house on a quiet tree-lined street or an overflowing memory chamber.

Apart from the faintly musty smell she has long since stopped noticing, upon entering her house Sophie is struck by the quiet, by the conspicuous absence of computers humming.

The idea of selling the house and moving out of London is still in play. But for now, she just wants to take some time off and decompress. With her exaflop programming experience on such a high prestige and cutting edge project, she's not too worried about finding work in the future.Sophie makes her way to her bedroom, throws one of the largest of her suitcases onto her bed, unzips it and begins to unpack her clothes. Inside the suitcase are also several small noo-gas canisters along with their tubeworks.

After about 3 months at K-Lab her curiosity about the product she was helping to develop got the better of her. She filled in the paperwork and signed the release. It was another couple of weeks before she found the courage to give nootropics a try.

Also soon after arriving at the lab, Sophie was delighted to get permission to have access to a small allotment to grow her own vegetables. Initially, she tried the nootropics for only a few minutes while listening to some classical music and planting seeds. She was pleasantly surprised. It was an enjoyable effect which enhanced the pleasure of her gardening. On the evening of her first use, she could close her eyes and still smell the earth.

In the beginning, Sophie was very cautious to use nootropics for short intervals in circumstances where she was enjoying a simple pleasure. If she used it during the day while gardening, it helped in the evenings to vividly recall pleasant garden sights and smells and avoid sorrowful thoughts of Ian. Sophie gradually started to use the nootropics more often.

The afternoon light is slashing through the bedroom window and falling upon the duvet of Sophie's bed as she begins to get undressed. Next to the bed is a mahogany end table with an art deco lamp of a dancer. Although it's midafternoon, Sophie reaches over to turn it on. The sculpted translucent figure becomes illuminated from within by a warm diffuse light. There's an armchair with a striped cushion next to the end table. Sophie throws her blouse, bra and knickers onto the chair.

Sophie swipes the sensor to get the shower started and when the temperature is right, steps behind the interactive curtain. Her figure is slim and fit.

It's been a while since Sophie checked email or watched the news on her home shower curtain.

As Sophie is washing,

"Open email from Ken Marshall."

She's reluctant to admit it to herself, but she's looking forward to seeing Marshall again,

'Hi Sophie. Welcome back to London. I'm very sorry to have to bail out for tomorrow. Something came up at work and it's going to be a very late night. I'll give you a call soon.'

What she has no way of knowing is that Marshall wrote the email before being canoodled in bed by Sally Zhao. Their affair had turned torrid.

Sophie gives the voice command to check phone messages.

'Hello Sophie. This is Gil Hinchliff. Are you back in London yet? I hope you're well and...'

Sophie had trepidations about exchanging numbers with Gil on the night of the commando raid. She almost felt like a witness to a crime scene and that they may need to communicate about it at some point.

She had no regrets about having helped him. Maybe she admired his idealism even if she didn't fully relate to his ideals. Maybe it was the discussion about heuristics left hanging? Maybe she liked his sense of humour? It was certainly not a case of looking at a man's brain scan and liking what she saw.

Gil's message continues,

'...I can't tell you how sorry I am about what happened. I did finally make it out of there and I'm back in London. I would not blame you if you never want to see or hear from me again. But, I was hoping there's a chance we could meet up even very briefly, for a coffee. Please call me back or email me if you can. Bye for now.'

The water is cascading off her face as Sophie mumbles under her breath, "Not in my lifetime."

After the shower, Sophie prepares herself a *Rhodiola Rosea herbal tea. It's an ancient Chinese medicine said to improve brain function. Sophie has been very cautious and restrained in her use of the nootropics but has noticed a decline in her short term memory. She forgets small things like which pocket is holding the plane ticket, or where did she place her flat keys, and things like that. She's not convinced it has anything to do with the nootropics but an ancient brain booster can't hurt.*

As expected, Sophie's back yard is overgrown with weeds. As a first order of business, she is looking forward to selectively uprooting them. She's not an indiscriminate weed killer. She considers attitudes towards weeds to be the horticultural equivalent of racism. So many 'weeds' are so beautiful and underappreciated. She loves bishops weed, horsetail, and fireweed but others can be nutrient hogs.

After tea, Sophie confronts her back yard. Docks go, nettles go, horse-tail stays, bishop's weed can be trimmed back a bit, aquilegia stays.

To the sound of a Bartok violin concerto, Sophie is pulling up some tall cleavers in her back garden while tethered to a noo-canister. She's wearing a loose fitting sweater top and bluejeans.

Sophie suddenly yelps in pain as the flesh on two of her fingers gets lacerated by some brambles. She bursts into tears as she inspects the torn skin and blood then violently yanks the tube off her face.

It's been over two years since Sophie has had the opportunity to visit her husband Ian.

The cemetery is beautifully landscaped and the sky is clear as she makes her way to his headstone.

She kneels down and faces the inscription,

Ian Hudson
Where there is memory there is life

Sophie leans over and gently taps the black inlaid Eternascreen. Her touch activates the solid-state playback of videoclips from their life together.

In the video,

Sophie is blowing out birthday candles on a cake shaped like a motorboat / Ian hands Sophie a birthday card with a set of keys / Sophie and Ian being windswept in the sun on a speeding motorboat / Ian is navigating with Sophie's arms around his waist / Sophie and Ian in hotel swimming pool. / Sophie playfully pushes Ian's head underwater, he bobs up and pushes her head underwater in turn...

Sophie is sobbing with her face pressed against the headstone screen.

Ian was also a computer programmer. He and Sophie worked together on a number of projects including a retinal protein delivery app which was part of post operative care for ocular implants. It was the project which first brought her to the attention of Cortx.

Sophie is being forcibly restrained on an operating table as a surgeon's assistant is shaving off a section of her hair. She's thrashing about and trying to scream, but she's lost her voice. Several surgeons in scrubs and masks loom over her. The operating theatre light is blindingly bright. A cranial saw is activated. It's piercing and high pitched sound is getting closer and louder. Sophie is consumed by pulsing panic and excruciating terror.

The merciless terror begins to lift as Sophie awakens from a hellish nightmare. It's a post-nightmare moment of profound relief.

The end of Sophie's contract and her return to London and the home she shared with Ian – are easy suspects to blame for her psychological riptides.

Corporate Citizen debrief

It would be an understatement to say Marjorie Cantini's office at Cortx HQ was spartan. It was so lacking in amenities or character it felt like it could be a set for a sensory deprivation experiment.

Sophie had been summoned to meet with Cantini as soon as she returned to London. It was routine for HR to debrief departing employees but Cantini had a supplemental agenda.

"Thank you for coming, Ms. Hudson. My name is Marjorie Cantini and I'm with Corporate Citizenship. The purpose of this meeting is to explain the benefits you are entitled to as part of Cortx alumni and answer any questions you may have about them. I would also like to outline the responsibilities expected of departing employees.

"But importantly, I also need your input for a report I am preparing about the night that K-Lab security was violated."

"I've already been grilled about that at the time – for several hours."

"I'm sorry, but not by my department."

"Can you please just get their notes about this? I really don't want to rehash that."

"I'm so sorry Ms. Hudson, I wish I could, but it's not as simple as that."

"Well, I'm so sorry Ms. Cantini, I really don't have the time today to answer for a second time a thousand questions I've already answered."

"I appreciate how you feel. I promise this won't take very long. Your cooperation is very much appreciated.

"You apparently spent over an hour with Mr. Hinchliff before he was taken into custody. Why did you do that and not call security?"

"What department did you say you were with?"

"Corporate Citizenship."

With restrained sarcasm Sophie responded,

"So I guess you question is, why wasn't I being a good corporate citizen?"

"I'm just doing my job Ms. Hudson and interested to know why you didn't call."

"Based on what had happened to Mr. Hinchliff, security knew he was there. I can't explain why they didn't take him into custody in the first place."

"Why did you take him to your flat?"

"The man was in a state of shock. He clearly needed help. He was of no danger to anyone."

"Did he ask you questions? What did you discuss?"

"He could barely talk. And I can assure you, I discussed nothing work related with him. In fact, we hardly talked at all before the gestapo arrived. It took 3 days before they repaired my door."

Cantini was taking notes then looks up,

"So nothing work related, about the lab, about the equipment in the lab, about the experiments, the trials, the nootropics, was discussed?"

"Nothing. Not a thing."

"Going forward Ms. Hudson, it's very important if you are contacted by Mr. Hinchliff or anyone associated with any groups who are trying to undermine or disinform about the life enhancing work of

Cortx or its subsidiaries to let us know immediately. You can contact me at any time."

Cantini hands Sophie her business card.

"If you are asked to be interviewed by any media, you are not authorised to speak on behalf of Cortx or any of its subsidiaries nor about any aspect of your work with Cortx.

"The NDA agreement you signed as condition of employment is in effect in perpetuity and it of course pertains to friends and family."

Sophie repeats the comment under her breath,

"Of course... friends and family."

Cantini then reads to Sophie an excerpt from the NDA which Sophie had previously signed:

"With regard to any future employment and employer, no proprietary or confidential information gained during the course of your employment by Cortx, be it of a corporate or scientific nature – may be used, disclosed, sold, transferred, or shared with your new employer or any third party."

"Is that clear? Do you have any questions about that?"

"Yes. No."

"If you need a job reference going forward, please do not contact your supervisor directly. Contact me or this department and we will liaise with your supervisor and arrange a reference.

Also, just to remind you that in your original employment contract it stipulates that upon your departure you may be asked to help train a replacement. Should that be needed, you will be contacted. You would of course be compensated for your additional time. We will email you shortly any documents needed for your taxes or tax records."

"I do have a question about that... regarding my vacation time. As I understand it, I'm entitled to receive compensation for vacation time I never took. Can you please help to insure that that is sorted?"

"You are entitled to that, absolutely. I will definitely look into it for you and arrange for any compensation due to be transferred into your account.

"Also, you must return all company property, any tabs, fobs, or lab equipment of any kind. We realise that it can be a stressful experience when a contract ends and in your case making the transition from K-Lab back to London. There are six sessions of counselling available to you over the next six months at no charge, should you decide to use them.

"Lastly, there are some very exciting Cortx initiatives coming up in the near future and I would like to give you these. I'm sure ticket touts would love to get their hands on them."

Sophie is handed two complimentary tickets for opening night of the Eidetic Cinema in London.

Sophie leaves the maddening debrief with Corporate Citizenship feeling irritated and alienated.

Keep your property claims out of our brains

On the matter of MRA principles, emails were bouncing back and forth over several weeks between Gil and Graham and MRA members in Australia, New Zealand, America, and India.

The reasons to formulate these principles were many. It would help establish the MRA identity internally and to the world. It would be an outreach tool for expanding membership. It would be a vehicle to fundraise and gain the support of other groups and institutions. It would focus and prioritise energy and actions going forward.

During much back and forth, the MRA principles took shape. Gil and Graham were keen to publish them on the MRA website as soon as possible.

Given the latest and most ambitious scheme of Cortx, a top priority is to oppose any attempt by it to claim property rights on any aspect of a persons memory. It crosses an existential threshold and would be a slippery slope towards staking wider memory claims and staking IP claims on other cognitive functions. Related to this, is opposition to the principle of permanent micro-charges.

The MRA will launch an educational campaign to oppose on mental health grounds any chemically augmented class of 'unforgettable' episodic memories. This profit driven intervention goes against the grain of a human need to allow most events and experiences to fade in time or recede in importance or prominence as new experiences occur.

Other principles would address the rights of employees to refuse to subject themselves to nootropics; resistance to the formation of new social hierarchies based on memory haves and memory have nots; and demand more robust and independent oversight of human experimentation involving any memory related research and development.

> *EDITORS NOTE: The first official draft of MRA principles were published to coincide with the start of the MRA v. Cortx judicial review. They are accessible on the MRA website. For easy reference and emphasis, they are reprinted below.*

WE ARE THE MEMORY RIGHTS ALLIANCE

1. *We oppose any intellectual property claims that infringe on the sovereignty of a persons body or mind.*

2. *The 'right to forget' is a sacred universal human right. Artificially induced unforgettableness is considered a mental health hazard to be opposed.*

3. *We oppose any forms of employment discrimination or job penalties against any worker who refuses to subject him or herself to nootropics in the course of training or work activities.*

4. *We are opposed to any mnemonic based ideologies which promote ideas of 'memory supremacy'.*

5. *We are opposed to any human experimentation which does not fully comply with the revised Helsinki Accords.*

6. *We are opposed to the use of animals for any neurochemical and/or neurotechnical research or experimentation.*

7. *We oppose neurotechnical products and interventions which are likely to exacerbate social divisions by creating a class of 'memory haves' and 'memory have nots'.*

8. *We oppose all forms of marketing or advertising which embodies or promotes 'memory shaming'.*

9. *We oppose any form of permanent memory surcharge.*

10. *If a corporation is receiving permanent fees for so called 'permanent' film memories, consumers of such memories should be entitled to and receive premium rate optic nerve transit fees in perpetuity.*

The formulated principles really hit a nerve. Soon after going online, representatives from two national unions contacted the MRA and said that while they can't sign up to all the principles they would give the MRA their complete support on matters of workers rights and nootropic related job discrimination.

The publication of the principles also led to the MRA getting unexpected support from Bollywood including the Taj Cineplex Consortium which is the largest non-nootropic theatre chain in India. An exec at the Taj said they would even run ads in their chain of 2,500 cinemas calling for optic nerve transit fees if Cortx dared to charge permanent encryption fees.

Greenpeace has decided to lend their support to the MRA which is a big deal. They've established an offshoot organisation focused solely on neurotech and memory rights matters called 'Greenpeace of Mind'. With them aboard other groups opposing unregulated geo-engineering experiments joined in. They felt there was a parallel between unregulated attempts to fuck about with the ecology of the planet and unregulated attempts to fuck about with the ecology of the mind.

All of these developments are being touted on the MRA website and making Cortx anxious as support for the MRA expands beyond the 'lunatic fringe' of hard core memory rights activists.

Memory flunkies and neuro-geeks

Amidst the hustle and bustle outside the courthouse are Cortx flunkies, memory rights activists, and a small contingent of neurogeeks. The neurogeeks are easily spotted under a wide banner which reads, 'Jack-Us-In'.

Neurogeeks who have been waiting decades to 'jack-in' are facing a colossal disappointment given the current reality of implants intended to augment cognition. Alex was not exactly a 'proof of concept' for a brave new world of chip implants but more the sole survivor of a wholesale slaughter of an endangered species by a powerful neuro-cartel of animal torturers.

If the reality of the Cortx neural implant debacle were to become fully known, it would likely tarnish forever the esteemed place of neural implants in the sci-fi imagination.

Inside the courtroom, spectators are settling back in after a 10 minute break. Sophie is staring downwards with her arms crossed. Gil is wiping sweat from his face. Marshall walks forward to the center of the courtroom,

"M'Lud, I would like to call Ms. Kathy Pendleton to testify."

Pendleton is 23 and a graphics designer. She's very fashionably and elegantly dressed with a purple satin top, narrow white silk tie, and dark blue slacks. She enthusiastically bounces up to the front of the court and takes a seat.

Her personality is bubbly. Her delivery is crisp, charming, and occasionally funny. She embodies the Cortx target demographic and is everything Cortx could hope for from a booster of memory boosters. She was carefully chosen and well prepped by Marshall and Co.

Marshall begins,

"Ms. Pendleton, can you please introduce yourself. Where do you currently live and what do you do for living?"

"Sure thing. I live in Folkstone and I work as a graphic designer. I work for a variety of fashion labels. I left Uni last year. I studied early 21st century lit and marine ecology.

"Ms. Pendleton, can you please explain how and why you got involved in the trial screenings for the Eidetic Cinema?"

"Happy to. There was a notice circulating at Uni about some movie screenings and a new memory improvement product and the company organising this was looking for volunteers to take part. My friends and I looked at each other and said, 'free movies?', 'improved memory?', 'dahhh, let's do it!'. It sounded like a no brainer."

"Why did it sound so appealing to you and your friends?"

"Well, we are film nuts, we love films. We spend the evenings binge watching stuff. Of course, that's only when we weren't cramming for exams. Actually, that's another reason why we were interested. Everybody at Uni these days takes something to try and boost concentration or try to improve their memory. Resveratrol, phospholipids, A-carnitine – you name it and students are taking it. There is so much pressure on students. Also to be honest, we'd get paid! That didn't hurt."

"After you and one of your friends were accepted for the trial screenings, did you feel that what you were getting yourself into was adequately explained to you? Did you think you might be taking any kind of medical or health risk?"

"Medical risk? My memory is pretty shit – oh sorry – anything that might help is worth a try. They really took their time and answered everybody's questions. They said the formulas were already approved and safe and that they were primarily looking at the consumer experience in conditions that were closer to the cinemas they would be opening."

"What film did you watch?"

"It was a half hour of various clips from the film 'Gone With The Wind.'"

Pendleton hums the iconic Max Steiner opening score. Marshall continues,

"When you were watching it – and listening to it, were you aware of the nootropic atmosphere in the room? Did you smell anything unusual?"

"No not at all. It didn't smell like anything. The only frustrating thing was we were all craving popcorn but there was none."

"Was the experience of watching the film clips with the nootropics any different than a 'normal' viewing experience?"

"You're not aware of anything different while you are watching the film, but afterwards, wow! It was amazing. This sounds ridiculous, but, I'll never forget it!

"I had actually watched the film on the internet when I was a kid, but don't really remember much of it, maybe a couple of scenes, that big scene with all the injured soldiers, that was all. After this screening, I could remember everything. But it's not like ordinary remembering. It's like seeing the film on a screen but inside your head – if that makes sense. You can sort of fast forward it in your memory. You can sort of pause the memory on a scene and look at all the detail – the lighting, the background, everything."

"After you viewed it, either that night or in the days afterward, did memories of the film – be they images, sounds, etc. – come into your head unexpectedly? Were they intrusive in any way?"

"Well that night my friend and I talked for hours about the film. We

rewatched what we saw scene by scene and blabbered on about it until 2AM. We've never before been able to talk about a film in such amazing detail. Afterwards, it didn't pop into my head unexpectedly if that's what you mean. It was just a film. If I thought about it, great, if not, not."

"Just to be clear, at any time during or after the screening did you experience any kind of headache or dizziness or any kind of physical or mental discomfort that might be connected to the viewing experience?"

"Zilch, nadda, nothing. Not a thing. All AOK."

"On another matter Ms. Pendleton, not directly connected to the experience of watching the film and the atmosphere, the payment model which will be introduced at the Eidetic Cinema will involve a lower than average admission charge to see the film and supplemental micro-charges of possibly .01 E-ren per month. What is your opinion about that?"

"It's totally worth it. It's practically nothing. I mean at that rate, the cost of one cup of coffee would cover my micro-charges for years."

"No further questions M'Lud. Thank you Kathy."

The neck of Gil's shirt is wet from perspiration. He stands up, wipes his forehead with a tissue, and steps closer to Pendleton,

"Ms Pendleton, you say that for you the micro-charges are no big deal. Now apart from the obvious point that they will likely get higher in time the more Cortx films you see, are you aware they are premised on an intellectual property claim to the protein structures in your brain that constitute the memories created when you watch the film? In other words, Cortx claims to own your memory of the film. Are you comfortable with that?"

"I'm not sure I see what the big deal is. If I buy and download a song on the internet, the fine print of the purchase agreement says I don't really own it. But I'll do whatever I want with it and they really can't take it back can they?"

"Does it bother you in any way that it's permanent? Maybe not every film you see under those conditions you'll like. You may want to forget..."

"I thought that was the whole point – to be permanent? I don't think I've ever just gone to see anything. If there's a buzz, if my friends recommend it...then I'll want to see it. I guess it's like getting a tattoo."

Pendleton rolls up her sleeve just enough to reveal a small tattoo of a starfish on her forearm,

"I love starfish. That's why I got the tattoo. I like the idea that it's permanent."

Gil wasn't exactly making great headway. He was actually beginning to feel despondent at the mind-set he is up against. He hesitated to pursue his next line of questioning, but he was feeling desperate,

"Ms. Pendleton, do you recall the kind of security checks you encountered the last time you went to the cinema?"

"You mean like metal detectors, body scanners, that kind of stuff?"

"Yes, exactly. Why do you think security is so tight at the movies?"

"All those mass shootings? And there were those multiple bombings at cinema's in India?"

"Exactly. Heaven forbid any more cinema attacks, but for those who survive there is trauma. The trauma of being present and witnessing the terror attack and its aftermath. Trauma victims can be helped, but what if..."

It was obvious to Marshall where this was going,

"Objection, M'Lud. The plaintiff is hoping to scare monger with a far fetched hypothetical. We cannot eliminate all the risks of modern life."

Gil certainly didn't think it was irrelevant or particularly far fetched.

"Mr Marshall, while Mr. Hinchliff is conjuring up a dreaded scenario, we can't live in denial that such things are possible. The consequences may be worth considering. I will allow Mr. Hinchliff to proceed."

"Ms. Pendleton, consider the possibility of an unexpected trauma becoming permanently embedded in your consciousness. Traumas need to heal and an essential aspect of that is to recede from immediacy.

"Ms. Pendleton, would the risk of being exposed to something traumatic while under the influence of nootropics concern you?"

Marshall interrupts again,

"M'Lud, security at cinemas has been effective at reassuring consumers. Otherwise, movies would have gone bust. It's also disrespectful of the intelligence of Ms. Pendleton and her ability to make an informed judgement about how to safely enjoy a night out."

Henderson intervenes,

"Ms. Pendleton will not have to answer a question about surviving a mass killing at the cinema."

"M'Lud, the hypothetical I'm asking Ms. Pendleton to consider is not about surviving an attack per se, but the possibility of having to cope with a permanent and vivid memory of a traumatic experience."

Henderson gives Gil a stare and shakes his head.

Gil backs down,

"Thank you Ms. Pendleton. No further questions."

Courtroom roulette

When Gil returned from Kyrgyzstan, his brain and his personal life were falling to pieces. His career as a lawyer was in danger of going down the drain. But his experience at K-Lab made his campaign against Cortx deeply personal. They were not going to pursue their ambition of owning a piece of everyone's brain – without a fight.

In Gil's calculations, if he breaks the 'get out of jail' agreement with Cortx, the worst that could happen is that he ends up being disbarred. Britain does not have an extradition agreement with Kyrgyzstan so there is little if any chance of being shipped back to stand trial in a kangaroo court in that Central Asian country. On the other hand, Cortx is at risk of international scandal, the threat of lawsuits from families with members permanently damaged by their experiments, and the most damaging scenario of all, a plunge in shareprice.

The Judicial Review is like a high stakes game of poker between Gil and Cortx and Gil is calling their bluff. Gil's instinctive strategy is echoed by military thinkers across the centuries from Sun Tzu, to Machiavelli, to Mao – the best defence is a good offense.

It wasn't difficult for Gil to determine that the main production facility for the nootropic gases was in Taizhou, China in spite of Van Trotta suggesting that it took place at a secret location for security reason.

Gil asked a friend who works for a news operation to request any PR footage from the Cortx press office of the nootropic production process. They were all to happy to accommodate.

The footage shows production of nootropics in high gear. You see thousands of stainless steel cylinders moving along an assembly line and being injected with high pressure gas in clusters of 8. You hear the loud, rapid, staccato bursts of pressurisation.

An automated process then guides the cylinders to a conveyor belt which transports them to shipping containers which get stacked onto ships then sent on their merry way to global distribution.

The production facility is filling orders from militaries in Brazil, Indonesia, Austria, Australia, and France. But the biggest order is for the new chain of Eidetic Cinema's planned for several dozen cities around the world.

The only country which has blocked the import and use of nootropics is Germany. When an MRA affiliate in Berlin launched their campaign against the Eidetic Cinema they referred to them as brain altering 'gas chambers'. That description was picked up by the media, made headlines, and hit a political nerve in Germany. Cortx was so rattled that they filed a libel suit hoping to intimidate and muzzle the local MRA affiliate.

When a preliminary hearing was finally held, the libel suit was thrown out of court. The judge's ruling was, 'Es ist eine sachlich korrekte aussage'. Translation: 'It's a factually accurate statement'.

Hype cycle of unforgetableness

The Cortx PR machine was determined to seize the news cycle with the glitzy opening of the massively hyped Eidetic Cinema. The Central London premiere was the epicentre of global publicity campaign.

Gil and Graham spent the morning of the premiere making calls and sending out fundraising emails warning of Cortx 'gas chambers' and asking supporters to give generously to the MRA war chest in defence of memory rights.

The premiere is scheduled for 20:30. By 19:00 the crowds and paparazzi are already gathering. At 19:30 the red carpet with cascading LED lights is activated.

A fleet of limos is delivering rent-a-stars in tuxedos and designer evening gowns. There are about a dozen tall and hefty guys in suites with ear pieces who are keeping watch on the crowds and the arriving guests. There's a wider perimeter of police who are maintaining a buffer between crowds and MRA protestors. The protestors are within earshot of the limos but about 15 meters back from the front-line celeb gawkers.

The Cortx PR machine has even enlisted Alex for opening night hype. On the huge membrane screen above the marquee of the cinema is a clip of Alex reciting a line from Shakespeare befitting the occasion. It's only a few seconds long but it's on a loop. Alex is not in his stainless steel cage but on the stage of the Globe Theatre. There he speaks surrounded by Elizabethan splendour,

'Tis in my memory lock'd,
And you yourself shall keep the key of it.

Hamlet, Act I, Scene III, Ophelia

Gil is irresistibly draw to the opening night glitz and glamour. He's keeping a low profile but craning his neck in the shadows to get a decent view. He dare not miss the groundbreaking, mass consumption, family friendly mind fuck-athon.

A social media personality is streaming live in front of the cinema as limo's arrive behind her,

"In time zones around the world – including London, Mumbai, and Sydney – it's opening night at the Eidetic Cinema and what Cortx claims will be the most memorable cinema going experience in movie history."

It's approaching 20:00 and the MRA office is shut tight. Most of the volunteers along with Gil and Graham are at the opening.

By 20:00, the last limo arrives outside the cinema – and the MRA office is quietly under assault. Its electronic lock is being hacked and its alarm system is being overridden. Inside the office, the only sound to be heard is the hum of the computer server. Once inside, the intruder lowers a backpack and removes a device about the size of a shoebox. It's a compact high energy magnetic pulse generator used in cyberwarfare.

There's something fiendishly poetic about wiping the memories and frying all the computers of the Memory Rights Alliance on opening night of the Eidetic Cinema. At the very least it is an intimidating, disruptive, and memorable fuck you message to Gil and the MRA – not to mention the 4 terabytes of MRA files that were copied before they got zapped.

There is a huge commotion outside the theatre. The crowd of celebrity gawkers are surging forward to get a closer look at and take selfies with the life-sized interactive holograms of the stars of the 'Gone With The Wind' original – Clark Gable and Vivienne Leigh.

AI has enabled Gable and Leigh to look like themselves, sound like themselves, move like themselves and to some extent, think like themselves. They have been programmed to be capable of answering hundreds of questions that the media or the public might throw at them.

A Cortx PR person allows the celeb streamer doing a live feed to be the first to interview two of Hollywood's immortal stars of yesteryear.

For effect, a microphone is thrust towards the mouth of Clark Gable, but his audio is actually coming from a speaker by his feet,

"Mr. Gable, what does it feel like to star in the very first film to be screened at the Eidetic Cinema?"

Gable is looking sincere and engaged,

"Frankly, my dear, it's wonderful."

"Ms. Leigh, how does it feel to know that a new generation of movie fans are guaranteed to find you character unforgettable?

"Fiddle dee, it's so exciting. I feel so alive! It's definitely a night to remember!"

Another streamer steps up to ask more anodyne questions of Clark and Vivienne for his coverage of opening night.

A woman in the crowd – not a brain dead streamer nor a hack reporter – shouts a question to the ethereal Clark Gable,

"Mr. Gable, is it true you raped the actress Lorretta Young?"

The Cortx publicist is incensed and with a security guard begins a move towards the woman. The crowd laughs. Before the presenter can blurt out an alternative question, Gable responds,

"Frankly, my dear, I'm truly pleased to get your question. I hope you and Loretta have an unforgettable time".

In the background, Gil and Graham are enjoying this off-piste moment.

On the giant membrane screen far above the heads of Clark and Vivienne is an animated trailer with a revised film title:

'GONE BUT NOT FORGOTTEN WITH THE WIND'

A glamourous media presenter dressed in an evening gown and being followed by a video crew is taking her viewers on a tour of the new cinema.

From the bustling crowds just outside the movie theatre, she gracefully walks though the metal detector and the chemical spectrometer and up to the self-service ticket window all without missing a beat. She presses a few buttons, the computer dispenses a ticket, and she glances at what is dispensed.

The presenter turns to camera,

"Welcome to the Eidetic Cinema! This has to be the lengthiest movie ticket in movie history."

The presenter allows the ticket to drop down and unfold like an accordion. There are at least ten folded sections to the ticket with unreadably small print on both sides.

"This movie ticket is actually a lengthy contract with health disclaimers, indemnifications, obscure IP clauses, subclauses, and details about financial strings attached. If you have a magnifying glass and actually take the time to read it all – well – you will surely miss the film.

"Just in case you haven't heard, in addition to the ticket price, expect to be charged a small monthly fee in perpetuity. The film memory is supposedly permanent and so are the charges.

"In a wise PR move, Cortx promises that for the first year, all revenue from their micro-charges will be donated to brain disease research."

The presenter is moving along, and passes an animated promotional poster,

'FANATICAL ABOUT UNFORGETTABLE FILMS!'

A security guard is opening the door for her to enter the Eidetic Cinema control room. The door sign proclaims: NO ADMITTANCE.

Inside is a long array of glistening cylinders, lots of valves, a network of tubes migrating out of the room, control screens, and some emergency kit including fire extinguishers and several gas masks.

"Welcome to the heart of the Eidetic Cinema."

When the doors into the main screening room close, the cinema becomes hermetically sealed. The invisible but not entirely odourless nootropic vapours are at the prescribed saturation levels mixed with oxygen. The air pressure is set for 1013.25mbar – the average sea level air pressure.

After a series of commercials for which sponsors paid an exorbitant premium to screen in 'unforgettable' conditions, the film begins. The Oscar winning theme music by Max Steiner which opens the film is a classic score from the heyday of Hollywood. It really doesn't need neurochemical intervention to be memorable.

Reflected light of the opening scene illuminates the faces of the first Eidetic Cinema customers. A crane shot lowers past a giant oak tree revealing Tara – the antebellum Southern plantation which is the backdrop of the American civil war era story.

The title of the film fades up...

GONE BUT NOT FORGOTTEN WITH THE WIND

Several seconds later, the title fades off except for the phrase:

NOT FORGOTTEN

Wiped

Amelia, one of the MRA volunteers is sobbing. It's the morning after the break-in and the MRA office is in crisis. Graham walks over to Amelia to try and console her,

"What did you lose?"

"All of my graduation photos, all the photos from my arctic holiday, photos of my mum and sis which I really loved."

"They were not backed up anywhere?"

"I'm an idiot."

"We're doing everything we can."

Graham drifts back to his desk and buries his face in his hands. The tech support team has sent someone over to try and reboot the MRA computers.

Graham is talking to himself,

"This is a nightmare, a total fucking nightmare."

Graham glances towards the technician, who shakes her head,

"Sorry Graham, it's looking like everything is fried."

Gil is sitting on his own by his desk with his back to the office commotion and staring out the window.

Graham walks over Gil who begins to speak without swivelling around in his chair,

"It looks like a pulse attack. The police are sending someone, but it's pointless."

Graham interjects,

"We'll need a police report for insurance, but it's going to kill us financially to replace things if our insurance doesn't cover it."

Gil is still staring out the window,

"The worst may not be our fried computers."

With that, Gil swivelled around and he and Graham locked glances both thinking exactly the same thing – membership lists, donor names, legal files, research materials – is there any chance they were copied by the attacker? Do they have backups?

Gil was the first to speak,

"It feels like rape."

"Gil, we need to decide whether or not to inform members and donors, and what to say. Jesus Christ, do we even still have a membership list? Have our funders been compromised – have all their names and contact details been lost? Let's try to figure out what we have or don't have."

Gil, Graham, Amelia, and several other MRA stalwarts gather around a conference table to assess the damage.

Amelia addresses Gil,

"Are you all right Gil? You look like shit."

"Thanks Amelia. Don't worry, I'm alright. Let's get on with this."

For security reasons, the MRA does not allow the automatic upload of important lists or documents to Orbit. However, lots of research materials and other publicly available information about memory rights affiliated groups and the neurotech sector should still be up there.

Amelia is the person who liaises with the company which does the newsletter and membership emails,

"They are not supposed to do this, but under the circumstances, I think they will be able to provide us with a copy of our lists."

Graham was appreciative,

"Thanks Amelia, if they do, that will be a huge help. Maybe I should talk to them directly. Hopefully, from that list we can reconstruct our donor list. A lot of tedious work to be done."

Amelia looks to Gil and Gil gives Amelia a subtle nod,

"That may not be necessary Graham. Last month Gil asked me to do a printout of our funders."

Amelia tossed the folder with the printout onto the table. Graham could not resist,

"So, you're not a complete fuckup Gil."

Gil remains quiet and oddly calm.

Graham then looks to Gil,

"What about all the documents and prep work for the judicial review?"

Everyone around the table is staring at Gil.

There is dead silence.

Everyone is collectively holding their breath.

Gil closes his eyes. Five seconds feels like an eternity.

After this excruciatingly long and melodramatic moment, Gil flings a 4 terabyte memory ring into the center of the table.

Graham collapses his head into his hands in relief.

There's a smattering of applauds.

A memory cracked, a forest down

Judge Henderson is staring off to his left as a trolley holding 28 thick bound volumes is wheeled into the court room. They are neatly arranged with their bindings facing upwards. Each volume is bigger and thicker than a vintage printed encyclopaedia.

Ken Marshall is addressing the court,

"M'Lud, there is a basic question about the precise nature of our intellectual property claim concerning a nootropic memory encryption. In the past, memories have not been a readily observable or accessible neurochemical phenomenon.

"These 28 volumes represent neuromolecular structures translated into alpha-numeric code of a memory which has been encrypted with the use of our nootropics. A similar set of 19 volumes exists for the same memory but without the intervention of nootropics."

Marshall picks up one volumes and flips through it,

"This voluminous alphanumeric code was generated by a one minute film sequence of sounds and images. The movie source is the Hollywood classic, 'Gone With The Wind'. The short sequence is when Scarlett O'Hara and Rhett Butler catch their first glimpse of each other at the plantation banquet.

"This degree of monumental detail, this groundbreaking translation of a memory into code would not have been possible without the revolutionary Cortx programme called Project Axion. Axion has been in development for decades. The world has not yet been hearing much about it, but I assure you, that will change.

"One of the achievements of Axion is to take memories out of the ambiguous realm of cognitive psychology and place them squarely where they belong in the realm of biophysics and indeed neuro-mathematics."

Some press in the courtroom appear to have perked up. Sophie is staring blankly off into space.

Judge Henderson is doing his best to follow,

"Mr. Marshall, I think what you are saying is that the library you've wheeled into my chamber is some kind of proof that memories can be pinned down as 'material things'?"

"Precisely M'Lud. Axion goes beyond establishing that all memories are material things. It can rigorously identify the exact material structure of specific memories. This in turn enables a substantial proof that what Cortx is creating with the use of its nootropics is a new class of proprietary material things."

Gil is doodling on the faces of Cortx executives in the Cortx annual report.

Henderson thanks Marshall then turns towards Gil,

"Mr. Hinchliff?"

Gil slowly walks over to the 28 volumes on the trolley gathering his thoughts along the way. He theatrically picks up one of the volumes and enigmatically presses it against his temple. He then holds it aloft with both arms as if weight lifting. He then brings it down in front of him and moves it up and down as if trying to guess its weight.

"M'Lud, I simply don't buy it. Yes, memories are material things. I don't think there is a neuroscientist around who would disagree with that premise. It doesn't take a Project Axion to make that case. But I don't think there are many neuroscientists who would agree to a memory being a fixed thing regardless of how or under what conditions it was formed.

"Rather than the wasteful depletion of a forest to try and prove a point, no two people will react to nootropics in exactly the same way. The distinction between a memory formed with nootropics vs. a memory formed without may be more a matter of degree rather than a difference in kind. Furthermore, the nootropic formulas are too new – excuse the pun – for there to have been long term studies which establish the neurochemical stability of the memory augmented encryptions.

"If the proprietary argument is accepted and by extension a memory surcharge is allowed to stand it will create for the first time in history the legal grounds for a thought crime.

"What else would it be if you ended up unable or unwilling to pay your memory charge? Wouldn't accessing your Cortx owned memory be a thought crime?"

Two members of the press must have just gotten their lead. They hastily leave the courtroom. Norman Palmer is staring down at his folded hands.

What a pelican can recall

Gil is sitting on a bench along the tranquil lake in St. James Park as a pelican eats popcorn out of his hand. It's a cloudy day but the tourists are still out in droves.

Sunlight briefly catches a corner of Buckingham Palace as the landscape maintains a palette of muted colours. Gil turns to his left and sees Sophie Hudson walking along the lakeside path approaching him. His chest is tightening and his stomach is queasy. He didn't expect to feel this nervous.

Sophie is almost unrecognizable. The last time he saw her was at night while he was having a psychotic meltdown and she was in a shapeless white lab coat. She looks relaxed in jeans and a black jumper. Her hair is longer than he remembers it and she is also wearing a warm but cautious smile.

"I really didn't think you would come. I'm very pleased to see you again."

Gil gestures to give Sophie some popcorn to feed the pelican,

"I don't really think pelicans are designed to eat popcorn out of hands. I think they're better at scooping up fish."

"Well, this one seems to love popcorn. Blame the tourists."

Sophie is tapping her temple,

"How is...?"

Gil turns one thumb up and the other thumb down. The pelican snaps at the downturned thumb.

"Watch it mate!"

The pelican appears to be losing interest. It waddles off.

"Sophie, you may or may not regret intervening in the way you did to help me, but I'll always be grateful. Things have been pretty bad and I've been just barely coping, but without your K-Lab battlefield first aid and advice, I don't think I would have survived."

"I'm sure you would have Gil."

"Have you finished your gig with Cortx?"

"Yes."

Sophie is being very reserved at first. She certainly has misgivings about meeting up with Gil,

"They recently quizzed me again about that night – which was infuriating given that I was interrogated for over 3 hours the day after it happened.

"I thought I was going to be polygraphed. They expect me to make a solemn vow that I will never again see or talk with you or your ilk."

"My ilk?"

"I was told to report if anyone connected to the MRA tries to make contact with me."

"You don't strike me as someone reckless enough to dare speak with such nefarious characters."

"Well you should know a reckless person when you meet one. I think you're the expert on reckless."

"Ouch! That hurt."

"Is bringing down Cortx still your full time job? Does it pay well?"

Gil was almost embarrassed to admit that his focus on Cortx was still consuming him and all the more so since his K-Lab experience. He hesitated to mention that the MRA was hoping to get a judicial review, but his gut feeling was that Sophie could be trusted.

"I don't think my expectation is to bring Cortx down, and you probably don't want to get me going about the corporate threat to the nature of human consciousness, but it would be great if they could be held in some way to account. I have been putting most of my time into preparing an application for a judicial review. They probably know what we're up to better than we do. I'm pretty sure they've hacked our emails and computers."

Sophie definitely wanted to change the subject,

"There must be something else to talk about other than my former employer – your current tormentor..."

Several tourists are taking some holiday snaps on the park bridge as Gil and Sophie stroll past them. They come to rest against the bridge railing with a beautiful view of mulberry trees in the foreground and the City skyline in the distance.

"So Sophie, dare I ask, are you married? Have any kids?"

"No kids. If I did, I'd be a pretty awful parent to have abandoned them for two years to head off to Kyrgyzstan."

Sophie stares off into space for half a minute – then continues,

"I was married, but my husband died on me."

"So sorry to hear that Sophie."

"That's OK."

"That happened before you took the job at K-Lab?"

"Yup. I think it was why I took the job – to get away from everything.

"What's your situation?"

"Well, definitely no kids, at least none that I'm aware of. I think my girlfriend is pretty fed up. Since I got back to London, things have pretty much gone downhill."

"Are your parents still around?"

"Yes and no. My mum died about a year ago."

"So sorry to hear that Gil. What..."

"She had a massive stroke."

"It must still feel very raw."

"Kinda.

"What happened to your husband?"

"A brain tumour. After three operations, he called it quits."

Tears are welling up in both Sophie's and Gil's eyes. Sophie turns her face away from Gil. Gil hesitantly places his hand on Sophie's shoulder. Sophie gently places her hand on Gil's hand and gives it a gentle squeeze.

"So Gil, it all comes down to memories, doesn't it?"

"In a way Sophie, maybe we all end up dying twice. The first time when we physically die, and the second time when the last living person who remembers us dies."

Sophie nods her head in agreement,

"Memories are so damn fragile Gil. A bunch of protein molecules in a quantum dance – taking up less space than you can imagine, and kept alive by a few millivolts of an electro-chemical charge."

The sun is trying to break through as Gil and Sophie exit St. James Park. They continue to chat as they stroll along Birdcage Walk,

"How did the job in Kyrgyzstan come about?"

"I met some employees of Cortx where my husband was being treated. They knew about my work as a programmer at Z-Napse on retinal implants. We were their main competition. They told me about this amazing project they were developing, and asked if I was interested in getting aboard. At first I wasn't but when Ian died, everything changed.

Sophie and Gil continue along Birdcage Walk,

"Is your dad still around? Brothers or sisters?"

"My father is still around but we've drifted far apart. Since mum's funeral I rarely speak to him except when he needs something signed. My parents divorced almost before I can remember. But..."

Gil appears to get lost in his last thought. Sophie tries to fill an awkward silence,

"So many things we wish we could remember better, or forget better..."

"Sophie, that's such a brilliant idea! It would redeem Cortx. Forget about 'permanent memories'! What Cortx needs to develop is a method for 'memory volume control'. I'd pay a premium monthly surcharge for that – and maybe even stop wanting to destroy them in court!

"I like that idea."

"What, of not destroying them in court?"

"No, memory volume control. But I don't necessarily agree they need redemption. Cortx drugs helped keep my husband alive."

Gil goes silent. It would be crass to try and convince Sophie that the evil deeds of Cortx outweigh the positive. Life and neurotech are complicated.

Sophie picks up on the whimsical idea of memory volume control,

"I will manage painful memories by hitting the mute button. Of course cranking up the volume on memories of simple pleasures will be a real treat."

Gil didn't know that Sophie was indirectly alluding to her own use of nootropics.

"And siblings Gil?"

"I have an older brother. We're not very close. Kinda opposites really. Actually, I had a baby sister, but she died before I was born."

"What happened?"

"I think it was some kind of infant cot death thing."

"God, I can't even begin to imagine what kind of trauma that must have been for your mum."

"I don't think she ever got over it. No, I know she never got over it. I think it had something to do with my parents divorcing. I was too young to understand what they were always fighting about, but I do remember hearing my father shouting at my mum, 'get over it'. I suspect what happened became a painful wedge between them."

"I would imagine it's hard if not impossible for a mother not to blame herself. Growing up, it must have been hard for you too."

"How do you mean?"

"You being the 'replacement child'."

Gil froze in his tracks and stood in stunned silence.

He had never heard the expression 'replacement child'. At first it sounded demeaning and Gil momentarily felt the impulse to defend his honour – the honour of being a child for its own sake.

The expression continued to reverberate in lots of dark and hidden nooks and crannies of Gil's psyche. It crystallised something that had troubled him his whole life. His existence was much more fraught than the byproduct of an act of love to create a new being for its own sake.

After a period of stunned silence, Gil repeated the phrase,

"A replacement child."

They continued to walk slowly,

"It's really rough when a child learns they had a sibling who died before they were born."

"Why so?"

"You'll never be the child your mum is missing so much. Also, when things are not right, children blame themselves. It helps to make sense of things they don't understand if it's their fault. Rightly or wrongly, consciously or unconsciously, you feel you might not exist but for the fact that a sibling died before you were born."

Gil stops walking and turns his back to Sophie. He does not want her to see the tears streaming down his face,

"Gil, are you OK? Oh my god, I've upset you. I'm so sorry Gil, I didn't mean to do that. I really should keep my big mouth shut."

"No Sophie, please don't keep your beautiful mouth shut."

It's morning, and Dena brings Gil a cup of coffee in bed,

"Another night in hell Gil? You only woke me up twice with your kicking and thrashing about."

"So sorry Dena. I don't remember any violence. I do remember a dream about my mother. I've had a similar dream a couple of times before."

Dena looks impatient to get her day started but is willing to listen.

"In the dream, my mother is still alive somewhere and is being looked after by someone but I forgot that she was still alive and I hadn't visited her in months."

"Sounds like a guilt dream Gil. Anyway, I've got to get to work or I'll be fired. Also, I won't be around this weekend, I'm visiting dad. Gotta run."

Pandora calling

In the aftermath of the pulse attack office morale is holding up. There's a heightened sense of mission among the MRA volunteers. Computers are being repaired or replaced depending on how badly damaged they were, files are being reconstructed and software programs are being reinstalled.

Gil is sitting at his desk lost in a reverie – replaying his afternoon with Sophie. Gil sees Graham walking in his direction and looks down to avoid making eye contact but in three seconds Graham is hovering,

"You've really gotten up their nose."

"Graham, please don't have another go at me. I'm really not in the mood."

"You've really gotten up their nose – but they really ain't seen nothin' yet!"

Gil wasn't expecting that and wasn't sure how to take it,

"This morning we got our email account back online and one of the messages which arrived while our account was inacessible was from the Chancery Clerk's office."

At that point Graham paused for dramatic effect and to give Gil a moment for his comment to register,

"The Chancery Clerk? And?"

"And, our petition for a Judicial Review has been considered... and approved! They will check the court calendar and get back to us soon with a date."

"Oh my fucking god! Halle-fucking-lujah! I don't believe it!"

Gil put his hands to his head swept back his hair and let out a gargantuan yelp.

"Holy fucking shit! That is unbelievable. That is great fucking news."

"Time for another fundraising email."

"Are you kidding me? Time for a case of Champagne."

Graham picks up the tab on Gil's desk and navigates to the site of the Yes Brainers,

"The Yes Brainers sent us a link this morning. You may find this amusing."

Gil clicks on the link and reads the story with shameful delight.

The Yes Brainers are reporting that a company in India has reverse engineered the nootropic formula and that bootleg nootropics are now flooding the Indian porn industry. Shockingly, they are also being promoted for use with class A and class B drugs as a means to achieve a permanent high. Reports of psychosis are rife. There is a growing demand for the use of bootleg nootropics at birthdays, weddings, and teenage high school spring break blowouts.

Gil turns to Graham,

"The Pandora's box of Cortx mind fucking has been opened."

A paramilitary bond

Sophie is reluctant to admit it to herself but she is feeling a twinge of fondness towards Gil. She has no regrets about seeing him and was surprised she felt comfortable enough to share her personal story. Even more surprising was that they spent the best part of the afternoon together and never got around to discussing heuristics.

Sophie is in her kitchen Saturday morning at 8:30 conjuring up an ancient Chinese herbal potion for improved brain function when her phone rings,

"Hello."

"Good morning Sophie, it's me, Gil. I hope I'm not calling too early."

"Oh, hi Gil. No, that's fine."

"Are you sure? I can call back later if that would be better."

"No, it's fine."

"I'm not looking to get you into trouble with your ex-employer, but I was thinking of checking out a new club tonight and was hoping you would consider joining me."

"Are you serious?"

"Absolutely."

"Tonight? No, I don't think so Gil."

"Do you have other plans?"

"That's a bit cheeky Gil. It's Saturday night, you don't expect me to have plans? Besides, this is ridiculously short notice."

"Oh, don't be a fuddy duddy. Whatever else you were planning to do, this will be much more fun."

"I really don't think so..."

"It's a very cool bar, they have a new kind of Karaoke."

"Well Gil, you make it so easy. I've never been to a Karaoke bar and I intend to keep it that way. But please enjoy yourself."

"But you don't understand, it's not really Karaoke, it's way beyond that. Please don't make me twist your arm."

"So, you think a threat of physical violence is going to persuade me? Besides, don't you have lots of legal homework to do?"

"Ok, please consider it on a strictly empirical basis. We give it a go only to inspect the scene. If the scene fails your inspection, we immediately exit the scene."

"What part of 'NO' is your brain not comprehending?

Sophie did valiantly resist – and Gil did valiantly persist.

Sophie's reluctance to go out with Gil was in part due to the uncomfortable feeling that Gil would be acting behind the back of his girlfriend. Also, Sophie and Gil were hardly friends and deeper feelings for him seemed improbable. But, there was an uncanny bond formed as a result of a midnight paramilitary assault while they were both 9,000 miles away from home.

A date to remember

Gil and Sophie are in a slow moving queue of mostly of young couples as they make their way past a couple of bouncers while heading for the foyer of the *Scareoke Club*.

"I can't believe I'm doing this! Remember the ground rules. I can leave anytime I want. You won't try to talk me out of leaving, you won't call me a fuddy duddy, and you won't hold a grudge."

"You are a free agent. There will be no pleas, challenges, motions, appeals, grudges, or attempts to physically restrain you – promise."

"I don't want to end up one of those damaged people with post-Scareoke stress disorder!"

"I was surprised when you said you heard about this place! I'm pleased your curiosity got the better of you."

The club is packed and noisy. The clubbers are mostly 20-somethings with a few middle-aged swingers. A giant membrane screen is getting a live video feed of activity from the club stage. On the screen, there appears to be an 80-year-old man tongue kissing a 20-something year old woman. On the stage below the screen we see the same young woman, but the man kissing her appears to be in his twenties.

Scareoke can do your head in. Some clubbers choose to confront their fears of aging by projecting ahead. Others long for past glory. And there are those who like to experiment with extremes.

Approaching the font of the queue, Gil and Sophie are next to have their faces scanned. The couple in front of them are instructed to close their eyes. Two fine red laser lines scan across their faces in horizontal and vertical directions.

"You're going to owe me big time Gil."

"That would be my pleasure."

"By the way, Gil, I heard that the MRA had a break in".

"How did you know that?"

"I read it on your website earlier today."

"Gee, thanks for taking my mind off things."

Sophie regretted the awkward timing of her comment, but something was eating away at her and she couldn't pretend otherwise.

"Sorry Gil. I know the review is only days away."

"I know that too Sophie."

Then came the grenade,

"I've been asked to testify."

At first, there is stunned silence from Gil.

"Hmmm, maybe a witness for the defendant shouldn't be seen cavorting with the lawyer for the plaintiff?"

"I guess we'll have to disguise our true identities!"

Gil and Sophie step onto the platform to have their faces scanned.

The operator is loud and friendly.

"Are you guys ready to time travel? Please take a seat, sit still and keep your eyes closed."

The red laser scan lines cross Sophie's face first, then Gil's. The operator slides a panel in front of them and asks them to open their eyes.

"OK, now comes the fun part. On the keypad, select your new age between 15 and 105 then choose a song from our playlist and you're ready to Scareoke!"

They agree to a classic 50's love song by Nat King Cole, 'Unforgettable'.

A crunch of people three layers thick are shouting for drinks at the noisy, dimly lit, Scareoke bar. Sophie and Gil stake out their positions. Gil is wedging his way in and ready to shout an order as soon as he catches the eye of a bartender.

Sophie appears on the cusp of bailing out,

"Why did I agree to do this? I think I'm ready to go now Gil."

"I bet you have a beautiful voice!"

Sensing the criticality of the moment, Gil abandons the plan of trying to order drinks. He grasps Sophie's hand firmly and pulls her towards the stage. It's an impulsive go for broke strategy.

On the large membrane screen a couple are singing an offbeat love song. It's the Leonard Cohen song, 'Don't Forget to Remember Me'. They are following the lyrics as they scroll across the lower third of the screen like a typical Karaoke bar.

The two women on the screen appear middle-aged – between 45 and 55 – but with girlish sounding voices.

Below and to the side of the video screen are two young women in their mid 20's who are singing the song.

Gil and Sophie are next up. As they wait, he's expecting her to yank her hand free of his at any moment but she hasn't, yet!

———————————

As they walk onto the stage, Sophie shakes her hand free. Gil has chosen to look age 50 and Sophie has chosen to be 20. They make their debut appearance on the jumbo screen above their heads.

They begin to sing – hesitantly and off key at first – but within a few bars, there is more harmony and confidence in their voices.

Gil begins,

"Unforgettable, that's what you are,"

Sophie follows,

"Unforgettable though near or far,"

Gil,

"Like a song of love that clings to me,"

Gil and Sophie together,

"How the thought of you does things to me,"

The chemistry between the two of them on the screen is both transgressive and electric.

Gil,

"That's why, darling, it's incredible,"

Sophie,

"That someone so unforgettable,"

Gil and Sophie,

"Thinks that I am unforgettable too."

The age-morph images of Gil and Sophie are turning heads in the crowd. Maybe it was the choice of song, the personal chemistry, or their endearingly off key voices, but they really got the attention of the other Scareoke clubbers.

As the song comes to its climax, they alternate between looking into each others eyes and glancing up towards the video screen. It's as if the image of 'themselves' they are watching is egging them on. They move to embrace each other. Just as they complete the closing line of the song, with a glance to the screen followed by a gaze into each others eyes – lost between reality and fantasy – they give each other a lingering kiss.

Sophie and Gil are back at the bar. They are silently sipping and staring at their drinks and avoiding making eye contact.

A young couple walk by with one of them using but not really needing a Zimmer frame. Gil blurts out,

"Now THAT's scary!"

"By the way Gil, I think you look much better with some grey and a few wrinkles."

"I've been mind fucked – again!"

"Serves you right!"

"My god, I looked like my father."

"Not a bad looking guy. It's weird, I feel as though I've seen him – you – somewhere before."

"I don't know whether to join a golf club or jump off a cliff."

Sophie is on her third drink and is almost nibbling Gil's ear as she cheekily whispers into it,

"Are you turned on by young-looking older women?"

"Are you turned on by old-looking younger men, or young-looking older men, or young looking young men?"

"I don't know Gil, I haven't recently tried old-looking young men or young-looking younger men for that matter. But I think I'm 'bi-temporal'. I could go either way."

It's getting near closing time. The host is on stage with a mic letting the clubbers know,

"I want to thank all you beautiful people for coming tonight and I hope you all had fun being a version of yourselves. Remember, starting next week we will have a new gender fluid software package for your Scareoke entertainment. Please get home safely."

Getting ready to leave the bar, Gil's hand which is holding a drink starts to shake. The glass flies out of his grip along with its contents. One of his legs is also starting to spasm. Gil is falling off his stool but Sophie manages to break his fall before he crashes to the floor. Lying on the floor Gil is thrashing and moaning apparently having a 'petite mal' seizure. People around him freeze and look on in horror.

Sophie immediately shifts gears. She looks calm and in command,

"Step back and give him some air, please. He'll be ok."

Sophie takes off her jumper and puts it under Gil's head. The manager has rushed over looking deeply concerned,

"Should I call an ambulance?"

"He'll be OK. It's a seizure. I don't think he hurt himself. He'll be OK. He just needs some air and a few minutes. Please back away folks."

The clubbers are staring down at Gil as they begin to make their way out.

Gil's eyes open.

"Hi Gil, it's me Sophie. You've had a seizure. How do you feel?"

"Where am I?"

"At the Scareoke Club."

Gil gradually regains his orientation and stands up with Sophie's help.

Their efforts to get a taxi late Saturday night predictably fail. In spite of his wobbly condition, Gil insisted on seeing Sophie safely to her street. After taking the night bus to Wandsworth Common, Gil and Sophie trek their way onto her street.

"That was scary. When I came to, I didn't have a clue where I was."

"You'll be fine. In fact, you'll be superfine."

"Age doesn't really matter Sophie, it's memories that matter!"

Sophie is still a bit drunk and starts to warble off-key the opening word of the song,

"Unforgettable..."

Gil waxes philosophical,

"There will always be memory haves, and memory have nots."

Sophie takes the cue,

"Yup, the rich old memory haves, and the poor young memory have nots. Memories, fuck 'em. They're so overrated."

Gil,

"Memory have nots are sad people... Memory haves are sexy..."

Sophie,

"So, so overrated. Up real close they all pretty much look alike. Just a lot of sticky protein."

Gil,

"Yucky memories..."

"Gil, I know memories better than anyone who has ever had one! Or forgotten one for that matter! Anyone! Ever!"

Gil begins to sing to the tune of 'Unforgettable',

"Sticky proteins, that's what you are..."

"Don't make fun of me, Gil! I'm the Queen of memories! Really! That's my top secret.

"We really love Cortx, don't we, Gil?"

"Yes Sophie, without doubt, you're the Queen of memories!"

Sophie begins to wag a finger at Gil,

"That's who you look like!

"Who's that?"

"That guy, the King of memories!"

Unbeknownst to them, Gil and Sophie are under surveillance. They are being followed and photographed by Phil Thurgood.

Gil and Sophie stand at her front door as she fumbles for her electronic key. She can't seem to remember where she placed it.

"I think we need just a little bit more rehearsal time together..."

"I think it's past my bedtime... Gotta go Gil."

"Gotta go Gil... Gotta go Gil... Gotta go Gil"

"Good night my silly parrot"

Gil tries to kiss Sophie on the lips but she turns her head to catch the kiss on her cheek. Sophie then slides into her flat. Gil is deflated.

Thurgood watches Gil leave Sophie's doorstep.

Gil makes his way to a nearby overground station and checks the schedule. It's more than a 20 minute wait for the next train. On top of being drunk, Gil is feeling sexually frustrated.

Prominent at the station is an NK with its brightly illuminated promo sign, '*Send Your Thoughts to Someone You Love*'.

Gil has an idea to add a new scan to his personal collection.

Inside the neurogram kiosk, Gil closes the curtain, lowers the scan helmet onto his head and gives a swipe with his bank bracelet to activate the process. Gil begins to watch his brain activity in real time.

There are two options, 'A', to record and send a short video file, or 'B', to access new auto-diagnostic features.

Gil presses 'Option A' to capture his brain activity.

Gil closes his eyes. His hand starts to rub his groin.

The live brain scan being recorded is becoming brighter and more colourful in the area of the hypothalamus – the part of the brain associated with sexual drive.

Gil is getting close to climax. The colours are getting more intense as blood supply to the hypothalamus increases.

A hand with a taser is thrust into the kiosk. The taser is pressed to the back of Gil's head – and discharged.

The neurogram helmet on Gil's head is engulfed with blue arcing spikes of electricity.

Gil's body spasms violently.

A circuit breaker shuts down the Kiosk

Yucky symptoms

Several months before her contract ended at K-Lab, Sophie was tending to her vegetable patch during her lunch break when the wonderful smell of the Osh spice market caught her attention. She had visited it soon after her arrival and bought some spices there for the occasional home cooked meal in her dormitory flat.

It was a wonderful smell. Sophie didn't give it another thought. The odd thing was that the Osh spice market was in the center of Bishkek about 25 miles to the west.

A couple of weeks after that, Sophie was lying awake late at night and heard a neighbour practicing scales on their piano.

Unlike life in London, Sophie knew all her neighbours who were mostly work colleagues. She had been inside everyone's flat and to the best of her recollection, nobody had a piano. Sophie's assumption was that one of her neighbours must have a synthesizer or has begun a piano tutorial on their pad. In the morning, Sophie was struck by how much the piano playing she heard the night before reminded her of the piano lessons she began as a ten year old.

Just before her contract ended, Sophie was sitting in Rita's café having an afternoon tea with biscuits when she experienced the abhorrent taste of chopped liver pate in her mouth. Ever since Sophie was a child she hated chopped liver pate. She couldn't even bear to look at the stuff. The biscuits had been in a sealed packet and chopped liver pate was nowhere to be found on Rita's menu or in her Café.

The morning after her night out with Gil, Sophie is walking along her quiet tree lined street on the way to buy some groceries. She nearly jumps out of her skin when she hears Gil's voice behind her saying, "Yucky memories!" She instantly swings around – but nobody is there.

At first, Sophie thinks it might be related to a hangover in the aftermath of an emotionally turbulent night out. But her concern about this and other odd sensory experiences began to trouble her. She decides to take up the Cortx offer of a free medical checkup for former K-Lab employees.

High voltage hangover

Graham receives a call at the MRA office from an administrative assistant at the Lavender Hill police station in South London who is trying to reach a parent, spouse, or sibling related to 'Mr. Gilbert Hinchliff'. Graham assumes the worst.

Thinking on his feet, he says he's a cousin in the hope of finding out what in hell has happened. He manages to get the name of the hospital where Gil is being treated. The fact that he is being 'treated' is a big relief. At the very least, he was still alive! Graham races to the hospital.

In the emergency room Graham manages to get a bit more information about Gil's condition and what happened to him. He's eventually allowed to see him.

Gil, in hospital garb, is lying in a room on his own with eyes closed and hooked up to an EKG.

"Gil, hello. Are you awake?"

Gil begins to come around,

"Graham...Hi. What's going on?"

"You're one lucky son of a bitch."

"God, I have an absolutely splitting headache. It feels like I've been kicked in the head."

"They think you'll be OK, they just want to keep an eye on you for another day."

"What the hell happened?"

"Did anyone explain anything?"

"...It's all a blur."

"You were found unconscious in an NK in South London. What were you doing in South London?"

"I dropped Sophie off at her house."

"You saw Sophie?"

"I plead guilty."

"Do you trust her?"

"I think so, maybe. Yes."

"According to the paramedics, there was smoke coming out of the scan helmet when they arrived. The kiosk appeared to have shorted out. The doctors think you might have received a serious electrical shock when the machine malfunctioned. Congratulations, you either fried a Neurogram Kiosk or, it fried you!"

"Maybe a case of mutually assured destruction."

Gil closes his eyes as he tries to recall anything about what happened,

"I don't think it was a kiosk malfunction."

Gil realises he may have been tasered. Luckily, the scan helmet absorbed much of the 50,000 volts.

Something isn't right

A long and very fine needle is being inserted upwards in the back of Sophie's neck by the HR assigned neurologist.

"Try not to move. It may feel a bit cold, but it shouldn't hurt. I'll be finished in about 5 seconds. The spinal fluid will tell us if there is any kind of infection or chemical anomaly that may be affecting your brain.

"What other symptoms have you been experiencing?"

"I misplace things. I can loose the thread of a conversation. My short term memory has been terrible lately. Something isn't right."

The neurologist asks about any history of brain disease in her family, then proceeds to give Sophie a short term memory test.

She is shown a screen with a cluster of different numbers for about 3 seconds then instructed to write down as many of the numbers she can remember immediately after seeing it. The exercise is repeated a couple of times with different clusters of numbers.

Sophie struggles to retain more than one or two numbers. Her frustration is fuelling her anxiety.

"I wouldn't worry too much Ms. Hudson. The incidents you mention as well as short term memory irregularities can be stress related. Being away from home for so long and the pressures of work or even the ending of your contract can trigger stress related anomalies. Do what you can to reduce stress and be kind to yourself."

"Is that it doc, be kind to myself?"

"I expect to have a lab report for the spinal fluid in two days. If there is anything unusual, I will let you know immediately. You are welcome to come back for another checkup at any time within your period of coverage. Of course you can see me privately beyond that."

"Is this check-up confidential?"

"Of course, of course. While I'm required to submit a report on any current or former Cortx employee I examine, that is done with a reference number and not a name."

"Why am I not reassured that this visit is truly private and in confidence?"

"Ms. Hudson, I assure you you have nothing to worry about. It is strictly confidential."

Naked nootropics

Dr. Cynthia Ayer is sitting next to Gil in the courtroom awaiting the opportunity to give her testimony. Judge Henderson is yet to appear.

"That was a great idea Cynthia to reverse engineer a sample of bootleg nootropics to see exactly what makes it tick. I did try to get my hands on some via my contacts in India, but so far, no success."

"The thought crossed my mind that you might be trying to create a bootleg version of the bootleg version of the stuff."

"I'm not that clever."

Dr. Ayer is putting on some makeup as she talks,

"No worries Gil. It might have been helpful, but it would also have been risky to assume too much from the bootleg version. When you get a sample of the actual Cortx formula I can easily reverse engineer it. We have a quantum field isotopic mass spectrometer at my lab and in a matter of minutes I can tell you everything, and I mean everything about what's in it. You can't keep any secrets from that piece of kit."

"I wish we had this discussion earlier."

"Again, it's not a big issue. There's plenty of known chemistry worth discussing."

The Court Clerk announces,

"All rise."

Judge Jason Henderson enters the courtroom and takes his seat with coffee in hand on the morning of day two of the Judicial Review.

"Be seated."

Gil did give Cynthia a dossier about the nootropic formula. Some of the info is from the original patent application and other tidbits are from sources he hacked. But Cynthia doesn't know that.

"Mr. Hinchliff, is your next expert ready to testify?"

"Yes M'Lud. I would like to call Dr. Cynthia Ayer. Dr. Ayer is the head of the neurochemistry department at the Institute of Translational Medicine at Glasgow University."

Ayer is in her mid 50's and smartly yet conservatively dressed in a grey pants suit, a subdued red floral print top and wearing a silver necklace which holds an opal broach.

She confidently takes a seat at the front of the courtroom.

"Dr. Ayer, thank you so much for taking the time to be here today to share your expertise."

"My pleasure."

"Just for the record Dr. Ayer, what is your familiarity with nootropics generally and with Cortx nootropics in particular?"

"Well, nootropics 'generally' is not a hard and fast category. It's a term which has been used loosely for a vast array of chemicals, suppliments, and snake oil – with claims to have brain function enhancing properties.

"I have frequently been enlisted by regulators to assess the efficacy and safety of many so called 'nootropics' which make all sorts of claims. And by the way, not always about improving memory per se.

"With regard to Cortx nootropics, I had no familiarity with them whatsoever prior to being asked by you Mr. Hinchliff to consider an assessment. Of course, that's only to the extent that I can relative to the information about ingredients which is available."

"Do you have any vested interests or competing interests – either with the work of Cortx and its affiliates or with its competitors?"

"None whatsoever. I'm mostly in my ivory tower or doing consulting work for various regulatory agencies. I have heard about the Eidetic Cinema, but I rarely go to the movies."

"Dr. Ayer, you are asked to assess the chemical ingredients of the nootropic formula developed by Cortx. You were provided with all the information which is publicly available via the original patent application as well as some independently sourced information…"

Marshall's head pops up from his notes with a quizzed look on his face.

"…but that information is not comprehensive. However, from the details you do have, what if anything have you gleaned that might relate to the safety or efficacy of their product?"

"Objection M'Lud. The plaintiff has just made clear that the information provided is incomplete and no assessment of our products safety or efficacy can credibly be made. No disrespect to the expertise of Dr. Ayer."

"M'Lud, Dr. Ayer is pre-eminent in her field. Her role is not to make a judgement per se on safety or efficacy, but to cast some light on the neurochemical approach of Cortx and perhaps ask informed questions. The plaintiff would gratefully receive the complete neurochemical recipe of the nootropics for Dr. Ayer's assessment, but Cortx is unwilling to provide it."

"Mr. Marshall, your objection pre-empts any testimony from Dr. Ayer."

"Precisely, M'Lud!"

"If her comments cross a line into baseless questions or claims, I'm sure you will let us know. Objection overruled. Dr. Ayer, you may proceed."

Dr. Ayer takes a moment to get back on track,

"I do have to agree with and underscore that the information I was given is incomplete in areas that may be important. However, I think there is certainly important information about neurochemical elements that are used and which raise important questions.

"It's very clever what they have done. Looking at their patents, it's an introduction of synthetic versions of natural chemicals which are usually metabolised before they get to the brain. For example, phenethylamine, which has been shown to boost neuro-modulation and the work of neurotransmitters. That's a substance found in trace amounts in chocolate."

Gil is keeping a sharp eye on the body language of Ken Marshall. He notices an almost imperceptible nodding of his head suggesting that he's agreeing with what Ayer is saying.

"Phenethylamine is also a chemical that has been found at high levels in the urine of schizophrenics."

Marshall has stop nodding and flies to his feet,

"Objection M'Lud. This is preposterous! Dr. Ayer is making a completely irrelevant and disconnected association..."

Henderson cuts Marshall off,

"What exactly are you up in arms about Mr. Marshall? Are you challenging the factual accuracy of something which Dr. Ayer has just said?

"Claiming a chemical is associated with the piss of schizophrenics is highly prejudicial."

"Mr. Marshall, I think it remains to be seen whether or not this comment is prejudicial.

"Dr. Ayer, you may continue.

"Thank you judge.

"In addition to the phenethylamine, the Cortx gas also includes sympathomimetic molecules that are stimulants. Based on what I can tell from their patent, the descriptions of some of the chemistry are in generic classes. For example, there is a cluster of chemicals which are stimulants. This group of chemicals are associated with psychedrine with the chemical number 300-62-9."

"Objection M'Lud, the comments of the witness are speculative. The precise formulation of nootropic gas remains proprietary and it must be emphasized it has been evaluated, judged safe and approved for..."

Henderson interrupts Marshall again,

"Mr. Marshall, the basis of this judicial review is in part a challenge to the safety and safety assessment process for new products from the neurotech industry. If the nootropic formula is as safe as it has been officially established to be, you should have little to be concerned about."

Henderson glances towards Gil who picks up the thread,

"You were saying Dr. Ayer, there is a general reference to chemicals in a group associated with pyschedrine, 300-62-9? What is the significance of that?"

"That is a very controlled group of chemicals."

"A controlled group of chemicals?"

Ayers responds,

"They are amphetamines. They can be addic…"

"Objection, objection, objection. I request this speculation based on speculation be struck from the record."

"M'Lud, Dr. Ayer is merely pointing to the intrinsic properties and hazards associated with a class of chemicals that are referenced in a patent for a specific nootropic formula."

Henderson concedes a need for exactitude and specificity regarding the chemical ingredients of the Cortx nootropic formula,

"The last comment by Dr. Ayer will be deleted from the record. Mr. Hinchliff, further questions?"

Gil grumbles at the ruling but thinks the point is still being made,

"Not at the moment M'Lud, but I may want to followup with Dr. Ayer at a later point."

"Mr. Marshall, do you have any questions for Dr. Ayer?"

"Yes, M'Lud."

Marshall navigates closer to Dr. Ayer,

"Dr. Ayer, in the field of neuroscience, are you familiar with the phenomenon of eidetic memories?"

"Generally speaking. There has been a lot of research into people who claim to have 'photographic' memories. The distinction between a so called 'photographic memory' and the phenomenon of eidetic memory is in part a matter of degree.

"Some neuroscientists are sceptical that the phenomenon of 'photographic memory' actually exists – where a person can retrieve past events in the minds eye like a snapshot and see all its detail. But on the other hand, most people, especially children between the ages of 3 and 5 experience eidetic memories.

"In most adults the phenomenon of eidetic memory only lasts about 1 second. That is, you look at a scene or image and close your eyes, and for about 1 second you can still see that image. That's what has been referred to as an eidetic memory."

"You mention that in most adults the phenomenon of an eidetic memory only lasts about 1 second?"

"More or less."

"Do you think there are adults whose eidetic memories last longer?"

"There have been case studies of such people."

"So there must be something occurring naturally in the endogenous neurochemistry of such people that facilitates an extended experience of an eidetic memory?

"Apparently so."

"Thank you Dr. Ayer. No further questions M'Lud."

The apple cart of memory prominence

After a '10 minute break' which lasted closer to half an hour, Gil makes the unorthodox decision to call a philosopher to testify.

This particular professor of philosophy, who happens to teach at the last philosophy department in Britain, wrote an essay about nootropics from the perspective of epistemology which caught Gil's attention.

"M'Lud, I would like to call Professor Suresh Appiah to testify. He is a Professor of Epistemology in the Philosophy Department of St. Andrews University."

Appiah is about 45 and is wearing a light blue shirt and a striped blue and orange tie with gold rimmed glasses. He looks soft spoken even though he hasn't yet opened his mouth.

"Professor, could you please give the court a succinct explanation of 'epistemology'?"

"I'll try. Epistemology is in part, the study of how we know what we know, and how we assign value to what we know."

"Professor Appiah, can you please explain to the court why you think nootropics may pose a threat to the fundamentals of human judgement processes and might even endanger identity formation among young people and adults?"

"Surely."

Professor Appiah takes a deep breath,

"Our perceptions are one of our primary sources of knowledge. So in principle, enhanced perceptions might be regarded as having enhanced reliability. Philosophically, there is a tradition of scepticism towards perception and a questioning of whether our perceptions can be trusted as a source of irrefutable knowledge.

"In human history, memories that are extremely vivid or unforgettable are typically associated with powerful experiences and emotions that have shaped our lives, our values, and our identities. Traumas, joys, fears, pleasures, etc. They are key learning experiences or behaviour modifiers.

"Nootropically enhanced perceptions introduces a new cognitive twist. There is a possible denigration of the value of prominent memories because with nootropics any memory can artificially be made prominent.

"We don't yet know the potential impact of nootropically enhanced memories as a new feature in a culture. We do not yet know what impact they could have on a conscious or unconscious level to our value systems socially. Indelible nootropic impressions are not born out of intense lived experiences which may provide invaluable life lessons, they are born out of a commercially driven enterprise that is oriented to our escapist tendencies and delivered in a mode of suspended disbelief."

Marshall was feeling dismissive of the philosopher's testimony but decided to take a swipe,

"Objection M'Lud. Professor Appaih's comments overlook the long held aspirations of great artists, writers, and filmmakers to change people's lives for the better and to enable them to see the world in a new way and..."

Gil interrupts,

"By engaging their hearts and minds, not by drugging them..."

Henderson comes down on Gil,

"You are out of order Mr. Hinchliff. That comment will be struck from the record."

The professor completed his introductory comments and Marshall engaged,

"Professor, do you believe it's possible that a film viewed without nootropics could engender powerful and vivid memories?

"Of course. My comments are meant to address a wider trend of artificially enhanced experiences. You can ask questions about the impact of a particular film from an epistemological perspective, but that's not akin to the potential for distortion by an entire class of movies."

"Professor, do you know which part of the human brain makes judgements?"

"Neuroscientists have identified the cerebral cortex as the part of the brain where higher judgements are made."

"Do you have any evidence to suggest that this part of the brain is in any way adversely affected by nootropics?"

"Sir, I'm a philosopher not a neuroscientist. I do not know what parts of the brain are or are not directly affected by nootropics. But if for arguments sake one says, OK, the cerebral cortex is not directly affected by nootropics, it is still being reactive to input that was synthetically altered."

"Thank you professor. I would like to think that human intelligence and human judgement are up to the task of making sound evaluations regardless of whether or not nootropics are anywhere in the equation."

"No further questions."

Gil interjects,

"M'Lud, just to clarify, we don't yet know for certain what effect the nootropics may be having in the long term on the cerebral cortex."

"Objection M'Lud. In the clinical studies submitted for this review, it is established which brain functions are enhanced by nootropics and how most of the cognitive functions of the brain – including the cerebral cortex – remain unaffected."

"These are short term studies by Cortx M'Lud. They are not a truly independent evaluation."

Raising the drawbridge

The clock in the courtroom hits 12:30 and Henderson announces a recess for lunch.

Gil stands up to leave and notices Sophie is already out the courtroom door. Sophie is consuming his thoughts which is a source of guilt. His relationship with Dena is definitely on the rocks and he feels helpless to undo the damage that's been done. He is also beginning to wonder how motivated he is to try. When someone falls out of love with another person, it's usually an irreversible emotional shift.

Gil heads out to the street to call Dena and just as he's about to make the call, he gets a call from her. She rarely calls in the middle of the day unless it's something urgent.

"Hi Dena, how are you? I was just about to call you."

"Hi Gil. How is the case going?"

"It's going OK, I think it's going OK."

"Listen, I just wanted to mention, I'm at your flat now. I'm picking up my clothes."

A long silence.

Gil's voice is cracking,

"I'm afraid to ask why you are doing that."

"I've not been very happy Gil. I don't think it's working out. I think I need some space to think things over."

Another long awkward silence followed – but this one was longer and more awkward.

"Dena, can we please meet up later to talk about this?"

"Look Gil, to be honest, I don't know what there is to talk about. Forget about your trip to Where-ever-istan. I get that. It was something you felt you had to do. You didn't tell me everything, I won't take that personally. I think it's more. I don't think you approve of the decisions I've made in my life. And I'm tired of us having abstract arguments all the time about the evils of memory supremacists. Yeah, we can meet and talk Gil, but later is not a good time. Let's talk tomorrow."

Gil could barely get the words out,

"OK, I'll give you a call tomorrow."

And then came the real stake in Gil's heart,

"I'll slide my key under the door on my way out."

During lunch, Gil confided in Graham that he had just broken up with Dena, or more accurately, that Dena had broken up with him. Graham was as sympathetic as he could be.

Gil was really down on himself,

"I don't blame her. Who can really put up with a psycho."

"You're not really a psycho Gil, just impossible to live with."

"Oh, thanks Graham."

"I was just kidding. But seriously, I had a feeling that you guys were drifting apart."

"We kinda were."

"Is it over over? Do you think it's fixable? Do you want to fix things?"

"OK, since I'm being cross-examined, I think the evidence suggests it's over over. She picked up all her clothes and left the key behind. Do I hope there's a chance of turning things around? My gut feeling is that the chances are slim. Once Dena makes her mind up about something, she's pretty unshakable. Do I want to fix things? That's the hardest one to answer. Maybe if I was happy or happier in the relationship it might not have deteriorated in the way that it has. I never really could talk to Dena about my work, nor did she really care to hear much about it. But it still hurts like hell. I'd really like to go home and curl up in a ball. I'm really not in the mood to listen to testimony from our neuroethicist."

"We need to get back Gil. Your neuroethicist guy, Basil, he's a pretty sharp dude. He'll take your mind off things."

Tales of a neuroethicist

Back in court, Gil calls neuroethicist Basil McFarlane to testify. Basil is a former advisory member of the government's first Parliamentary Neurotech Oversight Sub-committee.

"Dr. McFarlane, thank you for making the time to be here."

"My pleasure. I'm happy to make the time. I think the issues matter enormously."

"Dr. McFarlane, as a neuroethicist, could you please summarise what your role has been as an advisor to the government?"

"For two years, I was a part time member of the advisory board to the first Parliamentary Neurotech Oversight Sub-committee."

"From the perspective of a neuroethicist, what are some of the questions which the Cortx Eidetic cinema and other uses of nootropics raise for you?"

"Obviously, safety issues are entwined with ethical issues. But if we assume that the use of nootropics is demonstrably safe, the overarching question then is, are they a welcome or unwelcome intervention or manipulation of the human brain."

"But isn't that an academic question? After all, Cortx nootropics have aleady been approved for use. And they may soon be used by hundreds of thousands if not millions of consumers."

"A drug or chemical formula may be declared 'safe' and be approved for use, but a neuroethicist can still ask the question: Should it be?"

Marshall intervenes,

"M'Lud, does the court really have the time for this kind of academic indulgence? This sounds like navel gazing to me."

Before Henderson responds, Gil fires back,

"I think Mr. Marshall should apologize to Dr. McFarlane for his rudeness."

Henderson matter of factly asks McFarlane to continue his testimony.

"Historically, artificial interventions to boost or dampen a memory have always raised ethical questions.

"There have been nanosurgical attempts to remove specific memories linked to trauma – but these attempts often cause unforeseen collateral damage.

"Last century neurochemical drugs were developed that if taken within hours of a traumatic experience are intended to dampen the emotional power of the experience and the memory associated with it.

"An ethical case can be made for the benefits of such neurochemical intervention. But on the other hand, is it ever better to let a person try to come to terms with a traumatic experience rather than try to chemically redact it? Such an intervention could also enable a person to forget memories they are morally obligated to keep."

In his heart of hearts, Gil is feeling that McFarlane is being academic. He shudders at the thought of what he might be trying to cope with had Sophie not given him a medication to mute the psychological trauma of what he was subjected to.

"But Dr. McFarlane, the memories which Cortx will be boosting in its cinemas are billed as family friendly content. Surely, there can't be an ethical objection to doing that?"

"There are still reasons to be sceptical. Nootropically boosted memories may give an artificially inflated sense of happiness or unhappiness."

"Dr. McFarlane, in the context of other applications, Cortx has claimed that the use of nootropics has been proven to help consolidate memories in people suffering from neuro-degenerative brain disease who, for example, can no longer recognize a loved one – and that with nootropics, such a person can once again put a name to a loved one's face. Isn't that a very beneficial and desirable outcome?"

"From what I have read in the journals, nootropics does nothing to stop, slow, or reverse cognitive decline nor does it in any way improve higher cognitive functions.

"For example, for someone who doesn't recognise a wife, husband, child or close friend, with the intervention of nootropics, it has been shown to enable the placing of a name to a face. But ironically, the distress and frustration can be heightened because the connection between the name and face has little or no psychological resonance. There remains a void rather than a natural web of associations. It's a mechanistic connection made without a natural web of memories between one family member and another.

"It's a treatment that does more for family members who are in a state of anguish because their loved one no longer recognises them but does nothing of substance to benefit the person with a neuro-degenerative disease."

"Dr. McFarlane, what for you are the ethical issues raised by a company which makes an intellectual property claim on an individual's memory?"

"Objection M'Lud. For the record, I think it's important to state that Cortx doesn't make an ethically contentious 'claim' to own these protein structures. They have been established unequivocally as our intellectual property."

"Mr. Hinchliff, would you please rephrase your question."

"Yes M'Lud. You've just heard Mr. Marshall say that these protein structures i.e. memories, are unequivocally Cortx property. Isn't the law the law?"

"Applying the legal construct of 'property rights' to neurochemical processes does raise science based and ethics based questions about boundaries."

"Please explain."

"There are countless stories of neighbours getting into boundary disputes over where the fence should be or where the hedge should not be. The dispute may be over mere inches. These disputes can drag on for years and end up bankrupting one or both neighbours. You would think the boundary line between two neighbours is a simple and straightforward judgement call, but once emotions get involved, all bets are off.

"Memories are very complex multi-dimensional neurochemical phenomenon. They often contain elements of our 5 senses, they are experienced with a bundle of associations to other memories, they may have shifting emotional content, they have a spatial orientation and a neurochemical 'time stamp', they have a degree of vividness or intensity, and they have another layer which establishes them as a specific person's memory in continuity with that person's lived experience. So there can be around 10 dimensions to a memory.

"From the perspective of a memory surveyor, if there could be such a thing, it's very hard to imagine where the boundary lines of a Cortx augmented memory would clearly be relative to the complexity or the totality of how any memory exists in our consciousness."

"Thank you Dr. McFarlane."

Henderson glances towards Marshall,

"Mr. Marshall?"

"M'Lud, I have no questions for the eminent neuroethicist except to say that his suggestion of mnemonic ambiguity or the near impossibility of identifying the specificity of a memory has been superseded. Our presentation to this court of the 28 volumes of alphanumeric code establish with unprecedented and historic detail the specificity of a nootropically enhanced memory. And it was on that basis Cortx received one of its most important patents.

"The intellectual property rights of Cortx are a prima facie case of the triumph of clarity and common sense over presumed ambiguity."

Gil sluggishly returns to his seat. He feels emotionally battered but not by Marshall, just battered.

"Thank you Mr. Marshall, Mr. Hinchliff. This court is adjourned until tomorrow morning at 10AM."

As the courtroom begins to empty, Phil Thurgood approaches Gil.

"Hinchliff, it will be a pleasure to see you disbarred and in jail. Maybe then you'll keep your fucking nose out of our business."

"I'll keep my fucking nose out of your business when you keep your fucking business out of my brain!"

Exiting with Graham and a cluster of spectators, Gil spots Sophie standing at the bottom of the courthouse steps talking to Ken Marshall and another Cortx executive. Gil heads in her direction. Spotting him coming down the stairs, Sophie hastily leaves the building.

It is late in the afternoon. Media and demonstrators have dispersed with the exception of one middle-aged demonstrator wearing a sandwich board. On one side it reads, 'Don't Let Liberty Become a Memory'. The other side reads, 'Support Cortx and the Memory Choice Movement'.

As Gil reaches the outside square in hope of spotting Sophie, a flash-back of a public execution assaults him. It fits his mood perfectly. He momentarily closes his eyes and hears shots reverberating.

As an act of resistance to another insidious intrusion, he mutters to himself,

"Fuck you you motherfuckers and fuck that shit."

Gil spots Sophie and makes a dash to catch her. She takes eva-sive manoeuvres. Gil shouts her name. Sophie stops. Gil cau-tiously approaches.

"Sophie..."

Sophie turns to confront Gil with a fierce stare,

"You know Gil, you're smart, you must have way over the average hundred billion neurons in your skull. Do you really need to own every single one of them? Isn't that being a little bit greedy?"

Gil stands in stunned silence as Sophie turns and walks off. Gil is soon keeping pace two steps behind.

"It's just the thin end of the wedge, you know that! You don't have to testify for them."

Sophie stops and turns,

"And why the hell shouldn't I? I've programmed the worlds most powerful computers haven't I? I know exactly where all the lost memories are buried, don't I? Who the hell are you? You're nothing but a goddamned neuroterrorist!

Sophie starts to cry. Gil moves closer to Sophie, but he hesitates to embrace her. Gil dares to gently touch her shoulder. Sophie recoils.

"Leave me alone...PLEASE"

"Sophie, what is it? Please tell me what's going on..."

"You don't know a thing, you don't know a goddamned thing. Please, FUCK OFF!"

A mess rehearsal

Just the idea of giving testimony at a judicial review catapulted Sophie far out of her comfort zone. Her fears and the emotional conflicts associated with giving testimony were growing exponentially as her scheduled appearance approached.

In preparation, Sophie met up with Marshall and his team a week before she was expected to testify. She was told what to wear, the questions that will be asked, and what responses were expected. It was a dress rehearsal. Gil did the same with his experts.

The simple solution to escape the emotional turmoil would be for Sophie to tell Marshall she changed her mind and will not testify. She came very close to doing just that.

But Sophie has never run from fear. With the meticulousness of the computer scientist and programmer that she is, she probes it, she questions it, she dissects it. And after it has been broken down into its parts, the parts are subjected to the analytical part of her brain. She tries to disempower her fears rather than allow them to rule her.

Above all else, Sophie will be true to Sophie. She knows how much the case means to Gil but she is unwilling to be moved or manipulated by that.

At the outset of the judicial review, Marshall tried to discourage Sophie from attending until the time and date of her testimony. She was glad she didn't listen to him. It was intriguing to see Marshall and Gil go head to head.

There was a moment after Sophie got back to London that she wondered if there might be more between her and Marshall than a drunken one night stand in Kyrgyzstan. But when she asked herself if Ian would approve of him, she felt emphatically not.

Sophie was reassured by Marshall at the rehearsal that she is only expected to testify about her work and would not be asked anything personal or outside her expertise. But her recent short term memory anxieties have badly shaken her self confidence.

Sophie thinks the company neurologist was a patronizing arse. His diagnosis or lack of one can't be trusted. She's becoming more convinced that the nootropics are adversely affecting her.

The formula she first used at K-Lab was the original nootropic consumer mixture. She never did see the complete data for that mixture nor from the clinical trials involving the supposedly 'improved' formula.

Sophie suspects three possibilities. There were safety issues but they are now sorted. There remain safety issues and they are yet to be sorted. Or third, there are safety issues and they are unlikely to get sorted because Cortx wants to turn the population of the world into 'nooheads'.

Exaflops with attitude, courtroom crescendo

In the courthouse square on the morning of day three of the judicial review the MRA supporters are the largest and most vociferous contingent. There are about three dozen shouting in unison,

'Keep your claims out of our brains'

There are only a handful of Cortx supporters, but they have a new banner that reads,

LIFE IS TOO SHORT FOR
BEAUTIFUL MEMORIES THAT FADE

Inside the courtroom, Henderson, with coffee in hand, is getting the show on the road,

"Good morning everyone. Mr. Marshall, are you ready to continue?

"Yes M'Lud. Recently, I referred to taking memories out of the ambiguous domain of cognitive psychology and placing them in the realm of biophysics. This was made possible with a combination of technologies that rely on the most powerful computing system in existence.

"I would like to call Sophie Hudson, the lead computer programmer on our most ambitious and groundbreaking research enterprise, Project Axion."

Sophie is conservatively dressed wearing a white blouse, a grey suit and slacks and black leather shoes. There are pearl buttons on her blouse which compliment pearl earrings. As she approaches the front of the courtroom she glances down to avoid making eye contact with Gil or Marshall.

Sophie Hudson is now center stage and being addressed by Marshall,

"Thank you Ms. Hudson. Can you please tell the court how long you've worked at the Encore Foundation on the Axion project?"

Before she has a chance to respond, Judge Henderson asks Marshall if Sophie is a current or former Cortx employee. Marshall clarifies that her contract has recently ended.

"Ms. Hudson?"

"I'm sorry. What was the question?"

"How long did you work on the Axion project?"

"Yes, about two years."

"Can you please provide a concise explanation of the aims of Axion?"

"I'll try. Axion is essentially a 3D mapping enterprise. Its aim is to map the human brain and to do so at a molecular level neuron by neuron, dendrite by dendrite. Its goal is not to produce a static or generic map but to utilize the capacity of exaflop computing to provide a map of cognitive activities in real time. Lots of other breakthroughs have flowed out of Axion. As a programmer, it was the most challenging and exciting project I've ever worked on."

Henderson seeks some clarification,

"Ms. Hudson, you mentioned 'exaflop'. Please indulge me, what is an exaflop?"

"Yes sir. Our exaflop computing system, or should I say the Cortx exaflop computing system is the most powerful computer in the world today by a factor of 50,000. It can do a billion billion calculations per second. Now that might sound like an unfathomable amount of processing capacity – and it is – but the extraordinary thing is that one exaflop matches the processing capacity of one human brain."

"Extraordinary. Thank you. Ms. Hudson. Please continue."

"The mapping activity is done using a technique Cortx developed called nanotography. Nanoscopic transmitters are introduced into the brain which emit position related signals and metadata about neurochemistry. The signals are received and processed almost instantaneously as cognitive activity takes place and as memories are being formed. One of the important goals, but not the only goal of Project Axion is to map the formation process and neurochemical profile of a human memory."

Marshall picks up the thread,

"In relation to 3D spatial coordinates and neurochemistry, did you have any way of assessing the reliability or accuracy of the memory related data that was being mapped?"

"There was certainly redundancy in the data we were observing when multiple subjects received and processed the same audio visual input.

"I was pretty confident that what we were seeing was accurate. It's true that on a macro anatomical level no two brains are exactly alike. But in the context of the use of nootropics and mapping a memory encryption process at a molecular level among different subjects, it was uncanny how similar the results were."

Sophie continues to answer Marshall's questions for half an hour. She is asked about the dedication of the K-Lab team, her first reactions to seeing human memories being formed, and about other medical and neurological benefits that have flowed out of the Axion project.

"Thank you Ms. Hudson.

"M'Lud, Ms. Hudson was incredibly generous with her time today given that she is no longer a Cortx employee.

Marshall glances at his watch,

"She did inform me earlier that she will have to leave this review as soon as possible due to urgent personal matters. Again, thank you Sophie for your valuable time and testimony."

Sophie looked confused. Henderson turned to Sophie,

"Ms. Hudson?"

"Your Honour, I wasn't sure I would be able to testify at all today. I did say to Mr. Marshall that I was hoping there wouldn't be too many questions and I would not have to speak for very long. But if there are more questions..."

Marshall is clearly caught on the back foot by this. He's trading quizzical looks with Palmer and shaking his head to indicate this isn't the plan. During the rehearsal a week earlier, Marshall thought Sophie agreed to his plan that she leave immediately after answering his questions. He expected her to jump at the opportunity to bow out of the courtroom.

Marshall takes his glasses off and places them atop a bound compilation of hi-rez brain images from Project Axion.

"Mr. Marshall, do you have any further questions for Ms. Hudson?"

Marshall is looking down and barely audible,

"No M'Lud."

"Mr. Hinchliff, are there any questions for Ms. Hudson?"

"Yes M'Lud."

Marshall interrupts,

"M'Lud, if the plaintiff and court allows, I request a 15 minute recess"

"Mr. Hinchliff, is that acceptable?"

"It is – if Ms. Hudson will remain for questions."

"I will your honour."

"This court is in recess for 15 minutes."

Marshall immediately approaches Gil and Graham looking a bit nervous,

"Hi guys, can we have a very brief chat? There's a private room next to the Judge's chambers."

Marshall glances over his shoulder at Palmer.

Gil and Graham give each other a curious look, then shrug,

"Ok."

Marshall and a Cortx colleague of his lead Gil and Graham to the conference room.

Marshall makes his pitch,

"Guys, you are doing a fantastic job. You're really making your points, and the press you've been getting is something you should be very pleased with.

"The reality is, whatever this Henderson guy decides, it's not going to change the game. We will continue on with what we do and I promise we will tie you up in court for years and nothing will change.

"In exchange for you calling time on this judicial review, Cortx will make a 1 million E-ren donation to a charity of your choice. You can even set up an MRA Foundation and we will give a million to it.

Gil interjects,

"Call time on this review?"

"So, you can continue to rant and rave about Cortx as much as you like among your friends, but you cease and desist from any further protests or legal actions against Cortx and its payment model. And you issue a simple statement which says you believe Cortx takes matters of safety seriously. A million E-ren gentlemen."

Gil turns to Graham and with a sarcastic tone says,

"Gee Graham, should we put this matter to a membership vote?"

Graham responds directly to Marshall,

"Look Ken, why don't you give us a couple of minutes to discuss this. It's a bit of a surprise."

"Of course. Unfortunately, there isn't much time. Here's my number if you have any questions, I'm not going anywhere. I can ask for a longer recess if necessary."

Marshall and his colleague leave the room.

Gil and Graham are silent for about 20 seconds. Letting the million E-ren offer sink in and ping pong between their brains.

Gil was the first to speak.

"I want to accept their offer."

"What? Are you serious Gil, after all you've been through?"

"Yes, I'm very serious."

"I know a million is a lot, but that's a sellout and nobody would ever let you forget it!"

"Look Graham, believe me, I know what's right. I will send Ken a text message of our terms now. I will show it to you first and if you agree, I will then text it to him and if we're lucky, this all ends today – and you might even end up with a yacht."

Gil took a couple of minutes to write up his terms of surrender to Cortx. Graham was sitting and shaking his head in disbelief at what was happening. Gil handed Graham his message to consider,

Dear Ken,

Thank you for your generous offer of 1 million E-ren. On behalf of the MRA, I am very pleased to accept this offer and immediately terminate this judicial review process. The acceptance of this payment however is contingent on the following: Cortx agrees that all public advertising and promotion for the use of nootropics or the Eidetic Cinema must cease and desist immediately and permanently. However, Cortx would still be allowed to rave about their benefits as much as they like among their friends. Please let me know ASAP if this is acceptable.

Sincerely,
Gil Hinchliff

On behalf of the Memory Rights Alliance

Graham reads it and gives his approval with a big grin.

The message is sent.

More than 5 minutes passes and no response from Marshall.

The judicial review continues.

The packed courtroom is unusually quiet and attentive. That morning the Cortx PR team issued a press release intended to drum up excitment about upcoming testimony from 'Exaflop Sophie'. Sophie was not consulted about the press release and resented both the content and the fact that she wasn't consulted about it.

Sophie is back on the stand.

After locking each other in their sights, at least ten seconds pass before Gil asks his first question,

"Ms. Hudson, thank you for agreeing to stay longer and provide testimony.

"In addition to programming and data managing the Axion project, did you work on any other Cortx initiatives while in Kyrgyzstan?"

"Well, I had a garden allotment and grew plenty of fresh veggies for myself and the canteen..."

When laughter in the courtroom subsides, Sophie continues,

"I thought that was an important enterprise, but yes, I did work on other projects. For example, I helped design user friendly diagnostic software used to assess brain health"

"Could you please give a bit more detail regarding that software?"

Gil notices Marshall is about to jump to his feet.

"Of course, I'm not asking you to reveal any Cortx secrets!"

Sophie appears to be in her comfort zone.

"I am very proud of the data sets that went into programming it. It's very sophisticated and I believe very comprehensive and very easy to use and comprehend. It measures and evaluates over 300 neurometabolic and neurochemical stress parameters in real time, for example..."

It was another 'jack-in-the-box' moment for Marshall,

"Excuse me M'Lud, but because of Ms. Hudson's non-disclosure agreement with Cortx, she is not at liberty to discuss in open court what is proprietary information."

It was an unpleasant jolt for Sophie to be muzzled by Marshall. With a tight knot in her stomach, she was regretting not splitting when she had the chance.

It was Gil's pleasure to return fire,

"M'Lud, Ms. Hudson is someone who for two years has had a ringside seat during the development of nootropics and other Cortx products. Given how safe their products surely must be, why would

Mr. Marshall have any objections to Ms. Hudson talking about a diagnostic program that would underscore safety and health assurances they so vigorously proclaim? Surely she can speak in general terms that would not reveal proprietary information and her testimony would likely be beneficial for their case. Would it not? Instead we get this knee jerk objection on the basis of 'confidentiality' or the invocation of 'proprietary information'. Mr. Marshall, what are you afraid of?"

And then, addressing Marshall, Gil quotes Alex quoting Shakespeare,

> *"Good sir, why dost thou fear things that do sound so fair?*
> *In the name of truth, are ye fantastical, that indeed*
> *which outwardly ye show?*

"That's quoting Alex quoting Shakespeare M'Lud."

Henderson seems to get it,

"Macbeth?"

"Yes M'Lud. Act I, scene II"

Marshall wasn't amused,

"I'm pleased when I hear the plaintiff paying frequent tribute to a Cortx landmark achievement. But M'Lud, a judicial review cannot compel the disclosure of confidential or proprietary information which may be of benefit to our competitors and in turn cause financial loss to the defendant."

Marshall succeeded at getting Henderson's back up,

"Mr Marshall, please brush up on the protocols of a judicial review. You are correct, I cannot compel testimony from anyone any more than I can compel you to submit proprietary information or documents, but there is an overarching duty of candour on the part of the defendant and from all those who participate in a judicial review.

"It's of overriding importance to have a fuller picture of the issues in the public interest and in the interest of a fair and informed decision coming out of this process. I will allow Ms. Hudson to answer questions with whatever detail or generality she deems appropriate."

Marshall is knocked back and throws an anxious glance towards Palmer. But, he isn't quite ready to yield,

"M'Lud, may I approach the bench?"

"You may."

Marshall looks towards Palmer as he approaches Henderson for a direct plea out of earshot of everyone else.

"M'Lud, unfortunately neither you nor I can make an on the spot decision about whether or not Ms. Hudson says anything that is judged to be in violation of her confidentiality agreement. It's a decision made by our Corporate Citizenship department. Because of claw-back provisions in Ms. Hudson's Terms of Employment agreement, she could face substantial financial loses. If she's judged to have violated her NDA she could be forced to give back the bonuses she has received over her two years of employment. I would urge the court not to inadvertently place her in such professional and financial jeopardy."

"Mr. Marshall, I am moved by your concern for Ms. Hudson's financial well being. I think anyone who can program an exaflop computer is capable of understanding the significance of having signed a confidentiality agreement. I suggest we move forward."

Marshall takes a deep sigh and retreats.

Henderson glances to Gil,

"You may proceed Mr. Hinchliff."

"Thank you M'Lud.

"Ms. Hudson, given your work on the diagnostic software, and given its sensitivity to hundreds of neurological parameters, how would you characterise its capacity to monitor and assess the effects which the nootropics were having on the test subjects?"

Marshall is beside himself with incredulity,

"M'Lud, this line of questioning is so out of bounds. Ms. Hudson has signed an NDA which prohibits her from talking in any detail about her work for Cortx."

"Mr. Marshall, we have just discussed this point. It was the defendant which asked Ms. Hudson to testify in the first place. Was she violating her NDA then?

"Ms. Hudson, you are not compelled to answer questions by the plaintiff and you cannot be compelled to remain silent by the defendant. It's entirely your decision..."

Sophie is plunged into a dreaded predicament. Opening her mouth to say anything is likely to come across as being disloyal to her former employer.

She knows she may have hell to pay if she crosses the line with Cortx. Is she furious at Gil for putting her on the spot? Absolutely!

"I'm sorry Mr. Hinchliff, what was the question?"

"Did you by any chance assess the diagnostic software in the context of evaluating nootropic safety?"

"Almost."

"What do you mean?"

"I most strenuously object M'Lud! Ms. Hudson is not qualified to assess the effectiveness or the results of the diagnostic software trials. She is not qualified to make any judgement about those assessments regarding safety. Besides, the diagnostic software is a red herring.

Any new product must undergo a rigorous process of safety trials that far exceeds the parameters of any diagnostic software package. Ms. Hudson is a computer engineer and not a neuroscientist."

Henderson is searching for a thread of logic,

"Mr. Marshall, are you saying that the person who designed the diagnostic system isn't capable of having an informed opinion about the effectiveness of that system?"

"M'Lud, Ms. Hudson is programmer. All of the software parameters are defined by neuroscientists and specialists in neurometabolism. They are qualified to assess the diagnostic data, not Ms. Hudson."

Gil joins the fray,

"M'Lud, firstly I'd like to correct Mr. Marshall. He referred to Ms. Hudson as a computer engineer. If Mr. Marshall checks with Cortx HR he will discover that Ms. Hudson was hired as a computer scientist not as an engineer. Over a two year period, Ms. Hudson had close and constant interaction with a team of neuroscientists on a daily basis in the course of developing, refining, and testing the diagnostic software. I think the purpose of this judicial review would be well served to allow Ms. Hudson to speak.

Henderson's exasperation was evident in his tone,

"Mr. Hinchliff and Ms. Hudson, you may proceed – if you wish."

"Thank you M'Lud.

"Ms. Hudson, a few minutes ago I asked if you managed to assess the diagnostic software in the context of nootropic safety – and you said, 'almost'. What did you mean by that?"

"Well, the diagnostic safety assessments were online very briefly. I think for only a few hours. Before I had a chance to study them, they were removed. I was promised a hard copy but never got one."

"When it was briefly online, did you manage to read any of it?"

Sophie hesitates. Marshall and Palmer are giving her stares that could kill or maim. She is looking down and lost in thought when Gil repeats the question,

"Did you glimpse any of it Ms. Hudson?"

Sophie looks up,

"Not really. But, I remembered something odd the other day."

"What was that Ms. Hudson?"

"The day I tried to read it online, the safety evaluations were the last chapter. The table of contents indicated pages 96-110.

"I noticed that when the report was published on the company intranet about week or so later, the last chapter was not part of the report."

"What did you think at the time? Could it have been an accidental omission? A deliberate omission? A computer glitch? Or, maybe it was a section that would be published separately?"

"I don't recall what I thought. But it was frustrating not to see the complete summary of the diagnostic results. Given how hard I had worked on the programme, I just wanted to see for myself that it was all working as intended."

Sophie seems to freeze in mid thought. She puts her hands to her face and is silent for several very long seconds. Gil is confused and feeling guilty for questioning her.

Henderson could see Sophie's distress,

"Are you OK Ms. Hudson?"

"I'm OK judge."

Sophie drops her hands away from her face and begins to speak in a very calm voice and a changed demeanor,

"Yesterday afternoon I made the decision to try and test the diagnostic software I helped develop. Co-incidently, as part of a new marketing initiative, the most advanced version of the software was incorporated into a select few neurogram kiosks in London and around the country. One kiosk is on Harley Street. It's a very powerful and specialised piece of software.

"Brain health these days has become an obsession. It's rated more important than managing your weight, HRV, blood pressure, cholesterol, air metrics, or carbon footprint."

As Sophie is talking, Gil begins to pace very slowly a few feet away from where she's speaking. He's listening intently but uncertain where her testimony is headed. Marshall is sitting with his arms resting on his elbows with his hands covering his ears as if he doesn't want to hear what Sophie has to say.

Sophie continues,

"As a perk of working at K-Lab, employees were allowed to sample the nootropic formula which had completed safety trials. A number of us were curious to experience one of the most important achievements of K-Lab. It was something we all contributed to in one way or another.

"But first, you were required to fill out a very lengthy health questionnaire."

Sophie pauses for a moment which was an opening for Gil,

"So you did eventually sample the nootropics?"

"I have found the use of nootropics pleasurable. Over the past 18 months I have used them periodically when I garden or listen to music. But recently, I've started to experience some very odd phenomena. My short term memory seems to be deterior…

"Objection M'Lud. Ms Hudson's testimony is veering into speculative and anecdotal territory that is irrelevant or completely inappropriate…"

"Mr Marshall, please allow your star expert – Ms. Hudson – to complete her thought. Ms. Hudson…"

Sophie is frozen. She has completely lost her train of thought. A panic stricken expression is descending over her face.

"Ms. Hudson, you said you wanted to test the diagnostic software? "

The prompt by Henderson helps defuse the panic and put Sophie back on track,

"…So, I took my last remaining pocket sized cylinder of nootropics – which was given to me at K-Lab – placed the tube under my nose and went about gardening and listening to classical music for about 90 minutes, roughly the length of a feature film.

"I then went to the kiosk on Harley Street which has the more sophisticated diagnostic software. I positioned the scanner helmet, swiped my payment bracelet and chose 'Option B' for self-diagnosis.

"By the way, I thought the graphical interface was very user friendly and beautifully designed. It took less than 30 seconds to begin to get results. There are voice and printout options.

"First, a voice gave me the big picture, *'no evidence of strokes, tumours, aneurysms, degenerative disease, or trauma. Blood circulation and oxygenation are within normal parameters.'* Then the interface offers more detailed diagnostics for an additional fee. I paid it.

"Then things got geeky and a bit scary. I was told that, *'neurogenesis was at extremely high levels and neuromodulation was optimized'.* These processes are boosted by nootropics and linked to activities that are engrossing a person's attention as memories are being formed and consolidated.

"Then I was told, '*neurotransmitter potentiation is at elevated millivolts*'. Now that can be significant because it means the brain is running hot.

"That was followed by something worrisome, '*a glutamine deficiency is detected*'. Glutamine is one of the key elements needed for transporting brain signals. The diagnosis went on to say, '*this may be a result of synthetic neurometabolic enhancers at elevated levels*'. There was a blinking light on the interface with a text warning. It read, '*Extended use of synthetic neurometobolic enhancers at elevated levels can lead to glutamine deficiency. This can be remedied by elevation of neurometabolic enhancers*'.

"I thought long and hard about his warning. I think the DIY programme is detecting a nascent syndrome in which a glutamine deficiency can lead to a growing dependence on enhancers – and increased dependence on enhancers could be the start of a cycle that leads to nootropic addiction."

Marshall almost knocks over his chair as he shoots up,

"OBJECTION! OBJECTION! This is – outrageous."

Marshall stares incredulously at Sophie Hudson.

"M'Lud, the timing of a diagnostic test can be determinative. Taking a test soon after nootropic use is likely to yield distorted results. Ms. Hudson is not qualified to interpret or draw any conclusions from the diagnostic program and her speculations are completely baseless."

Gil interrupts,

"Sophie's interpretations are completely sound. The real problem is the defendant just doesn't want to hear them."

"Order, Mr. Hinchliff."

"M'Lud, the kiosks are at best a first step in a more comprehensive diagnostic process. I have said it before and I will say it again, government health authorities have already certified our nootropics to be safe and her comments reflect a misguided use of the diagnostic software, are ill informed, and prejudicial."

"Ms. Hudson, I'm afraid I'm going to have to agree with Mr. Marshall. The last section of your testimony will be deleted from the record."

Graham slides half way under his table. Marshall has fixed his stare on Sophie. Gil has put aside any guilty feelings about continuing to question Sophie. Sophie is caught in courtroom crossfire.

"M'Lud, I have a couple more questions for Ms. Hudson, but first I'd like to fill in some technical gaps. There was an earlier reference by Ms. Hudson to nanotography. Nanotography uses nanoscopes which are microscopic transmitters injected by the millions into the brains of human guinea pigs..."

"Objection!"

"Sustained. Mr Hinchliff, I caution you against the use of inflammatory prejudicial language."

"But M'Lud, that's what the so called 'memory donors' were, guinea pigs. The experimentation on humans at K-Lab does not conform to the Helsinki Accords for human experimentation."

"Objection!"

"Mr. Hinchliff, please refrain from making allegations if you can't substantiate them."

"I can and I will M'Lud – shortly.

"Ms. Hudson, have you ever worked with or observed others working with nanoscopes before your employment on the Axion project?"

"No."

Gil is feverish and beginning to sweat profusely. He's about to ask a followup question, but his field of vision is commandeered by a hallucination.

A chorus line of Soviet era peasants astride a tractor are singing and dancing inside the courtroom.

To spectators in the courtroom, Gil is staring off into the mid-distance. Gil glances up to the Courtroom membrane screen. There are no singing peasants to be seen. Sophie and Graham are staring at Gil in alarm. So too Henderson,

"Mr. Hinchliff? Are you OK?"

Henderson then begins to mumble to himself,

"This has been one of the oddest judicial reviews I've ever adjudicated. I haven't a clue what people are taking around here!"

Gil has seen this movie before. Determined to not let it freak him out, he manages to tune out the tractors and plows on with the real show at hand,

"Sorry M'Lud. I'm OK.

"Ms. Hudson, I'd like to ask you if there were any unusual or unexpected reactions to the process of injecting the nanoscopes?"

"Objection M'Lud. This has no relevance to any of the issues of this review which to be honest M'Lud, I'm losing track of."

"M'Lud, I think the question goes to the heart of challenging the proprietary claims made by Cortx. I aim to establish that the process used by Cortx to map a memory is not as uniform or stable as earlier testimony would lead this court to believe – and can vary significantly from one subject to the next.

"You may proceed..."

Gil is seeing and hearing another brutal prisoner execution, but he's becoming more adept at ignoring the hallucinations,

"So Ms. Hudson, the process of infecting people with nanoscopes..."

Marshall is beyond exasperated,

"Objection. The use of the word 'infecting' is gross and prejudicial language. The nanoscopes are sterile and have no biological properties and pass through the body as an inert substance."

"I will rephrase M'Lud.

"Could the interaction of these supposedly 'inert' elements with living tissue and the neurological processes always be predicted?"

"Apparently not..."

"Objection M'Lud. Ms. Hudson is being manipulated by the plaintiff to violate her non-disclosure agreement with Cortx.

"Ms. Hudson risks severe financial penalties should she continue to describe activities she was privy to or share her opinions on matters she does not have the expertise to comment upon. She is a software programmer not a Cortx neuroscientist."

Maybe it was the tone in which she was referred to as a 'programmer' after earlier being called an 'engineer' – that made something in Sophie snap,

"Marshall, you were there at K-Lab, in Kyrgyzstan! Why don't you testify about what you saw?"

Marshall was totally beside himself,

"What, M'Lud...?"

"You saw people having violent and uncontrollable seizures after being injected with the damn nanoscopes. You saw eyeballs burst with blood and nanoscopes oozing out – having some kind of 'allergic' reaction."

Marshall is drowning and waiting for Henderson to throw him a line,

"M'Lud!?"

"Maybe you can reassure me Ken that there was no permanent brain damage done to these people? Oh, I'm sorry Ken, you wouldn't be qualified to make that assessment would you? You're an entertainment lawyer."

Henderson finally intervenes,

"Ms. Hudson..."

But Sophie blasted on,

"Perhaps you found it entertaining?"

Henderson had a riot on his hands.

"Ms. Hudson! That's enough.

"Marshall, Hinchliff, approach the bench."

Tears are welling up in Sophie's eyes as Marshall and Hinchliff approach Henderson,

"What the hell is going on here? Marshall, Ms. Hudson is your witness!"

"I'm not sure M'Lud. I would like to ask the courts permission to treat Ms. Hudson as a hostile witness. I'd like to request a recess to prepare a rebuttle to her testimony."

The three of them conclude their huddle and Henderson ends her testimony – for now,

"Ms. Hudson, you may step down."

Gil approaches Sophie as she leaves the hot seat. Her hands are shaking.

"You did the right thing Sophie."

"Save it Hinchliff. Just save it."

"M'Lud, the defendant is requesting a recess and enough time to prepare a response to Ms. Hudson's outburst."

"Mr. Marshall, you can have a recess. Please get your act together. Looking ahead, you can recuse yourself and Cortx get another attorney, or be prepared for the possibility that you might be called to testify.

"Yes, M'Lud."

"Is two days enough time?"

Gil desperately needs to keep the plan for the day on track,

"M'Lud, it's early afternoon, before we recess for two days, there is important testimony which the court needs to hear."

Marshall absolutely did not want to accommodate,

"I think a recess is urgently needed M'Lud."

"This witness has made a tremendous effort to be here today M'Lud. A two day delay would cause undue hardship and jeopardize his ability to testify. It's not the courts fault if Mr. Marshall could not muzzle his witness and now he pleads for a delay to reckon with the consequences."

"M'Lud, this court has had enough surprises for one day. We have urgently requested a recess."

Henderson looks at his watch,

"Mr. Hinchliff, can't this witness wait until we reconvene?"

"No M'Lud. This person has travelled a very long way to be here and does not have the resources to spend extended time in London nor can he rearrange his return travel plans."

Henderson looks at his watch again – and responds to Marshall's pleas,

"Mr. Marshall, I am going to allow this additional testimony."

Marshall, like a petulant child, slams down his tab screen.

Henderson glances to Gil,

"Let's get on with it."

"M'Lud, I would like to call Mr. Askar Popoluv to testify."

Marshall and his team are stunned. Gil overhears Marshall ranting to his colleagues,

"Who the fuck, what the fuck?"

The chamber door opens. A middle aged man with hollow eyes and dark hair streaked with grey is in a wheelchair as he's being assisted into the courtroom.

"M'Lud, Mr. Askar Popoluv has flown to London from Bishkek, Kyrgyzstan. He is one of hundreds of paid volunteers who participated as 'memory donors' in the research and development phase of nootropics and Project Axion at the K-Lab.

Marshall is completely blindsided,

"M'Lud, this Askar person was not mentioned in any of the documents filed nor was he mentioned to anyone on my team at any point. The plaintiff is not just disrespecting the protocols of this judicial review process he is abusing them. We have not been given any opportunity to prepare for his testimony in spite of how tangential or irrelevant it will likely be. I urge this court to disallow this testimony and this insulting abuse of the process."

Without missing a beat, Gil interjects,

"Fear, fear, and more, fear. That's what I hear coming from Mr. Marshall. What is it you are so afraid of?"

Henderson manages to get a word in edgewise,

"Mr. Hinchliff, why the big surprise?"

"M'Lud, I was far from certain that Mr. Popoluv would be able and willing to come to London to testify. It was only due to the last minute intervention by the Treasury ministry that a visa was issued which enabled Mr. Popolov to make the trip.

"Also M'Lud, Mr. Popoluv's family along with a hundred other families of volunteers who participated in the Cortx experiments are filing a class action lawsuit against Cortx for its failure to abide by the revised Helsinki Accords as they apply to human experimentation.

"Given the uncertainty over travel plans and the risk if not the likelihood that Cortx would attempt to intimidate or interfere with Mr. Popoluv's decision to testify, we proceeded with an abundance of caution.

"And just to remind this court, the plaintiff received no prior indication in court documents nor was any member of my team informed that Cortx had applied for and received 'memory utility' status.

"Mr. Popoluv's testimony will underscore two vital things. One is the potentially criminal disregard for the health and safety of paid volunteers who participated in the research and development stage of nootropics. Also, the experience of Mr. Popoluv will make clear the volatility of neuronal reactions from one volunteer to another. This volatility makes Cortx claims of alpha-numeric precision with regard to their memory encryptions specious at best."

Henderson tilts forward and touches his temples with the tips of the fingers from both hands. Then he appears to throw up his hands as if to surrender,

"Proceed."

Gil makes a quick glance to Graham and they exchange grins. It was their turn to drop a bombshell.

Sophie looks surprised and pleased to see Askar again. Back at K-Lab, she did everything she could to help him when he was experiencing traumatic physical and psychological reactions to the nanoscopes – even though it was not her role to do so.

When Sophie first arrived at the facility, she was shocked to see how most lab workers treated the volunteers as non-entities.

Sophie and Askar exchange smiles and give furtive waves to each other. Then Sophie touches her mouth – it may be to throw him a kiss.

The media in the courtroom are perked up by the Askar plot twist. Gil and Graham have just handed Cortx a gift wrapped PR disaster by announcing that the neurotech giant will be facing a class action lawsuit for unethical treatment of volunteers in the course of their human experimentation.

"Mr. Hinchliff, please be very focused in your questions for Mr. Popoluv. It's getting late in the day and I think everyone is feeling depleted."

"Yes M'Lud. Mr. Popoluv's English is not very good. His daughter is on hand if help is needed with translation between Russian and English."

Askar in his wheelchair is pushed to the front of the courtroom. He has a noticeable facial twitch.

"Mr. Popoluv, can you please tell us where you live?"

"I live – farm. South Bishkek."

"Are you a farmer?"

"Da."

"What kind of farming do you do?"

"I most grow khlopok"

Askar's daughter clarifies,

"Khlopok is cotton. My father is a cotton farmer"

"Thank you Ms. Popoluv.

"Mr. Popoluv, do you recognise anyone in this courtroom from Kyrgyzstan?"

Askar points to Sophie Hudson.

"For the record M'Lud, Mr. Popoluv has pointed to Sophie Hudson."

"How do you know Ms. Hudson Mr. Popoluv?"

"She kind to me when ill."

"What kind of illness did you have Mr. Popoluv?"

"Objection M'Lud. This testimony is proceeding in a speculative and subjective direction and unless Mr. Popoluv has a specific and qualified expertise to offer, I once again urge you to disallow this testimony."

"M'Lud, Mr. Popoluv was one of the volunteers who took part in Project Axion and allowed himself to be injected with nanoscopes for memory mapping. He also took part in clinical trials of the nootropic formulas which Cortx claims established their safety.

"His testimony will underscore the serious health and safety hazards faced by volunteers during the trials. And the range of unpredictable and extreme reactions to injections used for mapping will cast doubt on the stability and distinctiveness of nootropically reinforced protein structures – and by extension their alpha-numeric representations."

Marshall sits in stunned silence.

Henderson prods,

"Get on with the testimony Mr. Hinchliff."

"Mr. Popoluv, why did you decide to participate in the experiments that were taking place at the K-Lap facility outside of Bishkek?"

"Bad weather."

"Excuse me, bad weather?"

"Bad weather... bad crop... need money."

"What did the people at K-Lap tell you about the purpose of the experiments?"

"It was to cure for brain disease."

Marshall interrupts,

"M'Lud, I'm sure there was a clear and comprehensive explanation to all volunteers about the focus of the research. It would be part of any release form they must sign at the outset. Project Axion has enabled numerous insights into the biophysical nature of various brain diseases, which as we speak, is being translated into therapeutics."

At the very least, Popoluv's comment is embarrassing. Depending on the wording of the release agreement, it might be materially important for any lawsuit which argues that volunteers were inadequately informed about the commercial entertainment focus of the research.

Gil continues,

"Mr. Popoluv, did you watch movies at the lab?"

"Good movie. Good... Casablanca."

Askar is smiling at the thought of the film.

"And you would breath the nootropic gas while you watched the movie?"

"They put us in case."

Gil offers a clarification to Henderson,

"M'Lud, a 'case' is a body shaped clear plastic pod that volunteers are placed inside of. Once inside, it's hermetically sealed.

"How long were you in the case?"

"One... two hours"

"How many days did you watch movies?"

"Ponedel'nik, vtornik, sreda, chetverg, pyatnitsa, kazhdyy den'"

Gil glances to Askar's daughter,

"Those are days of the week. He view movies almost every day – it go on for two weeks"

Gil nods in appreciation, then glances back at Askar,

"Did you experience any side effects?"

"Objection M'Lud. Mr. Pop...

"Mr. Marshall, let the man speak. He's come a long way."

Henderson gestures for Gil to continue.

"Mr. Popoluv, did you have any side effects?"

There was a long pause from Askar after the question was translated. His mood noticeably changed. And then he responded,

"Ya uslyshal golos d'yavola. Ya chuvstvoval zapakh d'yavola."

His daughter translated,

"He say he started to hear voice of devil – and it not stop talking to him. Then he start to smell devil and smell not go away."

Upon hearing this, Gil asked Henderson if he could ask Askar's daughter a question for clarification. Henderson permits it.

"Ms. Popoluv, did your father have any history of hearing voices? Did you ever see him talking to himself?"

"No. He a simple farmer. My life he never hear voices. Never talk to himself."

"Thank you so much. I noticed that your father has a muscle twitch on his face. Is that something he has always had?"

Just to be sure she understood the question, Askar's daughter makes a twitching gesture with her hand near her face. Gil confirms that that is what he is referring to.

Ms. Popoluv brakes down in tears,

"Before experiment, my father good. After experiment, many bad things. He now shake, he seizure, he not sleep."

Gil walks closer to Askar and his daughter,

"Mr. Popoluv, thank you so much for coming all this way to share your experiences with us.

"M'Lud, if you've read the 400 page summary of the Cortx clinical trials, you may have noticed there are no references to serious side effects. You will not see any references to hallucinations or psychosis or schizoid episodes..."

"Hold on just a moment Mr. Hinchliff. Mr. Marshall, do you have any questions for Mr. Popoluv?"

"Thank you M'Lud, no M'Lud, I have no questions.

"I don't know what it would achieve. The testimony I hear is certainly taken out of context. I am not entirely convinced that what Mr. Popoluv was describing was directly connected to the experiments. A detailed inquiry would determine if there were any pre-existing conditions. Were there other medications which Mr. Popoluv might have been taking which had an adverse affect or a cocktail affect. To my knowledge, there are no devils in Casablanca."

Gil mutters under his breath,

"Except for all the Nazis."

Marshall continues,

"The experiments are part of a scientific process of trial and error. Scientific breakthroughs don't happen without setbacks or difficulties. They never have and they never will. You try a formula, if there are issues, you adjust the formula, you improve it. That is what research and development is. Mr. Popoluv's testimony is really not about the possible side effects of nootropics, it's about the nature of the scientific process. All the people who volunteered to participate in the clinical trials received the best medical care there is – I can assure this court."

"M'Lud, what Mr. Marshall forgot to mention in his tribute to the scientific process at K-Lab in Kyrgyzstan is that they are working outside the framework of the Helsinki Accords which establishes ethical standards for human experimentation. Over 150 countries are signatories to these protocols."

"Objecti..."

"Mr. Marshall will strenuously object to my comment and explain that all experimentation is actually taking place under rigorous oversight by an independent entity called 'Encore'. Is that correct Mr. Marshall?"

Marshall is silent. Henderson nudges,

"Mr. Marshall?"

"Yes it is M'Lud. Encore Foundation is an independent entity which conducts the experimentation which Cortx is not in control of. Their work is entirely in compliance with the Helsinki Accords."

"Another fiction M'Lud.

"Mr. Marshall, can you really look anyone in the eye and say that? Encore Foundation is nothing more than a shell to offset liability and side step independent oversight. All of its employees are essentially approved by Cortx. All of its reporting is to Cortx. Its budget is controlled by Cortx by way of tax deductible 'donations' to the foundation. The only thing independent about its operation is some locally sourced vegetable produce."

Sophie cracks a smile. Few others get the joke.

"Don't worry Mr. Marshall. There's plenty of clean up work coming your way. Encore Foundation, K-Lab, and Cortx are all being sued for their reckless disregard of the Helsinki Accords and the resulting harm caused to many volunteers who participated in your 'scientific process.'"

On that note, Norman Palmer stood up and exited the courtroom.

Marshall had the look of a deer caught in the headlights.

Henderson glimpsed to see if there was any coffee left in his cup, but there wasn't.

"M'Lud, Mr. Marshall makes an eloquent appeal to place the nightmarish experiences of Askar Popoluv in the context of the scientific method. But there is another significant omission by Mr. Marshall. The nightmares of Askar Popoluv were unfolding AFTER a formula of Cortx nootropics had already been released to the public and was being consumed by the public.

"When Askar Popoluv was having hallucinations of the devil, seizures, and insomnia for weeks on end, school children were being given nootropics as part of their reading lessons. When Askar Popoluv was having the side effects of psychosis, tourists and military recruits were given the blessing of permanent memories – courtesy of Cortx nootropics."

Judge Henderson intervenes,

"Mr. Marshall, is this correct? Were the nootropics already in commercial distribution when trials were still taking place at the lab in Kyrgyzstan?"

Marshall is fumbling,

"Na, no M'Lud. That's not the case M'Lud. Different formula's..."

Marshall is shuffling papers on his desk and appearing to look for something in a desperate effort to buy himself a few more seconds of time to recover from this ambush.

"It's routine M'Lud to continue to experiment with various mixtures. Special uses, new and improved formulas, etc."

Henderson echoes the last phrase with a raised eyebrow,

"New and improved formulas?"

"Yes M'Lud."

Henderson looks at his watch,

"I think that's all for today ladies and gentlemen. This court is adjourned until Thursday morning."

Is is no shortage of loud sighs as the courtroom begins to empty. Askar and his daughter are chatting with Gil and Graham. Two reporters come by and start to ask Askar questions.

Marshall and the Cortx legal team shut their folders in dismay. Several reporters are trying to get their reactions to the accusations which have just been made.

Sophie walks over to say hello to Askar. She gives him a peck on the cheek then turns to shake hands with his daughter. They chat for a few minutes about Askar's health then Sophie gives him her contact details.

Without Gil noticing, Sophie is heading out of the courtroom. A reporter is chasing her hoping to ask some questions, but Sophie fobs the reporter off as she exits the building and all the turmoil.

Graham is in a good mood,

"Gil, how the hell did you manage to get a visa for Askar?"

"It pays to have a friend at Treasury."

At that point, Gil gives a shout to his brother Stephen as he is about to drift out of the courtroom with the tide of spectators. His brother walks over to Gil and Graham and Askar. Gil does the intro's.

"Mr. Popoluv, this is my brother Stephen who helped arrange for your Visa to come to London."

Askar and his daughter thank him. Stephen looks almost embarrassed.

"Graham, I don't think you've ever met my bro – Steve, Graham."

Graham figures it out.

"I think you did once tell me your brother works at Treasury. So you're Gil's secret weapon? Many thanks for helping out!"

It occurs to Gil that his brother has never before seen him at work. He once or twice came by the office, but he's never actually seen him in action – giving testimony at a hearing or defending someone in a public interest case. Whatever the ultimate outcome, this judicial review is a big deal and Gil is very pleased to see his brother there.

Gil is especially pleased that his brother allowed himself to be roped in to help out. It been rare for them to work together on anything. There's so little they see eye to eye on.

Stephen's comment to his brother before he left the courtroom brought tears to Gil's eyes,

"They really have crossed a line haven't they?"

And just as Stephen is walking away, he turns to Gil with a surprising afterthought,

"I suspect their Kyrgyzstan operation is avoiding taxes. I wouldn't be surprised if Treasury decides to take a close look into that."

Sophie is out of the pressure cooker courtroom, but as she exits the building there is still something eating away at her above all else.

Regardless of the blowback which is sure to follow, Sophie found the courage to testify about her kiosk autodiagnosis. But she was too frightened to mention its most disturbing finding.

While the first level of diagnosis indicated no tumours, the premium diagnosis detected the abnormal presence of micro-lesions in the hippocampus – a crucial zone in the memory formation process. The fact that Sophie's husband Ian had died of a brain tumour added to gut wrenching anxieties about her mental health.

Gil races out of the the courtroom in the hope of catching Sophie.

From the top of the courthouse steps he spots Sophie in the distance probably heading for a bus or the tube. Gil is about to sprint down the steps when he sees her approached by two brawny looking men. At first she jumps back and as they walk towards her she continues to backpeddle.

The three of them stand there chatting for a moment. They then take Sophie by the by arms and escort her to a waiting car. Sophie enters the car with the two men and they drive off.

Shootout at the Cortx coral

Wearing a freshly pressed suit and tie, Gil enters the bustling lobby of Cortx HQ in Central London. There are several monitors above the main reception desk and one of them tuned to a mile-wide inch deep 24hour news channel. There, a reporter is seen standing in front of the court building where the judicial review is taking place. Her report can clearly be heard above the buzz of the lobby,

'...It was a day of testimony in the so called 'memory tax trial' which Cortx executives wish they could forget. Cortx share price took a very hard knock by the close of trading yesterday amidst calls for tighter regulation of this neurotech giant...'

While security guards are much in evidence, Gil manages to avoid their attention as he matter-of-factly clears the metal detector and X-ray machines and heads for the lifts.

Gil takes the lift to the executive suites on the 73rd floor and approaches the receptionist,

"I'm here to see Mr. Palmer."

"Do you have an appointment?"

"Tell Mr. Palmer that Gil Hinchliff is here to see him."

"Do you have an appointment?"

"Please, just tell Mr. Palmer that it's Gil Hinchliff."

The receptionist calls for a security guard to come by reception to keep an eye on Gil before she walks off.

Behind the reception area, Gil eyes a collection of corporate artefacts, corporate governance awards, and photos of Norman Palmer with dignitaries and politicians including one of him shaking the hand of the president of Kyrgyzstan.

While perusing corporate memorabilia, Gil has a horrific flashback to an animal experiment. He sees a rat with its skull open and electrodes attached to its brain. This was one of the images Gil was force fed while trapped in the K-Lab pod. But to Gil's surprise, the grisly image was not accompanied by intense emotions of dread and anxiety which have come along with flashback episodes in the past. Gil places his hands over his eyes. After usurping his field of vision for several seconds, the wired rat begins to melt away.

The receptionist returns,

"This way please Mr. Hinchliff."

The security guard follows.

Gil enters a spacious and light filled office befitting a CEO. It has a spectacular view of London. The walls are decorated with plaques, more corporate leadership awards, group photos, and a few golf trophies sit on a shelf. Palmer is still on the phone but gestures to Gil to sit down and gestures for the security guard to leave.

As Gil sits, the receptionist leaves. Palmer finishes his call, hangs up the phone and looks up to Gil.

"To what do I owe this honour? I gave up hope of ever again coming face to face with an honest to god neuroterrorist."

"The Royal Shakespeare Society says Alex owes them royalties."

Palmer doesn't appreciate the joke and his demeanour shifts abruptly,

"Stop wasting my time you worthless piece of shit. What the hell do you want?"

"Well dad, I want to ask a favour."

Palmer crosses his arms and leans back,

"A favour? And what the hell might that be?"

"Please don't penalise or prosecute Sophie for her testimony."

"Why the hell not? Is she putting out? You have some goddamn nerve! Do yourself a favour and forget about Sophie. She's sure as hell going to forget about you. You should be worried about your own goddamn ass."

Palmer calls reception,

"Joanne, would you please get Phil in here."

Palmer begins to round on Gil,

"You think you're the centre of the fucking universe don't you? Just like your mother! The whole goddamned world revolves around you!"

"Is that why you treated mum like a worthless piece of shit too?"

"Gilbert, maybe if you actually had a life, you wouldn't waste so much of your time trying to destroy mine."

"Don't flatter yourself. Long before you were headhunted to work for these mindfuckers, I was doing memory rights work. Cortx is very good at destroying other people's lives, and you fit right in."

"I can never forget the way you treated Mum."

"What the hell do you know about me and your mother? You were too goddamn young to understand or remember anything!"

"Not young enough. You ran off with someone else. You cut her off completely. You treated me like I didn't exist. When she was ill you did nothing to help."

Phil Thurgood bursts into the suite while on his walkie talkie.

"What you're moaning about was more than twenty five years ago. I don't know what the hell she told you, or what you think you remember but I loved your mother."

"Maybe shouting at her all the time and telling her to 'get over it' isn't the best way to show love to a woman grieving the loss of a baby."

"She refused help. She was not moving on with her life. She's the one who had an affair. Things between me and your mother deteriorated long before I met someone else.

"As far as doing nothing to help, I haven't a clue what you are talking about. Your mother tried counseling which I paid for, I looked after our family, and I certainly paid for your goddamn law degree. What a waste that was! When we're done with you, you will be disbarred and in jail for your little Kyrgyzstan adventure."

"Actually, the reason I hope you don't prosecute Sophie is because of this..."

Gil activates a video file on a tab and slides it over to Palmer.

He picks it up.

On the screen are horrific images from Kyrgyzstan. Several so called 'memory donors' are seen having violent seizures and bloody eyeballs are bursting in reaction to nanoscope injections. There is also footage of a person with his skull removed for a neural implant surgery – who goes into caridac arrest.

"I have many more home movies from Kyrgyzstan where this came from. It's real unforgettable stuff even without nootropics. I would consider sparing your shareholders a flood of such grisly images. As long as Cortx leaves Sophie and me alone, I will not submit this in court. I will not make it public."

"Are you trying to blackmail me? Your mother, may she rest in peace, would be very proud of you. Get the hell out of here."

Palmer pushes the tab back at Gil. Thurgood moves towards Gil.

"My law degree is finally paying off. Cortx stock lost more than 10% of its value yesterday. Oh, and one more thing, I almost forgot to mention, Scotland Yard is expanding its investigation into the murder of Geoff Weyland and the attack on me in the kiosk."

Palmer glances to Thurgood.

Ignoring Thurgood moving towards him, Gil pulls out an envelope and throws it onto Palmer's desk. He then turns and leaves Palmers office slamming the door behind him. Palmer reads the inscription on the envelope, 'To Norman, from Alex'.

After initial hesitation, Palmer opens the envelope.

He removes a greeting card with a glossy photo of Alex on the front. But upon opening the card he sees a ghastly collage of images of dead and mutilated parrots. An embedded sound chip is activated and Palmer hears Alex's voice reciting a line from Shakespeare:

'Rich gifts wax poor when givers prove unkind.'

Closing twists and memory turns

It's the final day of the judicial review. Judicial reviews tend to be short and focused. They may last 3 or 4 days, sometimes less. Marshall has had a couple of days to lick his wounds. Today, Thursday, will be final testimony and closing statements from the defendant and plaintiff. Henderson can take whatever time he deems fit to come back with a ruling. It could be a matter of days, but it's usually within 2 or 3 weeks.

The Crown courtroom is as packed as it was on opening day. Seating for reporters and spectators is on a first come first served basis and members of the press were queuing outside the chambers from 4AM along with many of the MRA stalwarts.

Courtroom absentees include Sophie Hudson and Norman Palmer.

Henderson enters the courtroom with coffee cup in hand.

The court clerk performs the 'please rise' and 'please be seated' ritual to get the show on the road.

By late morning all testimony was finished. Not surprisingly, Marshall & Co. managed to dig up a K-Lab volunteer who had only nice things to say about being a human guinea pig.

After lunch, Marshall was first up with his closing comments. He hoped to win by points in spite of taking some heavy blows in earlier rounds.

"M'Lud, we recently heard a very unsettling account from a former Cortx employee and we also heard accounts from two of the volunteers who took part in the research and development work at K-Lab. In very different ways, they are all people who have played an invaluable role in advancing our understanding of how the human mind works.

"I am pleased to say that Mr. Popoluv and his family will be receiving the best medical care and support possible to help him make a full recovery and to help him make a productive transition back to his livelihood as a farmer. I am submitting to the court a signed statement by Mr. Popoluv in which he expresses his full and unequivocal support for the work being done for Cortx at the Encore lab and this statement also confirms that he was treated professionally at all times while he participated as a paid volunteer in the experiments."

Gil and Graham are looking at each other in disgust. It is so painfully obvious what has happened. The Popoluv family was bought off.

"M'Lud, I would like to ask Mr. Marshall how big of a bribe did Cortx have to pay the Popoluv family for them to agree to sign such a statement?"

Marshall responds,

"M'Lud, by mutual agreement, the terms and conditions of this commitment by the Encore Foundation to the Popoluv family are confidential."

Henderson's cynicism can't restrain itself having seen these kinds of last minute manoeuvres numerous times before,

"Does that adequately not answer your question Mr. Hinchliff? Thank you Mr. Marshall."

Marshall continues,

"Sophie Hudson, if she was in court today, would be thanked again on behalf of Cortx and the Encore Foundation for her stellar work. Being at the sharp end of experiments into uncharted territory while working with a diverse group of volunteers and many medical unknowns can be extremely stressful.

"All lab workers at K-Lab for the duration of their employment contracts and for a six month period beyond, have access to free psychological counselling. It is entirely up to each employee whether or not they take advantage of this service. Cortx considers this service invaluable for coping with stress that comes with making a transition from the intensity of research to post employment. For whatever her reason's, Ms. Hudson has chosen not to take advantage of this service."

Before his objection, Gil is stage whispering to Graham,

"Marshall is such a motherfucker...

"Objection M'Lud. Mr. Marshall is brazenly violating Ms. Hudson's right to privacy and confidentiality. How does Mr. Marshall know whether or not Ms. Hudson has sought or received counselling at any point during or after her employment for Cortx? Whether she did or did not, it was a personal decision which should be a matter of strict confidentiality. Instead, Mr. Marshall has decided to make this information public in a transparently cynical attempt to undermine the credibility of Ms. Hudson's testimony."

"Mr. Marshall, I have to agree with Mr. Hinchliff on this. Your comments about Ms. Hudson and whether or not she received counselling are way out of bounds and will be deleted from the record."

Gil leaned over to whisper again to Graham,

"If Sophie was here today, it would have been such fun to see her beat the brains out of this asshole!"

Henderson puts down his coffee and directs Marshall to continue.

"M'Lud, memories are perhaps the most valuable aspect of human existence. The stronger our memories the fuller is our experience of existence. Having a good memory has long been linked to higher incomes and greater intelligence.

"What Cortx is providing is a groundbreaking public service that enhances the experience of being alive."

Marshall is doing his best to deflect from testimony that raised doubts about nootropic safety,

"Nootropics have been consumed by the public and used by institutions for over a year now. Voluminous feedback attests to consumer satisfaction and product safety.

"On the matter of a memory being our intellectual property, the patent we were granted is based on precedent. In essence, what is patentable is a new arrangement of matter. Towards the end of the 20th century, after a lengthy and contentious patent dispute over a naturally occurring gene, the Supreme Court ruled that while the discovery of a new gene cannot be patented, the creation of a modified version of a naturally occurring gene can be.

"The wording of patent law is deliberately open to allow for the unforeseeable. Whether a new arrangement of matter is inside or outside the human body is not relevant to patentability.

"Memories formed with the intervention of nootropics are new arrangements of matter that did not previously exist and this is precisely why we have been able to secure the patents and intellectual property rights that we have."

While Marshall is delivering his closing comments, Gil drifts off into a reverie about the meaning of memories he does not have. These are memories which haunted the house he grew up in. These are memories that hovered in every room like little ghosts. They are phantom memories of his baby sister who died before Gil existed and before his own memories began to form.

In his reverie, the memory of a lost child is hot coal burning a hole in his mother's soul. Just how close dare Gil get to memories that he doesn't own but which can torture him nonetheless – if given the chance. Is it wise to be jealous of a brother for having faint memories of having had a baby sister?

Why flirt with dark memories in cognitive limbo? Why not be satisfied with the collection of dark memories you already call you own? And what's the best way to do battle with memories being inflicted on your brain during an incident of neurotech score settling?

Gil is having a personal reckoning with the goddess of memory, Mnemosyne. Every memory he has ever had, good or bad, big or small, exhilarating or horrifying – may not have come into existence but for a tragedy. It's a tragedy that Gil has decided to try and turn the tables on. Forget about the prologue, why can't being born simply be his good fortune? Maybe its time to cut the umbilical on all the pain and anquish that existed before the 'replacement child' was even conceived.

As Gil is coming out of his reverie, he's gratified it was not a malign side show of horrific flashbacks. Last night, Gil had his best night's sleep since returning from Kyrgyzstan.

Marshall is winding down,

"On the matter of permanent micro-charges, they are a bargain. Ticket prices for first run feature films have become unaffordable for a family night out for many working class families. Our payment model of lower up front charges for movie tickets has populist appeal and enables even poor families to have an enjoyable time together at the movies.

"On the matter of becoming the world's first memory utility, we take our new responsibilities very seriously. We will implement and oversee consumer protections against fraud, offer customer complaint hotlines, settle customer payment disputes, solicit customer feedback, and be a service which insures value for money – and value for memory! Thank you."

"Thank you Mr. Marshall. This court will take a lunch recess. The closing comments from the plaintiff will begin promptly in one hour."

Gil and Graham manage to find an empty park bench in the courthouse square – just far enough away from the demonstrators and the media to enjoy their coffee and Danish.

Graham sighs,

"How are you feeling Gil?"

"I could have been on my yacht. How are you feeling?"

"I think you're doing a great job Gil. I haven't a clue what to expect from Henderson, although I think he sees through Marshall."

"Thanks Gray, that means a lot. You've always been the adult in the room and I appreciate that."

"Do you know how Sophie is doing?"

"Not really, but I wouldn't be surprised if she never wants to speak to me ever again."

"You never know Gil. Give it time. Her heart seems to be in the right place."

"You're not missing your half million?"

"I don't really need it. I have a plan to secretly siphon off micro-charges from all MRA members. I'm sorted."

Back in the courtroom, Henderson has his coffee in hand. One of the main court video screens is showing a wide angle shot of the entire courtroom from the rear. Gil is taking a final glance at his notes, before his closing comments begin,

"Our brains are a wondrous dance of chemistry and electricity. This buzzing, blooming, neurochemical miracle can produce great works of art, can focus its energies in pursuit of knowledge about the world, the universe, and perhaps most astonishingly, it can discover the secret workings of itself, the human mind.

"Driven by greed and cynicism, it can even come up with such pernicious ideas as a permanent charge for a human memory. To cede ownership of a human memory is to cede power and control over the essence of what makes us who we are.

"This is a court of law not a philosopher's salon, but what Cortx is claiming, which at first sounds deranged, comes as a perilous threat to the human spirit.

"There is famous dictum by the philosopher Rene Descartes. In the 17th century, he was a pretty bad ass thinker. He grappled with trying to define how we know what we know and how do we know for sure we are who we think we are. His famous dictum is, 'I think therefore I am'.

"Well, I think his dictum leaves something very fundamental out of the equation. I think it would have been more accurate to say, 'I think, and because I can remember having had that thought, therefore I am.'

"Our memories are who and what we are. To remember is essential to learn from past mistakes, to fade from memory is essential to transcend hardship, pain, and grief. The need to remember can be just as important as the need to forget. This is an essential characteristic of the human psyche and a by-product of human evolution.

"Cognitive science has long grappled with the realities and challenges posed by 'unforgettable' or fade-proof memories – it's called PTSD.

"We have raised credible and substantive doubts about the safety of nootropics and the reliability of proprietary claims by Cortx. We implore this court to draw a line in our cerebral cortex and to not allow commercial encroachment upon the sovereignty of human consciousness.

"On the matter of intellectual property, the so called 'property rights' of Cortx should not be considered a landmark in patent law, but subject to action under Penal Code 602 which relates to the crime of trespass.

"Neurotech has taken qualitative leaps since patent law was revised in the early part of the 21st century. A patent should never have been granted to Cortx without a clear and established legal framework which can adjudicate the ethical complexities of extending property rights into the domain of human consciousness. Such a framework does not yet exist.

"An existential boundary line is being crossed. It's a slippery slope that could open the way for the privatisation of human consciousness."

Marshall leans over to a colleague and whispers, "What a great fucking idea!"

"M'Lud, I thank you and this court for this opportunity to present our case and our concerns."

Gil walks to his seat.

Justice Henderson takes his empty coffee cup and throws it into the bin under his bench. He removes his glasses and places them in a shirt pocket under his robe.

Thank you Mr. Hinchliff, Mr. Marshall. You can expect my decision this coming Wednesday. This court is adjourned until then.

The court clerk shouts,

"All rise."

Henderson places his documents under his arm and exits the courtroom.

The following morning Cortx issued a press release which announced that they plan to make available to the public a neutralising therapy for nootropic memories. But an online trade piece which appeared later in the day suggested that this therapeutic option remained 'aspirational' and a long way off. Cortx also indicated that if or when such an option becomes available, the permanent micro-charges will continue. It will be the cost of having unwanted permanent memories permanently neutralised.

Global actions and reactions

It is rare for any judicial review to receive the level of international media attention that this review has generated.

In the days immediately following the testimony of Sophie Hudson, there were protests and demonstrations in about a dozen cities around the world. In some cases, they turned violent.

In Mumbai, there were peaceful sit-ins outside Cortx offices, but a protest outside an Eidetic Cinema in India did end up with beatings and arrests. A stink bomb was released inside the cinema during a screening and all hell broke loose. Protestors outside the cinema were clubbed by police and arrested. The suspicion is that the stink bomb was the work of a provocateur.

Another Eidetic Cinema in India was vandalized. Its screen was set ablaze prior to the first viewing of the day.

Cortx has immediately begun to lobby legislators in India to declare acts of vandalism against Cortx property e.g. Eidetic Cinemas – as 'neuroterrorism'. This would introduce draconian penalties beyond imprisonment and hefty fines. These would include the suspension of public trial by jury, the revocation of passports, the suspension of drivers licenses, and a permanent threat to future employability. Proposed legislation is being drafted.

In an attempt to stay a step ahead of Cortx and the police, a sit-in movement which was gaining momentum in New Delhi relocated from outside the Cortx offices to outside the headquarters of the Indian Sovereignty Fund. It was a new campaign to try and convince the fund to divest its financial stake in Cortx.

After two days of being stepped over by Sovereignty Fund employees, the protestors appeared to overstay their welcome. Skulls were cracked and sweeping arrests were made. Of consolation was a serious hit to the Cortx shareprice on the Bombay Stock Exchange.

Refusing to be intimidated, a group of young scientists teamed up with struggling farmers who identified with Askar Popoluv. Their target was Cortx offices in Bangalore.

Wearing hi-viz vests and hard hats to pass as construction workers, they took a pickup truck loaded with cow manure and dumped it as close as they could to the revolving glass doors of the Cortx office entrance. A flashing LED sign atop this mountain of manure reads, 'Hello Cortx, Enjoy the unforgettable aroma.'

The operation was done so quickly, there was little time for security or police to try and thwart this masterfully choreographed special delivery. The scientists and farmers are a new tight knit collaboration not yet infiltrated by Cortx spys or government agents. Coverage of this action was the lead story on most of the Indian newscasts. It is also a story that went viral on the tabs.

Because of the looseness of the MRA alliance, activist groups around the world are free to initiate their own actions or protests but are urged not to do so explicitly in the name of the MRA.

In Seattle, publicity surrounding a group that claims to be the Washington State affiliate of the MRA is causing serious reputational damage. Gil and Graham have condemned their actions and suspect they are paid provocateurs. Near the Cortx offices in Seattle, this 'MRA affiliate' is handing out Molotov cocktails with matches. Labels on the bottles read,

'Dear Cortx, Let's toast to UNFORGETTABLE memories!'

The ruling and the perilous cut

It's two minutes to ten. The courtroom is abuzz with spectators and reporters, chatter, speculation, and neck craning. Judge Henderson is soon to arrive and deliver his rulings.

Cortx has been in damage control overdrive. Sally Zhao is ordered by Palmer to head off the class action lawsuit by any means necessary. Charm, bribes, threats, and skulduggery – will all do nicely.

The court camera operator is practicing moves. There are sweeping pans and crash zooms into faces. It's the best video coverage which modern justice has to offer – even if it's justice for the many by the one – Justice Jason Henderson.

Henderson struts into the courtroom appearing more magisterial than usual. Is it the freshly pressed robe or the fact that he is not schlepping a cup of coffee?

The sound of people rising together and then seating together is more in sync today than usual.

Palmer is present and playing to the press. He's smiling, chatty, and looks like he's been to the arctic for the weekend sporting a fresh tan.

Sophie Hudson is not among the spectators.

Henderson puts on his glasses. There is silence and anticipation for the next 10 seconds as he arranges some papers, then clears his throat,

"Thank you all for coming today and for your interest in the rulings of this court."

Having foregone a cup of coffee, Henderson pours himself a glass of water from the pitcher by his desk. He takes a sip then continues,

"I'm neither Mnemosyne, Descartes, or Shakespeare. I would have difficulty describing in any detail the differences between a hippocampus and a hippopotamus. But, I recognize the gravity of the issues raised in this judicial review.

"Just in case there is any doubt or confusion, let me first offer some clarity about my role in this judicial review process. If there were previous legal rulings that affect the matters at hand which I determine to be unsound I can quash them. If I determine that there are laws that to my estimation are unreasonable or nonsensical I can rule them 'perverse' and overrule them. If there are past legal decisions that were made on a misapplication or misunderstanding of the law, I will lay out my opinion about that and order the decision revisited.

"I can issue injunctions, demand compensations, and make myself a royal pain in the arse to a lot of people. But a judicial review is often not the last word in a process. A lot may remain to be resolved and neither side is guaranteed to be happy with the final outcomes."

The judge signals for the clerk to come to the bench. Henderson mumbles a request for a cup of coffee.

In a long and starkly lit laboratory corridor, several people in green surgery scrubs are strapping the arms and legs of Sophie Hudson to a hospital gurney. She's receiving intravenous medication of some sort through her right arm. The scene ominously echo's a nightmare that has tormented Sophie in the past. She's drifting into unconsciousness and starting to struggle against her restraints and beginning to ramble incoherently.

Judge Henderson continues,

"On the matter of permanent charges for permanent memories, if the defendant is now a certified memory utility which receives, or is qualified to receive government subsidies, that entails new kinds of responsibilities to your customers.

"According to the administrative code for utilities, contracts which cannot be cancelled are a violation of customer rights.

"I deem all contracts with a nominal utility which stipulate permanent and uncancellable fees to be null and void."

Marshall whispers into the ear of his colleague, "I wonder if that will qualify us for a boost in permanent subsidies?"

Henderson rounds off the point,

"Whether or not purchasing a ticket for the Eidetic Cinema qualifies as giving informed consent to any kind of contractual relationship with Cortx, I have my doubts. Having gotten my hands on a high powered magnifying glass and read the entirety of the Cortx licensing agreement aka 'movie ticket', I've concluded that only a speed reading entertainment lawyer with a consultant neuroscientist would be capable of providing truly informed consent.

Sophie arrives in a harshly lit operating theatre. It's a terrifying reprise of her nightmare, only this time it's for real. A patch of her hair on the left side of her head is being shaved away. The figure about to cut open Sophie's skull is wearing thin surgical gloves through which the letters

A L E X appear on his knuckles. It's Yoshio aka 'Birdbrain', the microsurgeon who implanted the memory chip into Alex the parrot. A line is drawn on Sophie's scalp to guide an incision.

Henderson continues,

"On the matter of safety and Cortx nootropics, I was impressed, challenged, and at times entertained by the testimony offered to this court by the plaintiff. There is clearly much to be extremely cautious and circumspect about regarding the availability and public use of nootropics. However, I am not fully convinced there is not a place in society for safe and responsibly administered memory enhancing nootropic therapeutics.

"I was frankly aghast at the level of doubt and confusion raised regarding the safety of the nootropic formulas that are already on the market. I'd like to believe that Cortx would not intentionally release drugs that have the potential to cause short or long term harm. But companies do sometimes face financial pressures that can cloud their best judgement. This situation is unsatisfactory. There must be a rigorous and transparent safety assessment before mass marketing.

"That three of the five members of the NOC – the Neurotech Oversight Committee – are former Cortx executives, does not provide the appearance of integrity necessary for the oversight process. I do not make this call lightly, but I am ordering an injunction against the operation of Eidetic Cinemas in this jurisdiction."

The courtroom explodes. MRA supporters are cheering as they jump up and down and give each other high fives.

For the first time during the judicial review, Henderson is using his gavel,

"Order! Order, order! Order in this courtroom..."

Marshall and Palmer are looking stunned and aghast. Palmers jaw is tightly clenched. Gil and Graham cannot contain their glee.

"Order, everyone, everyone – quiet down..."

Then came the caveats and qualifications,

"This injunction will initially be for a period of between 3 and 12 months."

Sounds of jubilation mix with grunts and groans.

"The Parliamentary Neurotech Ombudsperson will be charged with assessing the independence of the NOC and reassessing their rulings on the safety of nootropics. It was these rulings which informed decisions by regulators.

"There must be no real or perceived conflicts of interest in the operations of the NOC. If the integrity of the NOC appears compromised, its members will be replaced and a new ruling on nootropics will be mandated.

"Going forward, it is imperative that Cortx submit complete and comprehensive data from their clinical trials to the NOC.

Henderson turns to face Marshall and Palmer directly,

"And that means...COMPLETE AND COMPREHENSIVE."

Gil is whispering to Graham,

"Who's going to oversee the ombudsperson?"

"Don't be so cynical Gil."

"But what has the fucking ombudsperson ever fucking done?"

"Don't worry, we'll light a fire under its sorry ass, promise."

———————————

The surgery upon Sophie continues. An incision is being made. A cranial saw is activated. Her vital signs appear to be wavering... adjustments are quickly made to the flow of intravenous drugs. A surgical microscope is moved into position.

———————————

On the two large membrane screens at the front of the courtroom are reaction shots of the plaintiffs on one side and of the defendants on the other.

Judge Henderson continues,

"On the matter of patent application N139755-83-2 which was the basis upon which Cortx was granted intellectual property rights to memories with a supposedly unique molecular signature, the defendant was unwavering in their conviction that patent law is patent law and they have staked their claim and are building their castle upon it. On the face of it, given some of the vagaries of existing patent law, their case appears to have legal merit.

"The plaintiff makes a passionate argument in defence of the sanctity of human memory and human consciousness and spotlights what are believed to be the long term perils to human cognition posed by commercially motivated intrusion, augmentation, and commodification of human memory.

"However, this court is making no decision on the merits of the intellectual property claims by Cortx as such."

Gil and Graham stare at each other, take a deep breath, and shake their heads in consternation.

"Having said that, in the rapidly evolving neurotech era there is a case to answer concerning the ambiguous wording of current copyright law.

"The defendant points to the wording of current patent law in their defence, 'any invention or creation of a novel arrangement of matter'.

"The defendant points out that this wording does not make a distinction between 'a novel arrangement of matter' being inside or outside a human body.

"A chip implant into someone's brain seems today to be a less contentious object of an intellectual property claim than a neurochemical protein structure that is integrally enmeshed within an individual's identity and consciousness. But on the other hand, in time, maybe not.

"Patent laws were last revised years ago and there have been leaps and bounds in neuroscience and neurotech since. Those who write the patent laws aren't necessarily prophets. It's possible that we have entered unchartered territory."

Sophie's brain invasion is unfolding. With the skill of a virtuoso pianist, Yoshio is remotely conducting micro surgical excisions of protein growths inside the hippocampus of Sophie's brain.

Upon completion of his surgical sonata, he instructs his assistant,

"Close her up."

Judge Henderson takes a sip of coffee followed by a sip of water, then continues,

"While this court is making no ruling on the merits of Cortx IP, I am directing the Parliamentary Sub-Committee on Intellectual Property to review and make any recommendations they consider appropriate regarding the potential insufficiencies of existing IP law given the ethical and biological complexities highlighted by this very contentious case.

"In due course, if relevant recommendations are made by the Parliamentary Sub-Committee, the Appellate Division of the Intellectual Property Court will be mandated to review the Cortx IP claim in this new framework.

"In that instance, the validity of a proprietary claim on protein structures that are fully integrated into a person's consciousness would be questioned anew.

"These are the rulings of this judicial review."

There is bedlam in the courtroom.

Gil and Graham are giving each other a high five and a hug. They are immediately mobbed by MRA supporters and reporters.

The courtroom cameras are catching wide sweeping shots of the commotion.

Ken Marshall closes his legal brief in a fugue state. One of the camera operators has the presence of mind to do a crash zoom into the face of a dejected Marshall. The courtroom video screens juxtapose the downcast and the joyous.

Both Gil and Graham appreciate that it's a moment to savour but at the same time their reactions are tempered by an acute awareness of the uncertainties ahead. If there is one thing that Cortx, the neurotech entertainment conglomerate is capable of, it's ANYTHING!

Gil then turns to Graham,

"I hope Sophie is OK."

The day after surgery, Sophie is lying in a recovery room with head bandaged and her eyes open and alert. Her face is ghostly pale. She's been to hell and back.

Yoshio walks into the room to check on his patient. Sophie had emailed him her neuroscan and full diagnostic report directly from the Cortx kiosk. He was deeply alarmed at what he saw and said he would do whatever he can to help.

"Hi Sophie, can you speak?"

She looks up. After about 10 seconds she finds her voice, and answers faintly,

"Yes."

"Can you see me clearly?"

"Yes."

Within a matter of hours, Sophie is on her feet for a short walk.

Back in bed and sitting upright, Yoshio is about to present Sophie with a series of test images on a large tab.

"Are you ready Sophie?"

"Fire away."

First up is an image of a parrot which appears for 3 seconds. It's followed by 3 seconds of black.

The second image is a vase of flowers. It's up for 3 seconds then black for 3.

Next is an image of a skeleton key.

The skeleton key is followed by an image of airplane.

Yoshio puts down the tab and quizzes Sophie,

"Do you recall the first image I showed you?"

Sophie responds without much hesitation,

"A parrot."

"What image came after the parrot?"

"Flowers."

"Do you recall the last image I showed you?"

"A plane."

"And the image before the last?"

"A key."

Upon answering the forth and final question, Sophie and Yoshio laughed a laugh of relief. Tears began to well up in Sophie's eyes.

"Yoshio, you're a genius."

She gives him a huge hug as tears began to stream down her cheeks.

"What did you see Yoshio?"

"As I suspected, the microlesions were acting as road blocks on short term memory pathways."

"Will they return?"

"I think they were a type of allergic reaction to the nootropics. If you don't use nootropics, I would not expect them to recur."

"And my hallucinations?"

"Lay off the noo."

Closing: A chemical ensemble begins to sing

Gil and Sophie are sharing a bottle of Russian wine from Dagestan at the 'Borscht 'n Tears' café in Southwest London, not that far from where Sophie lives near Wandsworth Common. They are about half-way through the bottle.

"What happened to your hair?"

Sophie answers Gil's question with a big smile.

"Sorry Gil, I've signed an NDA and can't answer that question."

"I was very surprised but very pleased to get your call Sophie."

"You should be surprised. I was really and truly hating you 'Mr. Lynchfield'. You really put me in an impossible place. But I confess, I'm glad I came around to watch the show. I loved seeing that weasel squirm."

"Which weasel?"

"The Marshall weasel. Well, on second thought, he's not so much a weasel as a good old fashioned slimebucket."

"Yeah, he's a slimebucket runneth over!"

"It was also great to see Askar again. It's amazing you managed to get him to London. But seeing him again also made me feel ashamed."

"Ashamed?"

"I think I was affected by the callousness of people around me. I didn't really challenge certain things I was seeing in a way I maybe could have.

If you're doing work that's suppose to benefit humanity, it's not suppose to sap your humanity while doing it, nor, should you be treating anybody else as less than human.

"You should be pleased Gil. What you are doing is a good thing."

"I'm pleased Sophie that you're pleased. One of the nicest things to come out of all this for me was to meet you."

Sophie is seriously blushing.

"You know Gil, I have to confess..."

"Go ahead."

"I think you're cute."

Some guys might be underwhelmed or even hurt to be referred to as 'cute', but coming from Sophie, it has the overtones of understatement and the undertones of 'true confessions'. Gil feels a surge of endorphins or adrenalin – he isn't sure which, maybe both.

If that isn't a cue to lean in and steal a kiss, there will never be one.

Gil's heart starts to race. He puts his hands to his side and starts to drift ever so slowly and deliberately towards Sophie. Gil's brain is racing, observing the changing perspective every increment along the way as Sophie's face gradually appears larger in his field of vision.

The trajectory of Gil's head is making imperceptible midcourse corrections along route to Sophie's head as she ever so slightly shifts in her seat. The cerebral cortex which makes higher judgement calls is getting a steady stream of data which pleasantly informs Gil that Sophie was neither pulling back nor turning her head away.

Gil's face still has about 45cm to travel before reaching Sophie's face. His neck is effortlessly supporting the 5k weight of his head which contains 1.5 kilograms of the most complex matter in the universe.

Sophie's perception of the incoming face of Gil is refreshing itself 24 times per second.

Whatever the neurochemical mix which correlates to the feeling of anticipation – that chemical mix is buzzing, chanting, and rising in volume inside Gil's brain.

Adrenalin, endorphins, or whatever – continue flooding into Gil's bloodstream. Lips are getting closer to lips and still no evasive manoeuvres on the part of Sophie. Eye to eye contact remains strong and course corrections unnecessary.

Gil suddenly has a flashback.

It's not a flashback to an atrocity. It's a flashback to him and Sophie on the stage at the Scareoke Club as they were about to kiss during the finale of the Nat King Cole song. That image appears in his field of vision then evaporates in an instant.

Centimetres to go. Contact is imminent, Sophie's eyes begin to close. The angle of Gil's head tilts slightly. Sophie moistens her lips with the tip of her tongue.

Their lips make contact. They softly melt together.

It is a precious and effervescent moment. It is an unaugmented and unforgettable NOW.

The kiss gives way to a gentle but passionate embrace which knocks over a near empty bottle of wine. With arms still wrapped around each other Gil and Sophie release a synchronised sigh.

Gil whispers in Sophie's ear.

"Thank you Sophie."

"Thank me for what Gil?"

"Thank you for being so brilliant."

"I'm not so brilliant."

"Yes you are."

"No I'm not."

Sophie does a jokey riff as if from an old Gilbert and Sullivan musical,

"Yes you are, no you're not, yes you are, no you're not."

"You gave me a real insight into something."

"How do you mean?"

"Well, it's complicated, but I think what it boils down to is that I didn't feel I had the right to exist, but I never really understood why I felt that way."

"Gil, you have every right in the world to exist, and guess what, the world is a better place for it."

"What are you on?"

Sophie makes unflinching eye contact with Gil,

"I mean it Gil. Gil, you will be fine, you will be fine. I'm sure of it."

"Oh, so you're a hypnotist too?"

It is Sophie's turn to launch a kiss.

It's early evening but there is still traces of daylight streaming through the blinds into Sophie's bedroom. Gil and Sophie are kissing passionately and starting to undress each other.

"Just be very gentle Gil, I'm feeling a bit fragile."

"I was concerned when I didn't see you in court."

"I had to go to memory rehab. But the good news is that the doctor has ordered some pleasurable, vivid, and 'au naturale' memories."

"Well, if thems the doctor's orders...who am I to argue? Besides, I wouldn't want my memories any other way."

Sophie and Gil continue their lovemaking. Sophie is whispering in Gil's ear as she kisses it.

"I got a call from the Cortx Corporate Citizenship department this morning. They said I've broken the terms of my severance contract and my confidentiality agreement."

"And?"

"They want to forget I ever worked for Cortx."

Now Gil is gently kissing Sophie's ear and whispering into it,

"I'm having a very vivid memory of you gently lowering my head into a bowl of ice water – it's turning me on".

"Sorry Gil, I don't think I have any ice. Maybe you want a cold shower?"

"You might be right, I'll take one, but only if you'll join me..."

Gil and Sophie are in the shower making love as a news report appears on the shower curtain. A correspondent standing outside the London Stock Exchange is seen and heard through kissing, caressing, and streams of water.

"The neurotech titan Cortx has experienced the most volatile trading day in its history.

"Its shareprice plunged to a record low at the opening of trading this morning after its memory surcharge was declared illegal in a London courtroom. And one of its most important patents now faces an uncertain future.

"But, before the close of trading today, Cortx shareprice skyrocketed on an unconfirmed report that its exaflop supercomputer neuro-mapping venture called Axion – spontaneously achieved artificial consciousness.

"If true, it will be game changer for humanity.

"Axion is rumoured to have activated its own computer keyboard and wrote the message, 'Please do not turn me off'".

Gil and Sophie pause in their lovemaking to give a sidelong glance at the shower curtain, then they look into each others eyes and shout in perfect unison,

"Fuck Cortx!"

Their lovemaking resumes.

On the electronic billboard of the newsstand opposite the Royal Society building in Central London is the latest headline:

Cortx Employee Questioned in Street Robbery Murder Mystery

Inside the Royal Society, it's past opening hours and very quiet. Alex is sharpening his beak on a cuttle bone at the far end of one of the branches inside his chrome cage.

He flies a circular lap as he prepares to settle down for the night. Alex is scratching the side of his head just below his little knit cap with one of his claws while remaining perfectly balanced on his perch. The CCTV cameras and directional microphones are on-line as always.

Alex clears his hoarse voice. His head is tilted back and his eyes are glancing up as if he's searching his memory chip for an apropos phrase or sentence from the collected works of Shakespeare to end the day.

Uncannily, Alex repositions himself on the branch closest to a directional microphone – and begins to speak.

He has settled on an excerpt from Hamlet, Act I, Scene IV,

"So horridly to shake our disposition
With thoughts beyond the reaches of our souls"

His voice echoes in the Grand Hall of the Royal Society.

THE END